MAGIC
OF FLAME AND
SHADOW

WITCHES *of* MOONFELL
BOOK 1

KIM RICHARDSON

Magic of Flame and Shadow, The Witches of Moonfell, Book One

www.kimrichardsonbooks.com

MAGIC
OF FLAME AND
SHADOW

WITCHES *of* MOONFELL
BOOK 1

KIM RICHARDSON

CHAPTER I

The soft skin of his belly was torn open, marked by runes, symbols, and letters carved into his chest. The deep, jagged cuts told me this was done either by an amateur or someone in a hurry. Or maybe they just didn't care. Garish and unoriginal, if you ask me.

The victim's eyes were missing, and blood trailed down his wrists where he'd been cut. The scent of blood and entrails was thick.

I loved nothing more than to find a dead body before nine in the morning, before my second cup of coffee. Caucasian by the light coloring of the blood-soaked skin and male. He was just a kid.

Maybe seventeen years old. Possibly younger. And that—didn't settle well with me.

The sight was grim. The body hung from the wall like a painting, pierced and punctured by an iron rod through each clavicle. The corpse was pinioned out in the shape of an X, with cords stretched to hold the limbs apart. Blood had dripped from the body and pooled on the wooden floor beneath.

The runes and letters were carved into the victim in what I recognized as Latin. My Latin was a little rusty, but I knew this word. The letters said ANIMAE. *Soul.*

What the hell did that mean?

This wasn't my first experience with a ritualistic killing. In my line of work, these were as common as a sale at your local grocery store. I'd seen my share of dead bodies, even those carved up in runes, but no matter how many, when it came to kids, it brought some deep, primal rage up to the surface. I hated nothing more than the killing of kids. Nothing.

But that's not what had my blood pressure, or the hairs on the back of my neck, rising. Nor was it why I'd *requested* this particular case.

It was the fact that I'd seen *this* particular way of ritualistic killing, along with those strange runes and symbols, once before.

Exactly twenty years ago.

I could still see the face of the girl all those years ago, like it was yesterday when I'd ducked under Fallburn Bridge on my way to see my aunt, seeking shelter from the rain. She'd been strung up just like this boy, the same runes and symbols carved into her chest and her eyes missing.

And she'd been still alive.

I shook those thoughts away and focused on the scene.

It told me two things: one, the culprit who'd done

it wanted us to see it, to show off his masterpiece. They were seriously twisted individuals.

And two, they were paranormal.

I could sense the echoes of magic—not much, just a soft humming and enough to know that magic was performed here.

I yanked out my phone and began taking pictures of the body, the house, everything. It was always better to have too many photos I could delete later than not enough and miss something important.

After I'd done a quick walkthrough of the house, including the basement, I couldn't see any signs of a struggle. The house was clean, too clean, like no one had lived in it for a while. Possibly months. The lack of visible defensive wounds told me that the kid was brought here, probably unconscious or drugged, and probably didn't feel anything until they started to carve his chest and took his eyes. Yeah, I was sure he was awake for that.

Bastards. Bile rose in the back of my throat. It was too early in the morning for this shit.

A loud bang behind me made me spin around.

A thin woman in her early sixties walked through the entrance of the two-story house. Her straight gray hair brushed her shoulders as she marched forward, and red glasses sat on her thin nose. She reminded me of my fifth-grade teacher, Mrs. Spots, who loved to pick on me in class because I wasn't like the other kids. I hated her.

"Thank the cauldron you've arrived," said the stranger, her shoulders slumped as she stood next to me like she'd been carrying the weight of the world on her shoulders until this very moment. Her jacket was two sizes too big, as though it belonged to her husband, and her mom-jeans were held up high on her waist with a belt, again a size too big for her thin frame. "I didn't know what to do. So I called Jack. Said he'd send a Merlin to help us."

Jack Spencer was the assistant director of the Merlin Group in New York. The Merlin Group was an acronym for Magical Enforcement Response League Intelligence Network. They were like the FBI, like a sort of magical police force.

My nose tickled at the paranormal energies that rolled off her. Wild and canine. A werefox, if I had to guess.

"Got here as soon as I got the call," I said. "And you are?"

The stranger flashed a quick smile and stepped into my personal space—way too close. She stuck out her hand. "Helen Robbins," she said, her warm breath smelling of coffee as it brushed my face. "I'm the mayor of Moonfell. And you must be Katrina."

"Kat."

"You have no idea how *relieved* we are that you're here. We didn't know what to do. We're all beside ourselves."

"Who found the body?" I took a step back. It was too early in the morning for those close-talkers.

"The Realtor. Angie. Nasty woman. She came in to get the house ready for a showing this afternoon. Been on the market for a while. The price is way too high, if you ask me. Who can afford prices like that? No one will buy it now after they find out what happened here. Shame. It was such a lovely house when the Airds lived here."

"Do you know who he is?"

Helen sighed and nodded. "Tim Mason. Local boy. Smart. Good-looking. He had it all."

"Paranormal." It wasn't really a question since I already knew the answer.

"A werewolf, like his parents." Helen stole a look at the young man hanging on the wall. She quickly averted her eyes as though staring at it too long would somehow damage her sight. "What do you think happened here? Why would someone do this?"

Good questions. "Not sure yet. But it's why I'm here. To find out why this happened to Tim." I hated it when innocent lives were taken so brutally. And this was a ruthless killing, no doubt about that. No matter what Tim had done or gotten involved in, he didn't deserve to die this way.

"His parents still don't know." Helen pulled off her glasses and rubbed her eyes with the butt of her palms. "This is going to kill them. He's their only son. I don't have children of my own, and I can't imagine the pain they'll suffer. It's too horrible to imagine." She slipped her glasses back onto her face. "Do you know what the word means?"

I studied her for a second. I could lie to her and tell her I didn't know, but she was the mayor of this paranormal community. Sooner or later, she'd find out.

"Soul."

"Soul? As in *our* souls? Us paranormals? Do we have a serial killer in our town!" Helen's face flushed like her blood pressure was going through the roof.

"I'm not sure." My own tension rose at the stress of the situation. Helen's outburst wasn't helping. My body trembled as it always did under these conditions. A cold slip of energy rushed inside me, and I quickly pushed it down. This was not the time to display my magic.

Instead, I reached inside my pocket, pulled out a stack of gum, and popped a piece into my mouth.

"Is that nicotine gum?" Helen was back in my personal space, the scent of lavender shampoo brushing my nose. "You smoke?"

"Trying to quit." I showed her the stack of gum before slipping it back into my pocket.

"Do they help? With the cigarette itch?"

Not so much. "Sure." The truth was, I hated the taste of these things. But it did keep me from buying a pack of cigarettes. I really was trying to quit.

"Smoking kills," scolded Helen, looking at me like a disappointed parent.

Apparently, so did just being a teen kid.

"I'll keep that in mind." She was starting to annoy me, but I didn't dislike her. Not yet. She was one of those people who oozed goodness and dependability like she was the one you called when you were in a jam. Might come in handy while I was here.

Helen propped her hands on her hips, looking at everything except the dead teen. "So, do I alert the town that we have a murderer in our midst? This has never happened before in Moonfell. We've never had a murder."

We had, but I decided to keep this to myself. After all, Helen was a stranger to me, and I wasn't in the mood to share.

"Should we keep our kids inside until you catch the murderer? I mean, this was some sort of ritualistic offering. Right? Shouldn't you be looking for witches and wizards? A male witch moved in last year. He rubs me the wrong way, you know. Gives me the willies when he walks past me. He smells of incense. Maybe you should start with him."

"It's too early to start pointing fingers," I told her. "I need more to go on." And I happened to like the smell of incense. It calmed me.

"But this *is* a ritualistic killing?" prompted Helen. "Dark magic. Voodoo hoodoo. That sort of thing. To call up a Dark god?" Her eyes rounded.

I shrugged. "Maybe. Maybe not. There are many different types of ritualistic killings. This could also be something *posing* as ritualistic, but not. To try and steer us away from the real killers."

"So you don't know?"

"Not yet. No."

At that, Helen gave me a hard stare, like she was trying to lift the skin off my forehead to get a peek inside my brain. "Aren't you Merlins experts in these things?" she asked, waving her arms around like she was doing a backstroke.

I blinked. "I wouldn't know."

Helen's mouth fell open. "Aren't you a Merlin? You know, that group of investigative witches?"

Here we go.

"No. I'm not a Merlin." I didn't feel the need to elaborate on how I'd failed the Merlin trials and had brought great shame to my family, especially to strangers. "But I do work for them from time to time. Depends on the job. Contract work mostly."

"I asked Jack for a Merlin," said Helen. A frown twisted her forehead as she stared at me like it was the first time she set eyes on me.

"And you got me."

"Oh." Disappointment flashed on her face. Guess they were hoping for better, or maybe even the best.

I was used to that look. It had been my constant companion these last thirty-seven years, but it still stung.

An uncomfortable silence followed until Helen broke it.

"Well," she said with a forced smile my way. "Jack must know what he's doing if he sent you. It means he trusts that you're a capable Mer—person. So that means we will, too."

I appreciated her words, but they felt forced and fell flat.

"Thanks." *Thanks?* Why the hell did I say that?

"Wish Blake would have stayed," said Helen. "He kind of took off after seeing the body."

"Who's Blake?" Though the name did ring a bell.

"Our sheriff. He left in a rage."

"Understandable."

"He needs to work on that temper. It's going to get him killed. Mark my words."

"Will you contact the parents, or do you want me to do it?" It was the part of the job I hated the most, but someone had to do it. I'd done it so many times over the years that I was mostly numb when I had to do it. Still, it would be better coming from someone they knew rather than a stranger.

"Oh, I'll do it." Helen glanced at the body one last time. "How will you… get him down?" She blinked fast, and when she looked at me, moisture filled her eyes.

"I've got a cleanup crew on speed dial. They're very good at what they do. Very discreet. I'll be here and make sure they're gentle with him. Don't worry." I had a feeling this was what she wanted to hear.

Relief flashed on Helen's face. "Well, then. I should leave you to it. Please tell them to bring the body to the morgue on Birch Street." She started for the door.

I followed her. "I know where it is."

Helen opened the front door, stepped over the threshold, and turned around. "You do? You've been to Moonfell before?" Curiosity was high in her tone and her features. Her green eyes flashed behind the rim of her red glasses.

Unfortunately. "I was born here."

Moonfell was a haven in Upstate New York for various supernaturals who had decided to retreat from the world.

I grabbed the doorknob and pulled the door

9

toward me, giving her the message that it was time for her to leave and let me do my job. I still had lots of work to do here, and the sooner she left, the sooner I could get back to it.

But Helen just stood there, blocking the door with her body. "You were?" A smile spread on her face. "Why didn't you say something?"

"Because I'm not planning on staying for long." Nope. As soon as I found the bastard who did this and put a stop to them, I was out of here.

She squinted at me, and I could almost see the questions brewing in her eyes. "What's your last name? I'm sure I know your parents. I know everyone in this town. Well, except for you," she added with a laugh.

Here it comes.

"Lawless."

At that, Helen's eyes rounded, and she took a step back like I'd physically pushed her. "Lawless? You're related to Evangeline and Alistair Lawless? Noooo… You are?"

Another unfortunate product of my birth.

I could see the connections she was making fermenting behind her eyes. When I didn't answer, she added, "You're *that* daughter. The one they never talk about."

Bingo. "I have to get back to work. Nice to meet you, Helen. I'll call you if I need anything else. Jack gave me your number. If you need to reach me, here's mine. You can call me anytime." I reached into my bag and handed her a card.

She glanced at it. "Lawless Investigations. That's you."

"That's right."

Helen blinked her large eyes at me, and I could tell she wasn't about to let that information go, not when she had the bit between her teeth. "I never thought I'd ever meet you in person. Never even seen a picture. But now that I'm looking at you… you look just like your mother. Well, a younger version of her. I can't believe you're her."

"Believe it."

"Will you be staying with your parents?"

I shook my head. "I'll be staying at my great-aunt's house. She left it to me in her will when she died two years ago. I haven't had the chance to see it yet…" No. I'd left this town twenty years ago and never looked back.

Helen's jaw seemed to be dislocated as it kept opening. "But that place is run-down. Only the squirrels and raccoons occupy that house. No one has lived there since she passed. Not after Luna died."

"I'll be fine."

"Well, if you need help with the renovations, I can give you a few names."

"That won't be necessary."

And then I shut the door in Helen's astonished face.

Was that rude? You bet. But she was really starting to annoy me. And I wasn't here to discuss my personal life. I was here on a job.

Damnit. The news of my return would spread like

wildfire in this town. And guessing from that look on Helen's face, like she'd just won the gossip lottery, I gave it one hour before all twelve hundred inhabitants in Moonfell would know.

Yes, I was back in my hometown—a place I'd sworn I'd *never* return to, no matter what.

I let out a sigh. "Welcome home, Kat."

CHAPTER 2

To say that my aunt's house was run-down was the understatement of the year. It looked more like it was ready for the bulldozers and demolition crew.

I killed the engine of my Jeep Wrangler, grabbed my carry-on bag, opened the door, and stepped onto what was supposed to be the paved front driveway. It looked more like an extension of the front lawn, though, with so many weeds growing through all the cracks.

Back when I was in my teens, I'd visited Aunt Luna whenever I had the chance. She was the only relative I had who didn't treat me differently. She treated me like a person instead of the failure my parents continued to shame me as.

"You've brought shame to the family. To the Lawless name." My father's words still rang fresh in my ears. Though now, they didn't hurt as much. Now it just

pissed me off that an adult would treat a kid like that.

Twenty years ago, the three-story Queen Anne Victorian had gleaming light-blue siding and white trim with tall welcoming apple trees flanking either side.

Now, it looked like a house the Addam's Family would live in.

Heavy vines webbed the house, like living siding. Its paint was tarnished and blackened by age, peeling in many places, though I could still see streaks of blue. And an unbroken line of tall trees circled the house.

It gave off a hell vibe, and I could only imagine the dated velvet furnishings, cobweb-filled corridors, shadowy rooms, dripping candles, and hidden passageways.

I glanced around. The other houses were all immaculate, their freshly painted exteriors shining in the sunlight, encircled by white picket fences and tidy lawns without a single unruly plant.

The thick underbrush around my aunt's house made the place look abandoned and forgotten. I guess it was. Maybe I should have sold it; then, the new owners would never have let it go the way that I did. Regret pulled at my insides. My aunt would be heartbroken at the state of her beloved home. The only one to blame was me. I'd left everyone and everything behind and never looked back. That included this big house.

It was massive, bigger than I'd remembered, and

it was in dire need of repair. I'd never have the money for the upkeep on a place this big. No, I didn't have the income to fix it up, not on my contract jobs. It would take me ten years.

What the hell was I doing here?

"To solve a case," I told myself. "And to get paid."

Resolute, I hefted my bag on my shoulder and waded through chest-high grass until I made it up to the front porch. I probably picked up a few ticks along the way.

The wood was soft with age and had peeled back at the corners. I stepped carefully, testing the wood. Seemed solid, and seeing that I didn't go through the porch floor, I took it as a good sign.

Fishing through my pockets, I yanked out my keys, found the large pewter one that belonged to this house, and fit it in the keyhole. With a twist, the front door unlocked and squealed as I pushed it open.

The air stank of mildew and something else I couldn't place. With the windows covered in heavy drapes, I was left in darkness.

"Nice." I hadn't paid the electrical bill—or any bills, for that matter. But I didn't want to take a chance and open the door for some light and risk having nosy neighbors look in, so I shut it behind me.

If I were a White witch and drew my magic from the elements, I could have easily conjured some witch light.

I wasn't so lucky.

I rummaged through my shoulder bag. With my phone in my hand, I tapped the flashlight mode and pointed the phone. I could make out my aunt's furnishings, the same Queen Anne-style chairs, sofas, and side tables. Everything was the same as she'd left it. Surprisingly, I couldn't see any cobwebs or great amounts of dust. No squirrels or raccoons, as far as I could tell. Not that it would have bothered me. It wouldn't.

I went to the front bay window and pushed back the curtains. Yes, that let in a lot of light, but also dust that assaulted my nose.

Was I allergic to dust mites? I was about to find out.

In a coughing fit, I managed to make my way to the back of the house, where the kitchen was, and set my bag on the long prep island.

My skin prickled with the remnants of my aunt's magic. Even though it had been two years since she passed away, her power still lingered in the house. She had been a strong witch, after all.

Moving to one of the back kitchen windows, I pushed back the drapes and cranked open a window. Fresh air assaulted my face.

"Much better."

I looked around the kitchen with its white cabinets, white subway tiles, and iron pots hanging over the island. It looked exactly the same as I remembered, just a little dingier.

"Okay, so I need to get some cleaning supplies." I could do that, but only after I spoke to Tim's parents.

I'd probably get more from a close friend or maybe a girlfriend, but I only had the names of Tim's parents. It'd do for now.

Two hours had passed since Helen had left and the cleanup crew showed up. With the last of my collecting evidence, they took the body to the morgue, where the parents were told to wait and to identify the body.

Helen wasn't wrong about looking into the witches and all the magical practitioners in town. It had to be done, even if it was just to eliminate them from the list of suspects. Yet my gut feeling told me that wasn't the case. The markings were jagged, the words barely legible. Usually, when witches performed a ritual, they took care of the writings, ensuring they were well-scripted. One incorrectly written word could have disastrous effects on a spell or ritual, which was why I didn't think a witch did this. Nor a mage or wizard.

But that ritualistic killing, or whatever it was, was disturbing.

My insides tightened as the images of the young teen's eyeless face surfaced along with the ones that had haunted me for twenty years.

It was the same ritual. I knew it in my gut.

And I was going to find those responsible. Then I would make them pay.

"But first. I need to get the electricity back on."

I pulled out my laptop, connected to one of the neighbor's Wi-Fi without password protection (sorry, neighbor), and began to look up the local electrical supplier in town.

A knock sounded from the front door.

"Seriously?" That didn't take long.

I let out a frustrated breath and walked down the long hallway to the front door. I yanked it open. "Can I—" The rest of my words lodged in my throat.

Standing on the front porch was a beast of a man —a beautiful one, but still a beast.

Towering at an impressive six three, or possibly even six four, he stood before me with two hundred pounds of pure muscle. His dark hair draped down his neck and framed his handsome face. A short beard covered his features, but it didn't detract from the sexiness of his strong jawline.

Brown, intelligent eyes shimmering, watching me, studying me was more like it. His shirt only served to draw attention to his toned abs, and the tightness of his jeans revealed the strength in his legs.

From the sun-kissed sheen of his body, he smelled of pine, like he had taken a shower in the woods. His musk was pleasant and warm, and I started leaning forward until I caught myself.

Beautiful. Beastly. He looked just as I remembered him.

His eyes traveled over me, and I felt heat rush through me from my neck to my face. "I'm Blake Maddox. I'm the sheriff here."

"I know." I hadn't forgotten how gorgeous he had been in his early twenties. The type of guy all the girls daydreamed about and who had his pick of any girl he wanted. And, of course, back then, he didn't know I existed, but that hadn't stopped me from developing a major crush on him.

Now in his early forties, he was even hotter. How was that possible?

Paranormal energies hummed from him, wild and ferocious—a beast, a werewolf.

He stood with a casual and predatory edge, the way a person stands when they know they have the upper hand in a battle.

He was an alpha, a king among wolves. As far as I knew, he'd never lost a fight.

The indifference on his face made it clear he didn't remember me. In fact, he had no idea who I was.

Blake stared at me like he was trying hard to remember me but was coming up empty. "So, you're Katrina Lawless. Evangeline and Alistair's daughter."

"It's Kat. And yes. I'm her." I felt like a washed-up celebrity who'd had one hit movie in the eighties, but no one could remember a face or a name anymore.

Blake cocked his head to the side. "It's weird. Brad never talks about you."

Weirder for him than for me. "To my family, I don't exist, including my brother. And I'm fine with that. I'd like to keep it that way. So, I'd appreciate it if you wouldn't mention it to him." I doubted that would work since Helen had probably already spread the word of my arrival. I was certain my family would know soon but best to keep it from them as long as I could.

Brad and Blake had been close friends twenty years ago, and it seemed that was still the case.

"If you want."

"I do." That sounded strangely like a marriage vow.

A smile twisted his lips, and I found that I couldn't look away from those fine specimens. He was wayyyyy too handsome for his own good. And he knew it. "How long has it been since you've been back?"

"Twenty years." Why was he so interested?

He whistled. "Damn. Not even to see your family?"

Now, he was annoying me. I crossed my arms over my chest. "No." This was starting to feel like an interrogation—an interrogation by a walking sex god. I wasn't in the mood for sex. I mean, to be interrogated by the sex god. Why was I thinking about sex?

"You'll notice that things have changed since you've been gone," said Blake.

I didn't think so. "If you say so."

A slow, lazy smile touched his lips. "You're not much of a talker."

"I don't have much to say."

He was still watching me with that little arrogant smile. "I thought I knew all the pretty girls in town. But I don't remember you. Sorry."

My face felt like I'd stuffed it inside a hot oven. "I

was a forgettable teen. Not much to see." He'd been at my house multiple times. I was there. But he never *saw* me either.

"And you work for the Merlin Group?"

"I do."

"But you're *not* a Merlin."

I gritted my jaw. "No. I just work for them sometimes." *Please go away.*

He leaned his arm on the doorframe, and I spied some tribal tattoos peeking from under his leather jacket sleeve. He was coming across like a man who always got the woman—a player of hearts. I didn't have time for games. He didn't even have to work to get women. They probably threw themselves at him.

I noticed that his fingers were bare, no wedding band in sight. I had heard over the years that he'd gotten married.

"Wouldn't you rather be a Merlin? Your entire family are Merlins. Don't you want to be like them?"

"No. Is there an end to these questions?" I reached inside my jeans pocket, pulled out my stack of nicotine gum, and popped one into my mouth.

"Smoking is really not attractive."

"Thanks for the tip."

"Ah. You're angry with me." He leaned closer, his smile widening like he was really enjoying himself. His musky scent was intoxicating, and I felt a little thrill run up my spine.

Damn hormones. I hadn't had sex in over a year and a half, and things were probably covered in layers of cement down there. You'd need a jackhammer to get through. Why was he making me think of sex?

I looked into his eyes, and their intensity had that warmth pool in my middle. Damn. Damn. Damn. And why was he smiling like he'd just won a date with me. I would *never* date him. So, why was I thinking about it?

His eyes crinkled at the corners as though he could read my thoughts. "Sorry I wasn't there to meet with you and Helen. I… had some things to take care of."

Like running away. "Sure." I waited for him to say more. "Can I help you with something? Why are you here?" Apart from trying to melt my panties with that smoldering stare.

Blake lost all of his smile. "Do you have any leads on who did this to Tim?"

Ah. "Not yet." I chewed a couple of times. "I've got my buddy Melvin running samples of Tim's blood to see if he was drugged or anything else that can help explain why he didn't fight back."

"But it's something to do with magic. Right? The way he was killed?"

I nodded. "Could be. I did get a feel for some magical properties, but that might just have been there to throw us off. I still have a lot of work to do. I need to speak to his parents."

He clenched his jaw. "That's why I came here. They want to speak to you. I'll drive."

I snorted. "I can drive myself, thanks."

He frowned at me. "You don't know where they live."

"I can find out. I find things out. It's what I do." Aha. Now, *he* looked annoyed. Guess he wasn't used to females telling him no. Good. Let that sink in for a bit.

Blake stepped back and looked around, seemingly only to realize that a house surrounded me. "You can't stay here."

Was that an order? "I can. I am. And I certainly don't need your permission to stay in my own house." His sex appeal diminished by a smidgen. Damn him and all those muscles. Bet his ass looked great in those jeans, too.

His expression darkened. "I'm the town sheriff. If I think this house is a health risk, you'll have to look for somewhere else to stay."

Oh no, he didn't just pull the sheriff card on me. "Then I guess you'll just have to arrest me because I'm not going anywhere." I showed him my wrists.

Blake just stood there watching me, and I wasn't sure whether I went too far. He looked like he really was contemplating arresting me. *Whoops*.

And then, just like that, he turned around, stepped off the porch, got into his large black BMW SUV parked at the curb, and drove off.

"That could not have gone any better."

A prickling sensation tickled the back of my neck, the feeling I always got when someone was watching me.

I turned slowly and met three women's curious gazes across the street—a blonde, a light brunette, and a redhead, all eyeing me without blinking. Creepy.

My cheeks flushed some more. They'd seen my performance with Blake, and they probably loved every second of it.

I'd only been in town for less than half a day, and I'd already made an enemy. *Nice going, Kat.*

But his ass *did* look amazing in those jeans.

CHAPTER 3

I arrived at the Masons' house ten minutes after my little altercation with Blake. Their home was a quaint, two-story white cottage with a red door. A basketball standing post was positioned at the front of the garage. I could imagine Tim shooting hoops with his friends.

A pang hit my insides. I was going to find the killer, no matter what it took.

I sighed and turned off the engine. When I shut my car door with my hip, I noticed a black BMW SUV parked in the street, two cars down.

Well, well, well. Looks like Blake is here.

Crap. I pulled out my stack of gum and dropped one in my mouth. Then another.

I chewed. Hard. I chewed like a damn baseball player chomping tobacco. I wouldn't let this guy get under my skin. I had a job to do. I didn't have the time or the energy for this.

My annoyance returned, and I pushed it down

when I reached the front door. I knocked twice and waited.

Not long. A few moments later, the front door swung open. And guess who was standing there?

"Took you long enough," said the sheriff. He left the door open and walked back inside the house.

Hot and with good manners? A girl could only dream.

I followed the burly man-beast inside the house. He led me to a small living room just off the entrance. A middle-aged man and woman sat on a beige sectional. The man had his arm wrapped around the woman. Her eyes were bloodshot, puffy. A white nightgown adorned in pink flowers was draped over her slight figure, and she held a tissue in her trembling hands.

Mr. Mason looked up at me and gave me a nod. His eyes were filled with moisture, and I could tell he was trying his best to maintain control and not break down. As werewolves, they were made of hard stuff, strong as steel. But when you took away their only son in that horrible way, it would be totally normal and acceptable for the dad to lose it.

A sniffle turned my attention to the left. A pretty teen girl sat in one of the armchairs across from the couch. Girlfriend. Good. I didn't need to look for her.

Blake stood next to the couch, his muscular arms crossed over his wide chest. I ignored him and went straight to the parents.

"Mr. and Mrs. Mason. I'm Kat Lawless, and I'm here investigating the death of your son."

Mrs. Mason gave out a whimper and buried her face in her husband's chest. He looked up at me, tears brimming.

My throat tightened. "Would it be okay if I asked you some questions?" The last thing I wanted was to bring more pain to these poor folks, but I had a job to do. And they deserved to know why their son was killed and who had done it.

At Mr. Mason's nod, I sat on the edge of the only empty armchair. "Can you think of anyone who would want to hurt Tim?"

Mrs. Mason pulled her head from her husband's chest and just looked at me. But her husband answered. "No," he said, his voice rough like he hadn't used it in a week. "Everyone loved Tim. He was a good boy."

More sniffles from the girlfriend. "I'm sure he was. Did you notice any strange behavior coming from him recently? Did he act differently? Was he maybe nervous? Reclusive?"

Mr. Mason frowned as he pondered my question. "No. He was the same happy kid he's always been."

Hmmm. "Did he hang around with a new crowd? New friends?"

"I don't think so," said Mr. Mason. His eyes moved over to the girl sitting in the chair next to me. "Sarah?"

The girl named Sarah wiped her eyes with her fingers. "No. Just... Tyler and Phil. The usual. The three were inseparable."

I pulled out my phone and typed those names into a notepad app. "Did you two have a fight?"

Sarah's jaw dropped, and it took a moment for her to register the words. "No. Why would you ask that?"

"Just routine questions." I'd been fooled before by puppy tears from girlfriends and wives. I never really bought the stricken look. Wives, husbands, girlfriends, and boyfriends were responsible 90 percent of the time in my cases.

"You have any more questions for Mr. and Mrs. Mason?"

I looked up to find Blake staring at me, all the friendliness and, dare I say, flirtatious behavior gone, replaced by a stone wall, it seemed.

I glanced at Mr. Mason. "When did you notice that Tim was missing?"

Mr. Mason thought about it. "When he didn't come home last night. He usually comes in after eleven. But I went to bed and woke up around two to get a glass of water. That's when I noticed he hadn't come home."

I nodded and tapped down the information in my phone. "Did you try calling him? Texting him?"

"Yeah, we tried calling and texting him last night, but he didn't respond," answered Mr. Mason.

I looked up at Blake, who was still watching me intently. "What about Tyler and Phil?"

Sarah sniffled, wiping away more tears. "They swear they don't know anything. They said Tim left early last night. They were playing video games."

I made a mental note to interview Tyler and Phil next. "Do you know what time that was?"

"He texted me around ten thirty," said Sarah. "He was on his way home. He didn't text me after that."

So, whatever had happened to Tim, it had happened after ten thirty at night. After seeing his body and noting that he hadn't been dead that long, I figured he'd probably been killed sometime between twelve to two a.m. But I'd have to wait for the coroner's report to confirm that.

"Did you notice anything out of the ordinary around your neighborhood? Even if it didn't seem important or relevant, any minor detail can help."

"A van," said Mrs. Mason, speaking for the first time, her voice quivering. "I... remember it because I'd never seen it before."

"When was this?" Blake came around to stand next to me. He was like a damn giant with me sitting down.

Mrs. Mason dabbed her eyes with her tissue. "Yesterday afternoon. I came out front to tell Tim that lunch was ready. He was shooting hoops. And that's when I saw a van parked across from us."

I leaned forward, my pulse throbbing. "Can you describe it? Was it a delivery van or a passenger van?"

"Delivery. Black with tinted windows. That's all I remember."

"This is good, Mrs. Mason. Thank you." It was good. I always believed a woman's intuition was a powerful thing. Add the instincts of a werewolf, and

I was sure this black van had something to do with what happened to Tim.

They'd been watching him.

I met Blake's stare, and I could tell by that deepening frown on his stupidly handsome face that he was thinking the same thing.

"Do you think that van has something to do with what happened to my son?" Mr. Mason's face flushed, and I could see the muscles on his neck popping. His hands kept clenching and unclenching. He was upset. Devastated. And he looked like he was about to beast out into his wolf. Not that him shifting would be an issue, but having a mad-with-grief werewolf going berserk in town was. He might hurt people. And by the looks of it, I had a feeling I knew what he was going to do. He was going to try and find that black van on his own.

I'd seen this before. When people—paranormals—took matters into their own hands, it never ended well. Hell, it ended with more innocent dying, that's what.

"It might, and it might be nothing," I told him, trying to downplay the van. "We don't want to jump to any conclusions just yet."

Blake nodded, and I could see the gears turning in his head. He was already thinking about how we could track down that van. *We?* I was already thinking about us in terms of we. That wasn't good.

When I looked back at Mr. Mason's face, he was focused on a spot on the floor, and I could see the plans formulating behind those eyes. Shit. He was going to do something.

I'd have to find the culprits before the father did something stupid, like kill the wrong people.

I stood up. "Thank you for your time. If you think of anything else, please don't hesitate to call me." I pulled out another card and handed it to Mr. Mason. "Day or night."

"You're the Merlin Helen told us about," said Mrs. Mason, her voice weak and frail.

I didn't bother to correct her. "That's right."

"You look like her," said Mrs. Mason.

I knew who she meant. "So, I've been told."

Tears fell from Mrs. Mason's eyes. "Find who did this. Find who killed my boy."

My gut wrenched at the pain in that woman's face, in her words. And before I could stop myself, I blurted, "I will. I promise."

One of my rules when dealing with the family of the deceased, when working a case, was never to use words like "I promise" and "I swear." Because the truth was, sometimes, it just wasn't possible. It was giving them false hope. However, I'd never failed a case—yet. And I wasn't planning on it.

I felt for this couple. Their son had died a horrible, useless death. The only good thing was that they hadn't seen him strung up on the wall.

I felt Blake's eyes on me. He probably thought that had been a stupid move to promise the Masons, but I wasn't planning on breaking the promise. I was going to fulfill it.

I walked out, my legs feeling heavier than when I first walked into that house. If someone had been watching Tim, that raised all of my warning flags. It told me that the ritualistic killing was real, that someone had been stalking the teen for a reason.

Because he was a werewolf? Possibly. It meant I had some more digging to do.

"I'll look into that black van," said Blake as he shut the front door behind me and down the porch's steps.

My irritation rose anew. "I'm working this case. I was hired to do just that."

"And I'm the sheriff."

I glared at Blake, my fists clenched tightly. "I don't need you to babysit me, *Sheriff*."

"I'm not trying to babysit you. I'm trying to help," he replied calmly. "This is my town, and I care about these people. They're my people. I didn't run away twenty years ago and leave them behind, to pursue bigger dreams."

I gritted my teeth. "You don't know me. You know nothing of my life." No, he had no idea what I'd gone through as a kid, as a teen, even as a woman. How my own family, my own parents, basically disowned me because of my lack of magical skill. And how I had to fend for myself since the age of seventeen. The man didn't even know I existed.

"No. No I don't. But I'm not going to sit back and do nothing while a killer is at large in my town. You need me." Blake watched me, and I hated how, with just one look, my face flushed and my body reacted to him. Like he had some invisible pull. Did he know magic?

"I don't need anyone." Never have. Never will.

Blake's expression hardened. "Excuse me for trying to do my job and uphold the law."

"Your job isn't to meddle in my investigation," I snapped. "I work alone. I've always worked alone. It's how I do things. My job."

"Not this time." Blake raised a brow. "Your choice. Either you cooperate, or I'll give Jack a call and tell him you're not needed here."

I clamped my jaw shut. "You wouldn't dare." Bastard. He was not going to take this case away from me. Not when I'd waited twenty years to make amends, to finally catch those sons of bitches. I promised his parents I'd find the killer. Plus, I needed the money.

The muscles around his neck flexed. "Keep it up, Kate, and I just might."

"It's Kat." At his smirk, I knew he'd done it on purpose to piss me off. And it did.

My anger soared, and as it always did, so did my magic.

The energy within me began to simmer, starting low and erratically at first but growing stronger. However, in daylight, it wouldn't do much. I had to be careful and not reveal too much of myself. My magic.

I let out a breath through my nose and let go of my magic. Controlling my breathing, as I had taught myself at a young age, was a way to control my emotions, which in turn controlled my magic—or lack thereof. It wasn't that I didn't have *any* magic. It was that mine was different, which I had discovered and mastered over the years. And something I had to keep secret.

Blake was watching me, a curious expression on his face.

"What?"

"What was that?" asked Blake as he crossed his big-ass arms over his big-ass chest. "Your face got all… weird. Like you were struggling internally."

"Indigestion."

Blake laughed. "Fine. Don't tell me." The sheriff uncrossed his arms. "But just remember, we're in this together. You let me know if you find anything."

"And you'll do the same?"

"I will. I'll be watching your back whether you like it or not," he said, and I could see a hint of a smile on that face. "The more people we have on this case, the sooner we can solve it. I know this town inside and out, and you're an expert in investigating. Problem solving. We need each other."

"Whatever you say, Sheriff." I needed him like I needed a zit.

I knew he was right, but I didn't like it. I had a feeling Blake would get in the way of my investigation. He was the type to follow the rules, and I was the type to break them if it meant finding the truth. But for now, I needed to focus on Tim Mason's case.

Blake leaned closer, his eyes intense. "You know,

sometimes it's okay to accept help when it's offered. It doesn't make you weak or incompetent."

I scoffed. "Sure."

"We both want the same thing."

"I get it."

Blake's face got all serious. "You really should stay somewhere else. That house of yours is not safe. The roof could fall on you while you sleep. A wall could collapse. It could be infested with mold."

Here we go again. "I'll be fine. The house is fine."

"There's no electricity. Is there even running water?"

Shit. I didn't even check. "I just got here. And I've been busy with other more important things. But I'll have it running in no time. It'll be beautiful again once I'm finished with it." Wait—did I just agree that I was going to stay here while I fixed it up?

"So you're staying?" asked the sheriff.

Now, I'd jumped headfirst into the crapper. "Only until I've fixed it up. I'll probably sell it. I don't know. Haven't thought that far ahead just yet." It made sense. I had nowhere else to go. Might as well stay for a while. And working on a project like a renovation might do me some good.

The sheriff let out a long breath through his nose. "I've done my share of renovations over the years. I can help you if you want."

"Pass." Why did he even care? The man didn't even know me.

Blake shook his head. "Has anyone ever told you how stubborn you are?"

"Yeah, my ex-husband."

Blake's eyes widened at that, and he looked… he looked pleased.

I couldn't quite place it, but I definitely saw a glimmer in his eyes. It made me feel a little uneasy that he seemed to take pleasure in my past failures.

"Well, I'm not your ex-husband," Blake said with a chuckle, "but I am willing to help you out if you change your mind."

"I won't," I muttered, not really wanting to entertain the thought of getting help from him.

Blake held out his hand. "I'll take one of your cards."

I blinked up at him. Yeah, he was that tall. "Why?"

"I'm the sheriff, that's why."

Part of me wanted to punch him in the throat. I pulled out my wallet and fished out a card. "It's my last card—hey!"

Blake had my card in his hand before I could blink. Only paranormals moved that fast. Sneaky bastard.

He raised two fingers, my card stuck between them. "Thanks."

"Whatever." Why did I get the feeling he only did that to get my number? Nah. I was reading way too much into this. Why the hell would a man like Blake want anything to do with someone like me?

Now, I'd have to order more online.

"By the way," he said, walking toward his gleaming SUV. "You chew like a cow."

As he walked away, I had the foolish urge to kick him in the ass.

But having help might come in handy, so I resisted.

I watched him leave before turning to head back to my Jeep. The Mason case was becoming more complicated than I originally thought. It wasn't just a simple murder. Something else was going on here. Werewolves, black vans, and ritualistic killings—my mind was spinning with different possibilities.

I munched down on my gum, trying to control my temper. Of all the people in this town, why did *he* have to be the sheriff? I had a feeling he was going to make my life a living hell, but I couldn't let him take the case away from me. Not when we had a teen killer. Nope. I was going to have to *behave* around him. Easier said than done.

As I climbed into my Jeep, I couldn't shake the feeling of unease that settled in my stomach.

I was starting to question my decision to come back here after twenty years.

But I was already invested in Tim and finding his killers. His murder was connected to me.

And I would find them.

CHAPTER 4

By the time I'd made it back to my aunt's house —now my house—it was almost nine in the evening.

I'd spent most of the day interviewing and doing background checks on the local registered magical practitioners. I'd gotten the list from Helen, who was more than happy to assist me. So far, I'd interviewed twenty on the list. There were fifty in total, so I had a lot of work left. Then there were the "unregistered." Those who wanted nothing to do with the system or how things were done here in Moonfell.

"Do you own a black van?" I'd asked number twenty on my list, a senior witch with a mass of white hair piled on the top of her head like a crown of fluffy cumulus clouds. "Honey, I haven't driven a car or any automobile for ten years," she'd replied.

Of all the interviewees, none of them owned a black van or knew anyone who did.

Yes, I knew Blake was "in charge" of finding out

who owned that black van, but that didn't mean I couldn't do my own investigation. I couldn't rely on anyone. From what I could tell, he'd be pissed if he found out. It made me all warm and fuzzy inside.

I'd stopped off at the local hardware store to get a few supplies. I was surprised to see the original owner, Mack Blackfoot—a big werebear, whose dark hair was completely gray and whose jovial face was riddled in wrinkles.

And, of course, he didn't recognize me at all, even though I'd been to his store regularly on errands for my Aunt Luna.

After that, I contacted the electric company and paid the very late bill along with the late fees. Even then, they said they could only supply the electricity the following day.

Which was why I was cleaning the kitchen by candlelight. I had already done the bathroom on the second floor, which was connected to the master bedroom—my aunt's old bedroom—dusted the bedroom, and then cleaned the floors. The rooms were surprisingly clean, which made my job a lot easier.

I'd removed the old, dingy mattress, stuffed it in one of the other rooms on the second floor, and used the air mattress I'd brought with me and some clean sheets. It wasn't an exact fit on the king-sized, four-poster bed, but it was better than sleeping on the hardwood floors.

The room had the best view and was by far the largest of the five bedrooms. And well, since this was technically my house, I figured I'd get the best bedroom.

Thank the cauldron, the house was connected to the city water supply, so I had water. Just not *hot* water.

I cursed myself for not having those powers White witches were born with. I could have heated the bathtub full of water with some fancy spell. I was not looking forward to the cold shower waiting for me before I went to bed.

But I wasn't a White witch. I wasn't even a Dark one, where I could have borrowed some demonic mojo to heat the water and even get some more light in here. Nope. I was an anomaly—or a dud, according to my family.

That was a lifetime ago when I even realized the extent of my own abilities, and they had no idea what I could do.

My pulse throbbed at the thought of them, and I scrubbed the counter a little too forcefully. I knew coming back here would be a challenge on an emotional scale. But I was a grown-ass woman. I'd been through a lot, and they couldn't hurt me anymore.

A knock from the front door pulled my attention up.

"Blake," I muttered. Damn him. I tossed my rag on the counter and made my way to the front door, both annoyed and slightly excited at the prospect of seeing the handsome sheriff again. Maybe he'd found out who owned that black van.

I'd gotten a text from my buddy Melvin about Tim's blood. No traces of any drugs were found. Tim hadn't fought back because he'd been spelled. I hadn't told Blake yet.

I yanked the door open.

"Ah… yes?" Not Blake, but three women—the same three women who'd been watching me earlier from across the street. My stalkers had come to pay me a visit.

As they got closer, I could feel a wave of energy leave them and make its way to me. It felt like a million pricks on my skin. A combination of rose petals and lavender hung in the air, but underneath, I could smell the unmistakable scent of White witches —pine needles, wet earth, and freshly cut grass muddled with wildflowers.

Although they were all White witches, they varied greatly in their physical traits.

The blonde had that old Hollywood vibe in her tight white top that hugged her curves, leaving little to the imagination and requiring her breasts to fight for air. The matching mini white skirt barely covered her Lady V and clung to her toned legs. Her blonde hair fell in waves around her shoulders. Her skin was tanned as though she liked to spend all her free time tanning—or it could be a tanning spell. She was the tallest of the women and looked my age, possibly a bit older. Her blue eyes sparkled with mischief, and I could tell she was trouble.

The light-haired brunette was the shortest, but her fiery aura made her seem much taller. Loose yoga pants draped around her legs and her top was stained with green and brown spots. Her hair was styled in a messy bun, not the stylish type, but the type that said she didn't have time to do anything but grab her hair and stack it in a knot.

The redhead was sandwiched in the middle of her companions. She had an impassive expression that seemed like she was making a conscious effort to hide her thoughts. Yet her green eyes—the same shade of green as the ivy growing up the side of the house—were giving away her intense contemplation. Her hair was sleek and straight, hitting just the top of her shoulders. She wore a red leather jacket that matched her hair and had a fiery energy that seemed to radiate off her.

"Can I help you?" I asked, feeling strangely disappointed that it wasn't Blake. Huh? That was a surprise.

"Hi. I'm Annette." The brunette stuck out her hand, and I found myself shaking it. "We're your neighbors. I live in that messy blue house with the white fence over there," she said, hooking a thumb behind her. "And this is Tilly and Cristina."

"Hi," chorused the blonde and the redhead.

"We wanted to welcome you… *back* to the neighborhood," said Annette as she spied over my shoulder to get a glimpse of the house. Not that there was much to see in the candlelight.

"Thanks," I answered, not sure what else to say. Obviously they knew who I was.

"And you're the mysterious Katrina Lawless,"

said the redhead named Cristina, confirming my suspicions.

"Kat," I corrected.

"And you're the owner of this… house." Annette was on the tips of her toes, trying to see the inside.

"It belonged to my late aunt. She gave it to me when she died. I just… haven't been back since. Maybe you met her?" I doubted it since my aunt was a real hermit and kept to herself. But I'd been away for so long, maybe she got lonely.

Annette shook her head. "I only got a few glimpses of her when she'd get her morning paper… before…"

"Before she croaked," supplied Tilly.

"So, you used to live here?" Cristina eyed me. "We all moved to Moonfell about the same time, ten years ago. Your aunt's house didn't look as bad back then. Now it's…"

"A disaster," I said. But it will be beautiful again. That was a promise.

"It's huge. The largest house on the block. I've always wanted to see the inside of it," said Annette. "Are you going to sell it? I mean, what's the plan?"

"Yeah, are you going to flip it and sell it?" asked Tilly. "I'm a Realtor. I can help you with that." She pushed up her breasts. "My clients are mostly male, but I'll make an exception for you."

I laughed. "Thanks, I think. Well, that's the plan. It might take a while, though. I have a feeling it's going to cost me a small fortune to make it beautiful again."

"And then some," said Tilly, nodding. "Six digits, easy," she added. "Prices have gone up."

My heart slumped. I didn't even have five digits in the bank. How the hell would I come up with enough money to renovate this place? Looked like I'd be here for another ten years.

"We've been to your parents' Samhain soirées every year," said Annette. "I don't remember ever seeing you there."

"That's because I wasn't." I was tired and not in the mood to discuss my family with a bunch of strangers. Fatigue made me cranky, and when I was cranky, I was rude.

"It's huge for just one person." Tilly stared at me. "Are you married?"

"Tilly." Cristina slapped her friend on the arm.

"Divorced," I said, not that it was any of their business. Why was I even sharing this?

Tilly stared at me for what would be construed as too long, too personal. "Single?"

"Possibly." Where the hell was she going with this?

"Tilly," Cristina snapped again.

Tilly shrugged. "What? I'm curious. She's pretty and single. That means she's competition."

I snorted. "You give me far too much credit."

"We saw you and Blake earlier," said Tilly, raising a perfectly manicured brow. She pressed her hands on her hips. "Hands off, he's mine."

I forced a laugh. "He's all yours." Me and Blake? Yeah, that was never going to happen.

"He's *not* hers," corrected Annette. "She's just been trying to get inside his pants for the last ten years."

Tilly smiled proudly. "I have. I totally have. And this year, I can feel it. It's going to happen. He's not with Claire anymore. And I call dibs."

Claire must have been the wife I'd heard about.

Cristina looked at Tilly. "You're not his type. Give up and move on to another warm-blooded male."

"You mean…" Tilly rubbed her hands sensuously over her body. "The hot, sexy type?"

"No. He's not into sluts," said Cristina with a smile.

I bit my tongue, expecting the witches to start fighting, but Tilly just smiled. "I'm not giving up. You'll see. By the end of this week, I'll have him on his knees. You just wait."

These were some strange witches.

Movement caught my eye, and I was glad for the distraction. A creature stepped out from the bushes— and from the streetlight, I could just make out its shape—a cat.

The cat's black fur was a matted mess with leaves sticking to it and clumps of dirt. It was thin, and it looked sickly, limping while holding its front left paw. Its yellow eyes gleamed in the dark like two tiny suns.

Annette looked over her shoulder to see what I was staring at. "Oh. There's that cat again. Poor thing. I think it's a stray. No one can get close to it."

"Don't touch it," said Tilly. "It looks like it has rabies."

I wanted to tell her that wasn't what an animal with rabies looked like, but I stopped myself. "It looks in really bad shape. It doesn't have owners? Is it some witch's familiar?"

Annette shook her head. "No. All the familiars are accounted for. We started seeing it three months ago. It wasn't limping then."

My heart ached at the sight of the poor animal. The fact that it was injured bothered me, but when I looked over at the cat again, it was gone.

"We came here to invite you over for some drinks," said Annette, taking my mind off the cat. "My house is a mess, but Cristina said we could all go to her place."

"That's right," agreed Cristina. "I make a mean martini. And my husband's away at the Broom of the Year Witch Conference."

"Right." Never heard of it.

The fact that they wanted to invite a total stranger into their homes, that they took the time to come over, told me that they might be the meddling type but still kindhearted as well.

I smiled. "Thanks, but I'm tired, and I have a lot of cleaning to do before the night is over." Plus, I had to go over my list of names and track down those not on the list. I wasn't going to bed anytime soon.

Tilly stepped up beside me and looked inside. "You sure you want to stay here? No one's lived here for years. Didn't your aunt die in here? Bet it's haunted. You know, there's a special buyer niche for haunted houses. And they'll pay. A lot."

"It's not haunted." However, I would have loved to see my aunt again. Even as a ghost, that would have been awesome. But I hadn't seen or felt any ghosts since my arrival.

"I have a guest room you could stay in tonight if you want," offered Cristina with a smile.

"Thanks, but I'm fine, really." I was surprised at how genuine her offer was.

Annette crossed her arms and looked up at the house like it was giving her the creeps. Maybe it was. "Just doesn't seem right to leave you here all alone in this big house."

I laughed. "Trust me. I like being alone." Hell, I thrived on it. Yet I just realized that some of my guard was down. I felt strangely comfortable around this group of witches. Like coming back and meeting up with old friends.

"Want to join our coven?" laughed Tilly. "Just kidding. We don't have one."

"But we should." Cristina stared at her friend. "I've been saying it for years. Just better that way. And for protection. We're stronger together, not apart."

I searched their faces. "Protection? Protection from what?"

Annette looked at her each of her friends before turning her attention back to me. "Helen told us why you're here…" She leaned forward and whispered,

"To investigate Tim's murder. She said you work for the Merlin Group."

"But you're not a Merlin," Tilly said, in more of a statement than a question.

I shifted my weight. "That's right. I just work for them. Are you suggesting that what happened to Tim might happen to you?"

Annette wrapped her arms around her middle. "There's a lot you don't know about this town."

"A lot of crap's been going down," said Tilly.

I leaned forward, interested. "Like what? Do you know anything that might help explain what happened to Tim?"

"A week ago, a teen disappeared," said Cristina. "His parents think he ran away, but I know he didn't. He wouldn't do that."

"And you know this? How?"

"I knew him," she continued. "He was a shifter. A groundhog and my gardener. He told me he wanted to open up his own landscaping business here in town. He wouldn't just leave like that. Without telling anyone."

"Why wasn't it reported?"

"He's eighteen. He can do what he wants. His parents think it's an act of rebellion. He's a ground-hog. They go through phases with the seasons."

I had no idea what that meant. "And you think his disappearance and what happened to Tim are connected?"

"We do." Annette rubbed her arms. "But it's not just that. Lately, there's been a strange smell in the air at night. Like sulfur, but stronger. And a heavy feeling of… energy. Negative energy. I don't know what else to call it. It makes you feel off… scared."

"And our powers get all out of whack," said Cristina. "Like if I want to use my stones to summon a ball of light—which is easy, by the way—I can't. But then, in a few hours, I can again. It's weird."

"We did a locator spell," said Tilly. "Annette did. She does them for me all the time to see where my exes are, who they're banging. And it didn't work. It was as though something was stopping us from seeing where he was."

"That is weird." I'd never heard of something that would disrupt the powers of a witch on a scale like this. If what they suspected was true, and another young male was missing, presumably killed, it was worse than I thought. "What was your gardener's name?"

"Samuel Caddel," answered Cristina. "His parents are oblivious. But I know something happened to him. I feel it in my witchy instincts."

I nodded. "I'll look into it." I'd have to call Jack and tell him about the possible connection with the dead body. The black van, the dead teen, and now the missing one, possibly dead, were connected. I didn't believe in coincidences, and I, too, felt it in my witchy bones.

Should I tell Blake? He was probably aware of Samuel's possible disappearance. Still, I'd probably get more out of the sheriff. I'd have to talk to him.

Looked like I'd have to pop by his office in the morning.

"Well, we should go," said Annette, stepping back. "But you're invited to dinner tomorrow… and I'm not taking no for an answer. Besides, it'll be a great opportunity for us to fill you in on our little town."

I wanted to object, but she had a point. "Sure. Okay."

Annette pointed a finger at me. "Six o'clock."

I watched, half relieved and half disturbed as the three witches walked back to their homes. I felt a cold draft coming from inside, and I shivered, shutting the door and turning around, happy to be alone again.

Except that I wasn't.

A shape stood in the foyer. Not a shape. An old lady, bent with age and leaning heavily on a wooden cane with an infectious smile. I knew that smile.

"Aunt Luna?"

CHAPTER 5

"Finally, I thought they'd never leave," said the ghost. She glared at me. "I've been waiting for two years for you to show up. What took you so long?"

I rubbed my eyes. "I'm losing my mind." I was tired from having cleaned the house for the last few hours without any food in me and was experiencing some sort of lapse in judgment. But when I looked over, the apparition, ghost, whatever you want to call it, was still glaring at me.

Despite the years that had passed since our last meeting, she looked exactly the same as I remembered.

Her eyes were the same hazel color as my mother's; she wore a small red top hat perched atop her curly pink hair; a stack of several plaid coats rested on her shoulders, and a pair of knee-high zebra-patterned boots completed the look. Her skin was deathly pale, but her teeth were straight and bright white, and her lips were colored with the same shade of red lipstick I recalled seeing every day two decades ago.

Even as a ghost, my Great-Aunt Luna had some serious style.

The air was thick with the smell of earth and the distant scent of burnt matches. I felt a shiver run down my spine. I'd seen a few ghosts over the years in my line of work. But I never had to *deal* with them, not in the sense that I had to perform some ritual to send them away.

"I was beginning to think you'd never come," said my aunt, and I detected a bit of sadness in her tone.

"But… what happened to you?" I asked, stepping closer to her and realizing I wasn't dreaming, and it didn't look like she was going away. "Why are you still here?" I wasn't an expert on ghosts, but I knew when a person passed, they went on to the "other realm," whatever that was. Rarely did they stay on this plane.

My aunt gave me a look, the same one she used to give me when she was annoyed with me. "This is my house. Why shouldn't I be here?"

I moved closer still, and I noticed the closer I was, the more solid she looked. Weird. "I know. But why haven't you *crossed* over? You know. Step into that bright light and all that."

My aunt leaned on her cane. "Because I'm *not* dead."

"What?"

"I'm not dead."

I shook my head. "I heard what you said. But… how is this possible?" I moved to stand before her and then poked her shoulder with a finger. "Holy shit. You're solid."

She slapped it away. "I'm not a ghost, you idiot."

My jaw kept snapping open, the words not formulating. "But you had a funeral? I got a call from the coroner to tell me that you had passed."

My aunt shrugged. "Petra owed me a favor."

"You faked your own death?" Holy crap. Only my Aunt Luna could pull off a stunt like that.

"I did," she said matter-of-factly as if it was the most obvious thing in the world. "Sylvia, that tramp, cried. It was fabulous." She turned on me. "You didn't come to the funeral."

"I didn't want to see my parents. Didn't think you'd mind since… you know… you were dead."

My aunt snorted. "True. But you missed a great deal of fun."

"You attended your own funeral?"

"I wouldn't miss it for the world."

"How?"

"Disguised as my cousin Tammy. I hadn't been out in public in over ten years, so no one recognized me. I'm a master of disguise, dearest. Your mother didn't even recognize me."

"Not surprised." I stared at her. I had so many emotions running through me at the moment that it was hard to pinpoint one. "Why would you do this?"

My aunt had always been a bit eccentric. Scratch that, she was the epitome of eccentricity.

My aunt slammed her cane on the hardwood floor, making me jump. "Because I needed you here."

"You could have called. We did call. Once a week."

"But you never came. Twenty long years, Katrina. I kept asking you to come, and you kept coming up with excuses about your work."

"Not excuses. My work is time-consuming."

"Too much to see your own aunt?"

Ouch. "You know why I didn't want to come back. The way my family... well... you know all about that."

"I do."

I sighed. "I'm here now." A bit late, but better late than never. At the deep frown on my aunt's brow, I added, "I'm sorry. I just never looked back. I made a new life for myself. A new career."

"Lawless Investigations, I remember," said my aunt, and I was surprised at the proud smile on her face. She was silent for a moment, though her red lips twitched. "It's not a good enough reason. Not for twenty years."

Guilt hit me hard. "Fine. I'm a selfish asshole. So you faked your funeral in the hope that I'd show up?"

She pointed her cane at me. "Now you're catching on." My aunt glanced around the hallway. "Though I am disappointed you waited until two years after my death to show up. I wasn't planning on letting my home deteriorate this way. I can't pay the bills if I'm dead. But I had to keep up with appearances."

"You being dead."

"A bit of cleaning and upkeep a few times a year would have been enough to keep it spiffy."

"I get it."

My aunt turned around and headed toward the back of the house. "Come," she ordered. "We have a lot to talk about."

I hurried to catch up. She was surprisingly fast for a witch her age.

"But you've been alone all this time?" I asked, feeling a pang of sympathy for my dear old aunt. Two years stuck in this house was a long time to be alone. She was right and had every reason to be angry with me. I should have come back years ago.

"Not entirely," she said, a mischievous glint in her eye. "I still trust a few people in this town. I've had a few midnight visits."

"What did you do for food?"

"The basement's packed with enough food to last me another ten years. I plan ahead."

"Clearly." Before I could ask her more about her "fake death" living arrangements, she said, "What happened to you? You look like shit."

"Thanks."

"You're so skinny. You're practically a praying mantis."

"Thanks again." I didn't want to have to bring up the many reasons why I hadn't been eating over the last year. The divorce hit me hard, not that I hadn't expected it. I had, but it still made me feel like a failure —unwanted and worse. I'd been depressed for months, and luckily, I'd managed to bring myself out of it.

"Eat," ordered my aunt. "Eat before you fall over and die. I haven't waited two years for you, only to have you die on me now."

"You died on me. So to speak."

"That's different. I'm old. Old people die. It's part of nature." My aunt gestured to the bag of groceries I'd gotten earlier. "I saw that you have bread, salad, and tuna, enough to make a tuna sandwich. I have a hundred cans of veggie chili in the basement. If you want rice, I can boil some water for you with my elemental fire until the electricity is back on. You did pay the bill. Right?"

"Yes." I moved over to the counter and grabbed the ingredients. My stomach rumbled, telling me to feed the beast. "I'll just make a sandwich. So, have you been watching me this whole time? You couldn't come out earlier?"

A mischievous gleam sparkled in her eye. "I could. But I wanted to see what you were going to do with the house."

"I'm going to fix it up."

"So, you've said."

I grabbed a plate and a bowl from the cupboard, the ones I had washed in cold water, and started to make my late dinner. "But... why didn't you call me? If I had known you were here... I would have come back."

My aunt sighed and looked sad again. "I don't think that's true." She grabbed a wooden chair from the small breakfast table and sat. "I thought for sure dying would have made you come, but even that didn't work."

Shame wrapped around my middle. I gripped the tuna can, staring wide-eyed at my aunt. I let out a sigh, feeling a turmoil of emotions hitting me all at once. "I'm so sorry. I should have come back. I'm a total jerk."

"Yes, you are."

I laughed. "Glad to see that you're the same old Aunt Luna."

"Being dead doesn't change a person. They're just dead."

"But you're not."

"I'm faux-dead and fabulous."

I laughed. "You're crazy." I stared at the tuna sandwich that I'd made with organic brown bread. I was hungry, but I just couldn't eat.

"Why aren't you eating?" asked my aunt.

"Damnit. I need to do something first." I grabbed the second tuna can and a plate, peeled the top, and dumped the tuna in water on it.

"What's wrong with the first one?"

"Nothing. This isn't for me." I made it to the back door in the kitchen and popped it open. The air moved behind me, and I turned to see my aunt standing in the doorway, watching me.

I stepped onto the stone patio. The moon gave

enough illumination for me to see the tall grass and surrounding bushes. And two glowing eyes.

I hadn't expected to find the cat right away, but I was glad I did.

"Here you go, buddy," I told it and placed the plate on the grass without making eye contact. I didn't want to scare the poor thing. I needed to build trust. Then I'd take it to the local healer.

I stood and made my way to the back door.

"You always had a thing for the strays," said my aunt with a smile.

"That's because I am one." I shut the door and stared out the small window. Sure enough, the scruffy black cat limped slowly toward the plate piled with tuna. And only when it started to eat did I let myself relax.

Smiling, I returned to my sandwich and ripped into it, only then realizing how hungry I was. I grabbed a water bottle and washed down my bite. "You mentioned work. You do realize that restoring the house is going to take time and money. Money that I don't have at the moment. I'm not saying I won't do it. I will. Trust me. It's just going to take time." And possibly years of contract work for the Merlin Group.

My aunt walked over to the same chair and let herself fall into it. "I wasn't talking about the house. But now that you've mentioned it, I'm glad you're finally going to do something about it."

I wiped my mouth with a clean towel. "I'm sorry. Back it up. What work?"

My aunt clasped her hands on her cane. A troubled expression marked her face. "The work that you need to do here. In this town."

I leaned my butt against the counter so I was now facing her. "You're not making any sense. What work? What do you mean?"

"There's evil here in Moonfell. A great evil," my aunt began. "It started to spread again two years ago. And every day, it grows stronger and stronger."

"Are you talking about the dead werewolf teen?" I didn't know how she would have heard about that. Unless she overheard the witches who were here earlier or her midnight friends kept her in the loop.

She nodded. "Yes. But it's far worse than that. This evil has been here for centuries. It showed itself twenty years ago, but for reasons unknown, it disappeared. And now it's back."

I furrowed my brows, trying to make sense of what she was saying. "What kind of evil are we talking about? Rogue mages? Crazed vampires? A curse?"

"Worse than that," she said gravely. "It's not just those isolated incidents. They are a part of it, yes. This force is seeping into the very fabric of this town, infecting everything and everyone in its path."

"What you're saying is that there'll be more deaths? More dead teens?" I stared at my aunt. "Do you know who's doing it? Who killed Tim?"

My aunt shook her head. "No. That I don't know." Her eyes traveled over my face. "There's so much you don't know. And it's been so long. It would have been better if you'd come to see me years ago."

"We've already established that I was an asshole. What does my not being here sooner have to do with Tim's death?"

"Have you been to see your parents?"

I was not expecting her to ask that. "No. And I don't plan on doing so either. The plan is to do my job, fix the house, and then leave." I regretted the words that flew out of my mouth when I saw the sorrow in my aunt's face. Damn. I had to better control my word vomit.

"I'm sorry," I tried again. "Obviously I'm not going to leave."

My aunt dismissed me with a wave of her hand. "That doesn't matter now. What matters is that you prepare yourself for what's to come."

"Can we skip the Obi-Wan Kenobi talk and get straight to the point?"

My aunt blinked. "You must rid Moonfell from the darkness."

I barked out a laugh. "I'm sorry. Don't you know who I am? You know I can't do magic the way others do. Hell, it's why my family ostracized me. Why they pretend they don't have a dud witch as a daughter. I'm not a Merlin, Aunt Luna. You know this. I just—"

"Work for them," she interrupted. "Yes, I know. What does that have to do with anything?"

"Uh… everything?"

My aunt was quiet for a moment. "You have magic in you. But it's not the same as other witches."

I laughed. "Because it's nonexistent."

"That's not true, and you know it."

"Fine," I answered, recalling some events where I was able to perform some of my different magic in front of my aunt. "So I can do magic. But not the kind of magic that is needed here. I can't even summon a demon. Trust me. I've tried."

My aunt's jaw dropped. "What is this? You tried to summon a demon?"

I shook my head, remembering that time when I was nineteen and decided I had to be a Dark witch if I wasn't a White witch. The only thing I managed to summon was a blast of my magic that destroyed the top attic I was renting. I'd lost everything in that stupid attempt.

"The point is, it's… different. It's why I try to keep it hidden." Because we all know people are afraid of the unknown.

My aunt leaned back into her chair. "Katrina, listen to me," my aunt began. "Might as well start at the beginning. I realized something when you were twelve years old. The time your powers started to manifest themselves."

"You mean the non-powers."

"I knew then that something was different about you. Different from your brother. Different from your parents."

"Amen to that."

"Be serious. This is serious."

"Sorry." I clamped my mouth shut, doing my best to look serious. But the truth was, it had taken me a decade to mold my magic into something I could use. My aunt didn't know, so I figured I'd let her talk.

My aunt frowned as she rubbed her knee. "You see, our family, on your mother's side, we come from a long line of Merlins. Protectors. And if I were twenty years younger, I would go after this darkness myself."

"I'm not a Merlin," I said. "Can I get you something for your knee?"

She shook her head. "But even witches age. And so does our magic." She looked at me. "But yours is strong, Katrina. Very strong."

I folded my arms over my middle. "What exactly are you saying?"

My aunt adjusted her hat. "That you have great power in you."

Feeling my stress levels increasing, I reached into my bag and grabbed my stack of gum. I popped one into my mouth. If my aunt knew it was nicotine gum, she didn't say a word.

"This darkness you speak of," I asked, chewing. "Does it have a name?"

My aunt nodded, looking grim. "It has many names. But you can call them The Forsaken."

"Sounds ominous enough. So, let's say I can defeat this evil. How do I go about it?" As a faux-Merlin, maybe it was part of my job.

"Find those responsible for the death of that young werewolf, and you'll find your answers."

"That's it? That's all you've got to say?"

My aunt lifted her shoulders in a casual way.

"What more do you want? I've been cooped up in this house for two years, and my knowledge of the outside world is quickly diminishing. Isn't that what you do now? Investigate?"

"It is." I sat there, chewing on my gum and pondering my next move. It sounded too simple just to find those responsible, but maybe my aunt was right. Maybe that was the key to defeating this evil force that loomed over us, according to her.

"Fine, I'll do it," I said with a determined nod. That was why I was here anyway, to find those responsible.

My aunt pushed to her feet with her cane. "Good. I think that's enough for tonight. I'll speak to you in the morning. I'm going to bed." She raised her cane at me. "In my own bed, thank you very much. I'd like my mattress put back."

"Yes. I'll do that, too."

After that enlightening conversation with my aunt, I returned her bedroom to its prior state, old dingy mattress included, and opted for the second largest bedroom in the house to claim as my own. It wasn't as big, but it had its own bathroom—a rarity in my world.

Sleep was slow to come. I stared at a crack in the ceiling for hours before my eyelids finally felt like they were made of lead, and I slept.

I dreamed of hot, sexy werewolves coming at me from every direction, wearing only leather loincloths to cover their junk. It was a very good dream. Too bad I didn't remember much of it when I woke up.

CHAPTER 6

I woke to the sound of the doorbell. I peeled my eyes open with a groan and realized that the air mattress had deflated, and I was now lying on a hardwood board. My entire body ached, especially my back.

"Wonderful."

The doorbell rang again.

"Luna!" I yelled, and then realized she wouldn't answer her door, seeing as she was faux-dead.

The sound of the doorbell reached me a third time.

"Keep your pants on. I'm coming!" I yelled, though coming from the second floor, I doubted the person abusing my doorbell could hear.

With my new aching back, I made it to the hallway and stubbed my toe on the baseboard.

"Motherfracker!"

I peeked into my aunt's room. The bed was made,

and there was no sign of my aunt. Maybe I'd dreamed the whole thing.

Finally, I limped all the way downstairs and pulled open the front door.

"What the hell do you want?"

Shit. It was the man-beast—I mean, Blake.

I glanced up at him, taking in his towering figure and chiseled features. He was dressed to impress, wearing a black leather jacket and tight jeans. The V-neck gray T-shirt showed off his muscles beneath the fabric in just the right way. Despite my annoyance at being awakened from my uncomfortable slumber, my heart fluttered slightly at the sight of him. But I quickly pushed those thoughts aside and scowled at him instead.

The sexy-as-sin sheriff had a strange smile on his face as his eyes traveled over my front to linger on my breasts.

Of course, I hadn't had the time to put on a bra.

And, of course, my nipples were rock hard, twin torpedoes standing at attention. Swell.

I covered the girls with my arms. "What is it?" I'd slept in my yoga pants. Thank god for small miracles. Greeting him in my underwear would have been mortifying.

"Did I wake you?" Blake still had that grin on his face. He looked pleased with himself.

"No, I was in the middle of doing my taxes."

He cocked a brow. "You're very cranky in the morning."

"So are a lot of people."

"You look tired."

"Long night." I probably looked like hell, and now that I hadn't brushed my teeth, I most definitely had the breath from hell, too. "Why are you here?" I asked, moving my face away from him so I wouldn't kill him with my morning breath.

"Did something happen?" he asked. Was that concern in his eyes?

"No." From the corner of my eye, an apparition appeared. No, not an apparition, my Aunt Luna.

"My goodness," said my aunt, and she hobbled forward, her cane loud as she made her way next to me. "He's grown up and filled out. He's even more handsome up close. Look at those muscles. Did you touch them yet?"

"No," I told her, shocked that she would say such a thing.

My aunt waved a hand at me. "He can't hear or see me. Only you. I've doused myself with a glamour. It's like being a ghost."

"Yeah, you said that," said Blake, thinking I was still talking to him.

Shit. Now, this was awkward. People talking to themselves was never a good sign, even in our paranormal circles. Hearing voices was bad.

"Mhhmm," I voiced.

"But, my, my, my," said my aunt. "He looks a lot like his grandfather at his age. He and I... well... we got it on a few times. You know, he was especially skilled with his tongue—"

I smacked my hands over my ears. "I can't hear this."

The sheriff's expression turned suspicious. "I haven't told you yet. Are you sure you're all right?"

"Peachy." Damn. If I wasn't careful, I'd come across as a crazy person. "Sorry. Long night."

"Yeah, you said that."

"It's the truth."

My aunt winked at me. "Does he like older women? You know, sex at my age is kicking death in the face while singing."

God help me.

"What's that smell? Like lavender or something?" The sheriff sniffed.

Shit. My aunt might have used a glamour to keep him from seeing and hearing her, but she forgot to hide her smell. I assumed she wanted to keep her faux-death intact. We hadn't discussed that part yet.

"My soap." I covered my breasts with my arms again. "What can I do for you, Sheriff?"

Blake's eyes rested on my lips. "I thought you should know. I found the owner of that black van."

I perked up. "And?" This was very good news. Even if the van wasn't involved in the case, we could scratch it off the list.

"It belongs to a guy called Rus Grove."

"You know him?"

Blake shook his head. "No. I'm on my way there to question him."

"I'm coming with you."

Blake's lips pulled into that smile again. "Like that?"

I frowned. "Give me three minutes."

Blake raised an eyebrow, a sly grin spreading across his face. "Three minutes? That's quite specific."

I rolled my eyes. "Maybe four." No time for a cold shower, hell no. But I needed to brush my teeth, put on a bra, and change my pants.

"Four, it is." Blake's eyes flickered down my body and back up again, lingering on my breasts. "But if you're in a hurry, I can help you."

I glared at him. "Fine, I'll be right back." I closed the door, trying to ignore the hammering of my heart.

"What's this about a black van?" asked my aunt.

"It was seen parked in front of Tim's house," I said, rushing past her and doing my best to climb the stairs with my toe still throbbing. "It might be nothing."

I hobbled to my bedroom and grabbed a clean shirt from my dresser. I pulled on a pair of jeans and a sweater, making sure to grab a bra. I didn't need a repeat of earlier, with my nipples poking through my shirt. Very distracting.

"Tell me about this van." My aunt appeared next to me.

"I don't know yet. That's why I'm going to have a chat with this Rus Grove."

My heart raced as I made my way to the bathroom and splashed cold water on my face. Then I brushed my teeth, trying to get rid of the morning breath.

I grabbed my bag and phone before glancing up at my aunt. "I'll see you later."

She gave me a look. "Where do you suppose I go?"

Right. I made my way back downstairs to find Blake was gone. When I emerged outside, I saw that he was waiting for me next to his black BMW SUV.

"Ready to go?" he asked.

"Yes."

"Let's take my ride," said the big man.

I thought about it for a second. I didn't think I'd be comfortable riding with him, and if I had to leave for whatever reason, I didn't like that I would be dependent on him.

"I'll follow you," I said, not waiting for him to argue as I popped open the door to my Jeep.

Blake looked at me for a beat but said nothing before he climbed into his vehicle. The engine roared as he pulled from the curb.

While I followed Blake through the streets of Moonfell, I couldn't help but replay the information I got from my aunt. I hadn't told Blake about this group called The Forsaken. It's not that I didn't believe my aunt. But she had been locked away in her house for two years. How much of that information was real fact, and how much might be an old lady's tales of boredom? I couldn't tell. And before I made a fool of myself to the town sheriff, I would wait until I could make sense of it all. I would look into this group right after we talked to the owner of that black van.

When Blake took the next right on Lament Lane, I felt my pulse race. South on Lament Lane was the bad part of town, if you will. I hadn't asked Blake for the address, and by the looks of it, he was leading me to a place where we were told never to go as kids.

Tombstone.

So, of course, I'd been a couple of times. And I almost didn't make it back.

You see, Tombstone was on the wrong side of the tracks. Literally, my Jeep jolted over the railroad tracks, officially taking me to the wrong side as I bounced in my seat while driving south on the cracked asphalt.

To the rest of Moonfell's paranormal community, Tombstone was the slums or a very poor and unwelcome place to live. To them, the neighborhood was spooky and rumored to be filled with assassins and ex-cons; no doubt, no one wanted to cross over.

Tombstone was the nesting place for all the wicked paranormals who didn't fit with the rest of the community. They were the rogue vampires and werewolves, the wicked shifters that would cut out your tongue just because they felt like it. It was also the hangouts for Dark witches and mages, where they'd sell you a love potion, but it turned out to be acid, and they'd laugh as you died a slow death.

The Dark fae also roamed there, just as beautiful and mystical as vampires and just as wickedly deadly. They loved to pray on the innocent, the naïve. Loved to play games with your head and feed you some of their food and drink until you were completely under their spell and mercy.

It was also rumored that this was a regular hangout for crossing demons, the demons that had dealings with this part of town. I'd never seen one, though.

I'd heard so many rumors over the years of some of our community venturing into Tombstone and never coming out. Or coming out, but they were never the same again.

The memory popped up of a young me trying to prove to the other teen witches that I was just as good as them, so I'd ventured here on a dare. I'd never forget that tattooed fae male who had grabbed me and tried to pull me into an alley.

"I'm gonna show you a good time, my pretty," he'd said.

I could still remember his rancid breath on my face, the smell of booze, and his nasty body odor, like someone who didn't believe in bathing.

It was the first time I'd realized I had magic. Real magic.

The fear and overwhelming panic had been the combination necessary to construct an explosion in me—a dark explosion.

It was the only reason why the fae, startled, had let me go.

Then... then I ran like hell out of there and never went back.

I'd been both frightened and relieved. Frightened

that I had power I didn't know how to control and relieved that I actually had some freaking power. Go me.

I was surprised Blake was leading us here, but I wasn't a scared seventeen-year-old anymore. I could handle myself.

Blake parked his SUV at the curb, and I did the same. I reached inside my bag, tore out a gum, and popped it into my mouth.

When I got out, I noticed how dark and gloomy the streets were, like the bright morning sky had suddenly cast over with dark, ominous clouds, making it nearly like it was nighttime. This wasn't natural. I was certain this was something the Dark mages did to keep the sunlight at bay.

The noxious smell of sulfur and diabolical magic filled the air. It seemed to be everywhere—wafting through the atmosphere, soaking the ground and trees with its presence, and surrounding us like an invisible cloak. The cacophonous voices of powerful entities echoed around us, and a taunting laugh floated by on the breeze.

When I pulled my attention around, I found Blake watching me.

"What?"

"We walk from here," said Blake as he neared. "It's not that far. Two blocks."

I nodded. "Lead the way."

"Stay close to me," said the sheriff. "And you'll be fine."

I gave him an annoyed look. "I can handle myself, thanks."

Blake opened his mouth to say something but shut it as he turned from me and started up the street. Wise man.

A male vampire gave me an alluring smirk and glanced at me suggestively. Then he made a rude gesture with his tongue.

Of course, I responded with equal rudeness and flipped him my finger, prompting a snicker from Blake.

The sheriff walked with that confident gait, his large shoulders swinging as he looked every passerby in the eye like he was daring them to do something.

I followed his very fine ass up the street, trying to keep my focus on the issue at hand and not his perfect posterior.

Paranormals stepped out of their shops, their homes, and the local pubs. It was like we'd triggered some silent alarm or something. Like they all came out to see the new blood. Us.

An eerie feeling of déjà vu washed over me as I glimpsed Tombstone's vibrant carnival-like atmosphere. A group of werewolves battled in the middle of the street while ethereal nymph dancers entertained the crowds who came to see the fight.

"So, how did you sleep?" asked Blake, his head slightly turned my way as he kept his eyes on the street, on the onlookers.

"Like a baby."

He snorted. "You're lucky that roof didn't fall on your head."

"I'm a lucky gal."

"Do you have a decent mattress, at least?"

"Absolutely," I lied. "Paid top dollar for it."

The short laugh told me that Blake didn't believe a word I said. It didn't matter. I didn't care what he thought of me. I really didn't.

The pavement sloped downward, revealing a warren of ramshackle buildings clustered together due to lack of space. One could find shops selling poisons, potions, and charms on the street. Those seeking forbidden magic, whether a dark spell or demonic incantation, knew they'd find it here.

I caught some of the witches' gazes—cold and unwelcoming—while their Dark magic hung in the air, recognizable by its earthy and vinegar aroma.

"This is it," announced Blake suddenly.

A sign above a brownstone building read GROVE AUTOSHOP.

Blake yanked the front door open and hauled me inside with him. I heard the soft click of a latch as he closed the door behind.

The shop was mammoth in size, like a warehouse. Tall shelves stocked with a variety of auto parts and tools rose to the ceiling. The walls were pale yellow. The whole interior was dimly lit, and lanterns hung from the ceiling, casting a yellowish glow on the scattered parts and tools like pale shadows.

I breathed in a mixture of oil, metal, dust, and

burnt electricity that smelled of ozone. The thick scent of body odor and musk clouded the room.

A shiver ran down my spine as I felt a sudden chill that had nothing to do with the October air.

Sitting behind an old wooden desk at the back of the shop was a tattooed man with more piercings around his face and ears than in your local jewelry shop.

My heart skipped a beat. I recognized him. He might have a few more wrinkles and streaks of gray in his oily, shoulder-length hair. But it was him—the same fae who tried to take me all those years ago.

CHAPTER 7

Was this a coincidence? I had no idea. But the frown on the fae's face and the look of indifference when he moved past me told me that he didn't recognize me. it was clear that he recognized Blake, though.

"Get the hell out of my store," barked the fae. He snarled, revealing his sharp canines. Oh, yeah. Faes had similar teeth as vampires. But when they bit you, it was most likely because they wanted to see what you tasted like, not to drink your blood.

He stood up slowly. Tight muscles showed behind that dirty black tank top, and his pants were ripped at the knees. Every finger had a gaudy ring wrapped around it, and gold chains fell around his neck, too many to count. His hair was a shaggy mass of thick, black waves with streaks of gray. It was hard to tell a fae's age since they aged very slowly, again like vampires. He looked like he was in his early forties, but he could be past his hundredth birthday.

The fae's posture was such that he was ready to pounce, his muscles bulging like a jaguar about to spring from a tree. His dark eyes stared up at Blake.

The stench that came off the fae was a mix of BO and various bodily fluids. It had the hairs on the back of my neck stand on end. I'd never forget that smell.

Blake seemed to notice my tension. He looked at me with a semi-worried frown. I shook my head and ignored him, my eyes focused on that dirty bastard.

"You Rus Grove?"

The fae narrowed his eyes at the werewolf. "Yeah."

"Do you own a black van? KDE 3314?" questioned Blake.

The fae's dark eyes flicked to me, and for a moment, I thought he might have recognized me. But then his face had that same indifferent look about it again.

"Yeah, what about it?"

I perked up at this new information. Was this oily bastard involved with Tim's death?

"I'm investigating a murder, and your vehicle was seen at the victim's house," said Blake. I noticed how he excluded me from this investigation. It ticked me off. "Where were you two nights ago between ten and two in the morning?"

The fae hissed out a wet laugh, like someone who'd been smoking since they were a ten-year-old kid. Good thing I was trying to quit.

"Why should I tell you anything?" spat Rus.

"Because I'm the sheriff."

"Orik is the boss around here. Not you."

Orik? I never heard of him, so I committed that name to memory.

Blake took a step forward, a show of strength. "Where were you?" he asked. "Don't make me ask you again."

The fae mumbled something under his breath, and I felt a cold pulse of energy.

"Careful. He's drawing up magic," I told Blake. Yeah, the fae had magic, too. Magic that could take away your life force from you bit by bit, making you their servant for however long they desired.

The big man didn't seem fazed by the fae's threat. Instead, he stepped closer, and a wicked, terrifying smile spread over his face. "You will tell me. It's just a matter of whether I beat it out of you or you tell me willingly. Up to you."

The fae's face wrinkled in anger. "You're nobody here. No one gives a shit about you or your rules. You touch me, and you'll die."

Blake rolled his shoulders. "We'll see about that."

"Fuck you," spat the fae. "Fuck you and your bitch. I ain't telling you nothing."

Okay, now why the hell did he have to call me that? "Do you want to tie him to the chair and torture him?" I asked Blake. I had my own ways of interrogating suspects. Just not sure it was the way Blake did it in Moonfell.

A smile spread over Blake's lips. "Maybe."

In a blur, the fae produced a blade. "I'm gonna cut you."

"Not if you're unconscious," growled Blake.

"Hang on," I said, chewing. "We need him conscious. Remember? We have some questions that need answering."

The sound of the door opening turned me around. Three men, or rather, three more male fae, stepped into the store.

"You were saying?" goaded Rus, smiling victoriously at his backup. "You gonna regret coming here, *boss*."

My pulse raced at the three male fae who stepped forward. Their postures were bent, and they moved with animal swiftness, their faces pale and eyes a hungry black. Just like the owner of this shop, their clothes were marred with dirt and their hair hung in oily strands.

"Don't you people believe in showers?" I asked, totally grossed out.

"Kill them!" ordered Rus, flicking his knife at us.

I planted myself, not sure about how much of my power to show. This was a small town. The more people knew about my magic, the worse it would be for me. However, in this place, I couldn't draw much. But then again, I wasn't about to let these dirty bastards kill me.

But then I didn't have to.

In a flash, Blake pushed me behind him, none too gently, and I went sailing into the wall. *Ouch.*

My head smacked hard on something solid, and I swallowed my gum on impact.

Nice.

As I pushed off, I could see and feel power radiating from Blake, a white haze emitting from him.

I also saw his large canines the size of kitchen knives and claws the size of my fingers. It was like he was in between his beast and his human form, whichever form that was.

He took on the three faes at the same time, and he looked excited about it, like he'd been waiting all day for a fight. With his eyes intent, he snarled and thrashed at them with his claws. The faes shifted like shadows through the darkness, their movements rapid, reminding me of the way vamps moved.

But Blake was just as fast as them. Perhaps faster.

And for a larger male, that was seriously impressive.

Blake launched himself at the nearest fae in a blur of limbs and fangs as he crashed into his enemy with ferocious strength. With an earth-shaking collision, the massive male and the fae met in battle, unleashing their hatred and sharp claws.

I froze for a second, flabbergasted as Blake flew sideways, evading the talons of a mighty fae with a shaved head and muscles like Arnold Schwarzenegger. He snarled, causing his canines to shine in the light. He spun around and threw a solid kick in the chest of the bald fae, knocking him down.

But the other two charged. A cacophony of cries filled the air, a discordant blend of roars and screams. The wails thundered through my body, sending shivers of both fear and fury down my spine.

The fae were unrelenting, not giving Blake the opportunity to take control of the situation.

I was about to move in to intervene, but before I could, another fae somersaulted through the air and face-planted into Blake's chest. He stumbled backward yet managed to snatch hold of the fae's leg. With a snap of his arms, he sent the fae tumbling forward and smacked him hard on the side of his head. The fae's eyes rolled up, and he collapsed.

I was so enthralled with Blake's fighting skills that before I realized what was happening, something solid hit me across the jaw. The blow knocked me back, and black stars plagued my vision for a second.

Ow.

"Stupid bitch," spat the owner of the shop. "I'll teach you to come here uninvited."

I wiped the blood from my nose, blinking the tears from my eyes. "Doubt it."

I backed away and debated whether or not to use my magic. Blake was occupied at the moment. He wouldn't see. But that damn dirty fae was already there. He was dirty, stinky, yes, but fast.

I felt the heat of his breath on my face as he closed in on me. Memories of that night all those years ago came flashing back. The fear I felt, which I'd never felt before in my entire young life. I was alone and scared out of my mind. I'd never wanted to experience that kind of fear ever again.

I attempted to dodge his hit, but he was too quick. His punch landed in my side, and I flew into the air, eventually crashing onto the ground. An aching sensation raced through my body, and I fought for breath.

I screeched as the fae plummeted right on top of me, trapping me beneath him. I could barely breathe as his mass compressed my chest. He may have looked thin, but the bastard was heavy. Desperately, I thrashed around, trying to free myself from his grip. His face was close to mine, and his hot breath singed my skin as his eyes burned with a desire to kill me.

Yeah, not going to happen.

Rage was a useful emotion when it came to my magic. It was the match that lit the fire inside me, and I welcomed it.

I tapped into my magic, feeling its hard but pliable substance inside me. Straining, I reached out with all my might, pushing beyond the physical limits of my body to grab hold of those waiting shadows—my buddies. And as I did, I felt a wave of power surge through me like a river of warmth cascading through my veins. The shadows were mine now. Though limited during the day, this warehouse had enough for what I needed to do.

I pulled on my shadows and pushed out.

A blast of shadow energy hit the fae, and he sailed off me.

I rolled to my feet. "Told you it wasn't going to happen." I looked over as the fae struggled to stand. Fury flashed on his face, but something else flickered in his gaze. Recognition.

His eyes widened. "You!" he said. "It's you. You're the one."

Shit. He recognized me.

He bared me his teeth like a beast. "I'll kill ya, witch bitch."

"I don't think so."

A strangled cry came out of his throat—maybe it was a battle cry, I couldn't tell—as he rushed forward.

I could use my magic again, but it would be harder to control it this time. Whenever I released just a bit, it was as though the magic wanted out. Wanted more. I couldn't risk it. Not when Blake was so close.

So, I did the only other thing I could.

When the fae was close enough, I kicked him in his man berries as hard as I could.

He let out a yelp and crashed to the floor.

"What happened to him?"

I turned to the sound of Blake's voice, seeing his canines and claws retracted.

"He's suffering from a bit of penile dysfunction."

When I looked over the sheriff's shoulder, the three faes were splayed on the ground, unconscious.

I blinked. "What happened to them?" Truly, this guy knew how to fight and clearly enjoyed it. I liked it.

He rolled his shoulders and flashed me a smile. "Morning workout."

I laughed and walked over to the owner of the

shop, still hunched on the floor in pain. "Let's try this again. Shall we? Where were you two nights ago?"

"Fuck you," spat the fae.

Blake reached down, grabbed him by the neck, and shoved him into a chair. "Tell us. Or I'll break every bone in your body slowly, and I'll make sure you don't heal properly."

I whistled. "So violent." It was great.

The fae snarled, blood dripping down his chin. "I should have sliced that pretty throat of yours all those years ago."

Blake snapped his attention at me, but I kept my eyes on the fae. "I haven't had my morning coffee yet. And you know what happens when I don't? I get a little crazy. Crazier than my friend here." I leaned forward, pouring a bit of my magic through me, enough for the fae to sense it. "Tell us."

I really didn't expect the fae to talk and was surprised when he started to blab. Guess he appreciated the bones he had.

"I was here in my shop all night," said the fae.

"Bullshit," said Blake.

The fae pointed to the group on the floor. "I'd asked my friends to tell you, but they can't talk right now."

"Why were you spying on the Masons? Did you know you were going to kill Tim?"

The fae frowned. "Never heard of them."

Now I was getting pissed. "Your van was seen parked out front of their house two days ago."

"I rented out the van," said the fae. "I wasn't driving it."

For some strange reason, I believed him. I looked at Blake, seeing the same resolution in his gaze.

"Who did you rent it to?" asked the sheriff.

The fae started to laugh. "I ain't telling you shit."

Faster than I would have thought possible, Blake had the fae's neck in his hands. "Tell me. I won't ask again."

I saw real fear shimmering in the fae's eyes. "Don't know. They paid in cash. That's all I know."

"Can you describe them?" I asked.

Blake let go of his neck, and the fae replied, "Paranormals. The female, I remember. Witch bitch like you." His eyes roamed over my body, and I felt a chill roll up my back. "I will find you again, sweetheart. And when I do—"

Whack.

The rest of his words were lost with the thump of Blake's fist as the fae's head lolled forward.

"Well. That was fun," I said, walking back toward the door. The faster I got out of this place, the better. I felt like I needed to shower. Yup. A nice *hot* shower when I got home. Crap. No electricity. No hot shower. Bummer.

"We know that black van was involved," said Blake as the door to the shop closed behind him, and we moved toward our vehicles.

"We don't have names, but we know they're witches or mages," I said, feeling eyes on me from every dark shadow on this street. "I can work with that." Work with the list Helen had given me, but I felt like this group was the undisclosed kind. They weren't registered on any list. "They rented that van so they wouldn't leave any traces." And paid cash. It meant they were organized. They'd planned this.

"I'll have a team check it for prints. I doubt they left any, but it might be worth a try."

I nodded. "Yeah." I looked at Blake, wondering if I should tell him what my aunt said about The Forsaken, but then I thought better of it. Not until I had more proof than the ramblings of an old lady.

Blake was eyeing me, and I knew what he was going to ask before he did. "Did you know that fae? He seemed to know you."

I shook my head. "No. Never seen him before." I didn't feel good about lying to him, but I wanted to keep as much as possible about myself private.

The less he knew, the better.

"I have one of those faces," I said, hoping he'd drop the subject. I moved to the door of my Jeep. "Well, thanks for the tip." It had been extremely useful, but I wasn't about to tell him that.

"You're welcome," said Blake. The sound of a remote car door lock rang as he unlocked the doors to his SUV. "And I'll expect the same in return."

"How's that?"

"You discover anything I'd like to be told."

Right. "Seems fair."

He watched me a moment longer and then climbed behind the wheel of that large SUV.

Following his example, I slipped into the driver's

seat of my Jeep, locked the doors for good measure—you never knew in this neighborhood—and started the engine.

Coming here had been useful. Blake's intel had been correct.

But it left me with more unanswered questions.

CHAPTER 8

I didn't drive straight home. First, I stopped by to get some more supplies and some cat food for my little friend at the local grocery shop, The Produce Stand. I was thankful no one paid any attention to me. Then I drove to the mayor's office to speak with Helen, but she was out on an errand and wouldn't be back for another few hours, according to her secretary, a male shifter with misaligned eyes, his right eye on me while his left turned outward and stared at something off to the left. Creepy as hell.

By the time I arrived at my aunt's house, it was half past three in the afternoon.

I dropped my grocery bags on the front porch and made my way to the backyard, where I'd seen the cat.

The plate I'd left was still there. It looked licked clean, and I felt a pang in my heart. Poor little guy. As soon as I got him or her used to me feeding it, I'd try to trap it and bring it to our town healer. We didn't have vets like humans did, but we had different healers that specialized in different species. Some specialized in paranormals, witches, and vampires. And some with shifters and weres, those with a more of the "animal" type disposition, which was what I needed. And if my memory served me well, Dr. Carter was one of those shifter healers. Let's hope he was still around and hadn't retired.

Using the same plate, since it was clean, I ripped the metal lid off the can of wet cat food I'd gotten and dumped out the entire contents.

"Come on, buddy," I said to the bushes. "There's lots more. And it's grain-free. Yum." I waited another few minutes, and seeing that the cat was nowhere to be found, I straightened and headed back around the front of the house.

I unlocked the door and pushed it open. Then I looped the grocery bags with my fingers and waddled inside. I kicked the door behind me but misjudged the distance, resulting in a half kick, so the door stayed half open.

"Screw it." I made my way to the kitchen. "Aunty Luna? I'm back. Back with some information about that black van." I dropped the bags on the kitchen counter.

"The electricity is back," said a voice behind me.

"Ah!" I whirled around. "Don't do that."

My aunt shrugged. "Why? Aren't ghosts supposed to scare people?"

"But you're not a ghost."

"I feel like a ghost."

"So, the electricity is back?" Not waiting for her to answer, I hurried over to the wall and turned on the kitchen light switch. "And then… there was light."

A buzzing sound came from one of the four ceiling lights, and a warm yellow glow spilled from it.

"Well, one out of four isn't bad," said my aunt, staring at the ceiling.

"No. It means the bulbs need to be changed. You know what this means?"

My aunt blinked. "That you've finally paid the bill?"

"Hot water!"

"I've always said you were a strange one," said my aunt as I ran over to the sink and turned on the hot water faucet. I ran my fingers under the cold water.

Three… two… one…

"Damn. Still cold."

"What did you expect? It'll take several hours for the hot water tank to fill up again."

I turned off the faucet. "I'll wait."

"Whose cat is that?"

I turned around. The same black cat, dingy and looking like it had lived on the streets its whole life, sat at the entrance of the kitchen. It saw me and started to limp forward.

"How did it get in?" asked my aunt.

"I left the front door open."

"Oh dear, it looks in a bad way, Katrina. You need to take it to Dr. Carter."

"Is he still working as a healer?"

"Of course he is," said my aunt. "Well, I think so."

I moved carefully toward the cat, slowly, so as not to frighten it. "Hey, buddy," I said in my animal voice I used when speaking to dogs or cats, which was a high-pitched sort of girly voice. No judging. "You don't look so good." I knelt on the floor next to it. "We need to get you some help."

I reached out and scratched the poor animal's head.

And that's when things got weird.

The cat let out an odd meow that sounded strangely like a mix between an animal and a human voice.

And then the cat began to glow.

"What in the cauldron's name is happening?" shrieked my aunt.

"Hell if I know," I shrieked back.

The cat seemed to brighten, radiating an internal light that filled the space until his shape became fuzzy around the edges. My eyes burned, and I looked away from the sudden brightness. In just a few moments, the cat's body began to transform.

The cat's fur moved in a rippling way, making its features appear stretched and distorted. Its head grew wider, its body longer, and its tail shorter as it let out a low growl. In the blink of an eye, it was covered with dark fur. It snarled menacingly before a crunching noise broke the silence, signaling the breaking of bones.

And then, I wasn't staring at a tiny stray cat. I was

ogling a six-foot-two man with deep, penetrating brown eyes and ruffled dark blond hair, framing a strong face and full mouth that seemed to curl into a frown. The handsome face was paired with a chiseled body, long and slender, the muscles cut and defined, his abdomen rippling with a six-pack. But thin… way too thin.

"Cauldron help us. It's a boy!" My aunt clapped as though she'd been told one of her closest friends had just given birth.

"It's a man." This was not the body of a boy. "A *very* naked man."

Said naked man opened his mouth to say something. He staggered forward, his knees wavered as though his legs couldn't support his weight, and he crashed to the floor.

Crap. I rushed forward, grabbed a fistful of the tablecloth, pulled it off the table, and used it to cover him.

"But why is he here?" My aunt loomed over my shoulder.

Good question. I glanced at the man, the werecat, and saw that he was shaking. "Be right back." I pushed off and rushed into the den just off the front entrance. I grabbed the dust-covered but still in good condition wool throw my aunt had knitted, along with a throw pillow from one of the armchairs, kicked the front door closed, and hurried back. I covered him with the throw and gently tugged the pillow under his head.

"Good thinking." My aunt tapped my shoulder with her cane.

The stranger blinked a few times, like he was waking up from a dream, his focus far away.

"What's your name?" I tried, searching his face.

The man, the werecat, shook his head. "I... I can't... remember."

"That's not good," voiced my aunt, concern etched her tone.

"Yeah, I thought so." My eyes traveled over to his left arm. A nasty red and purple bruise wrapped around his forearm, and it was bent unnaturally. It looked broken. "What happened to you?" When he said nothing, I tried, "What's the last thing you remember?"

The werecat's face twisted like it was painful to try and recall his memory. "Dash," he said. "I think that's my name."

"Dash. Okay, well, that's something. I think your arm is broken." It looked like a bad break. It was swollen and bruised, and I worried the nerves might be damaged by the way his left hand was limp.

Dash tried to lift his arm but winced. "I think... you're... right."

"And you don't remember what happened to you?"

The werecat shook his head. "No. It's like... just a blackness. I can't... remember."

So it appeared that this werecat suffered from amnesia and wandered around until someone let him in, or rather until someone left the door open.

"Why haven't you shifted before? Why wait?"

The werecat stared at me, and it was hard not to look away from those unsettling eyes. "I didn't remember that I could. I thought I was just a cat."

Damn. My aunt and I shared a look. A werecat that didn't know it could shift to its human form was a sign of a curse. My witchy instincts told me something had happened to Dash, and he was cursed or hexed. Cursed to spend the rest of his life as a cat and to starve to death come winter.

"So, if you didn't remember, how did you happen to change now? And why here? At my house?"

"*My* house," corrected my aunt.

"You gave me food," said Dash. "No one else gave me food. They just… chased me away. After I ate, I felt… different. I started to remember."

I leaned back on my heels. "Do you know of a curse or a hex that stops working when a shifter eats?" I asked my aunt, who, to me, was as knowledgeable in spell work as the entire Merlin database.

She was silent for a moment, but I could see that big, witchy brain of hers working behind those eyes. "It's not about eating the food," she said finally, and both Dash and I stared at her. "It was about showing kindness. A good deed. Offering food to a scruffy stray cat broke the curse. Well, at least it seems to have lifted part of it."

"The part where he remembered he can shift back into a human," I said, but not all the amnesia. Cursing another paranormal in that way was illegal. We had laws and regulations to abide by. Otherwise, everyone would be cursing their neighbors for not picking up after their dog's business on their front lawn. You'd pay a fine for the hex or the curse, and if it was bad enough, you'd do jail time. This one was a jail-time kind of curse.

I wondered if what had happened to Dash was connected to Tim's death and what was happening to the town, according to my aunt. If someone was willing to use an illegal curse on him, maybe it was.

"I have a potion that can heal broken bones," said my aunt. "I might be able to help you with your memory, too. I can whip up a counter-curse, but that will take time. A few days to get it right."

"I'd be grateful if you could heal my arm," said Dash.

My aunt gave a grunt in response. She turned to me. "You haven't cleaned out my potions cupboard, I hope." My aunt stood next to a tall cupboard that reached the top of the twelve-foot ceiling.

I pushed to my feet. "I haven't gotten there yet. It was next on the list," I teased.

"If you threw any of my potions out, I would have strangled you."

I believed her.

I watched as my aunt grabbed a few things off the shelves and proceeded to the kitchen island, where she dumped her supplies.

"You're a witch?" asked Dash, curiosity high in his expression as he pulled himself up to a sitting position with some effort.

"I most certainly am," answered my aunt proudly.

"Have been for these past ninety-seven years. Give me that big iron pot," she ordered, pointing to the rack above our heads.

"Yes, ma'am." I grabbed the pot and handed it to her.

Dash narrowed his eyes. "You don't look a day past seventy."

My aunt straightened. "Why thank you, Dash. I knew I liked you from the first time I laid eyes on you." My aunt dumped some ingredients into the pot.

"You just met him."

My aunt ignored me as she sprinkled a blue powder into the mix, and I heard a small popping sound. Next, she poured some green liquid from a container, moved the pot over to the stove, and turned the knob on.

"And you?" asked Dash. "Are you a witch, too?"

"In a way. And in many ways, I'm not."

"Don't listen to her, Dash. She's a witch. She's my grandniece, so I know." From a small leather pouch, my aunt pulled out what looked like small bones.

"Are those bones?" I asked, a little taken aback.

My aunt glared at me. "How do you suppose I grow back bones? With straw? I need bones to mend the broken ones. Like a glue."

"Right." No idea that's how it was done. And I didn't want to know what bones belonged to what creature.

As I watched my aunt preparing whatever potion was required to heal bones, I couldn't help but feel anxious and worried about what was happening. I needed to solve Tim's murder soon and catch those responsible. And now I had Dash to think about. I had to find out what had happened to him.

Feeling a bout of stress coming my way, I hurried over to my bag and yanked out my stack of gum. I broke the package, popped one into my mouth, and started to chew.

"Those things will kill you," shot my aunt. "Do you even know what's in them?"

"Nicotine," I replied. Lots and lots of nicotine. "It's better than smoking." I had no idea what I was saying. I just needed something for my craving. I hated that I'd developed an addiction to cigarettes, but there you had it. I wasn't perfect. Far from it.

"It's not."

"You're trying to quit smoking?" asked Dash. His face was very pale and pasty.

"Yeah. You look like you need to eat more." I grabbed the chicken wraps I'd bought earlier and a water bottle and gave them to him. "Here. Eat this. It'll give you some more strength." And from what I knew about potions, it was better to take them when you had something in your stomach.

Dash regarded me with those intense brown eyes. "Thank you. Why are you being so kind to me? You don't know me."

"Because she loves to help strays," said my aunt, stirring her pot. "You should have seen her as a kid. Every week, she'd come to my house with a new pet project. There was the three-legged dog, the white cat without a tail, and then that blind frog."

"Thanks, I think he gets the picture," I said, feeling a flush on my face. I didn't want to talk about me right now. We had more important things to discuss.

My aunt mumbled a few words of an incantation as she kept stirring, and I wondered if she could still do potions at her age.

A sudden blast of blue light came from the pot.

Guess that was a stupid question.

"It's almost ready," my aunt called over her shoulder. "It just needs to cool down for a minute or so."

While I waited for my aunt's potion to cool, I decided to fill her in on the black van and its owner. I could have pulled her aside and told her in confidence since Dash, a stranger, was on the floor, but seeing as he'd been a cat for at least a few months, I didn't consider him a threat in my investigation.

"I told you," she said after I'd shared everything. "It's The Forsaken. Mages rented that van, and they killed that boy. I'm telling you."

I nodded. "Maybe you're right."

"Of course I'm right. Here. Drink up." My aunt walked over to Dash, one hand on her cane and the other clasped around a small glass. She tipped the glass with blue liquid at the werecat.

"Looks delicious," said Dash, a frown on his face, and I had a feeling we were getting a glimpse of the real him.

"Drink it up. Every last drop," instructed my aunt.

Doing as he was told, the werecat tipped the glass to his lips and drank the entire contents of the potion. He winced. "Just as delicious as I suspected," he added with a cough.

"Good boy." My aunt snatched the glass and moved back to her stove.

I watched as Dash's face started to get some color back, and then the flick of his eyebrows shot up as he stared at his left arm. I could see a soft, bluish glow emanating from his skin where the break was the worst. Then I heard a sudden pop, like the sound of a bone popping back into place.

Yikes. Glad it wasn't me.

"I can move my arm," said Dash, wiggling his fingers and bending his arm to test it.

I smiled. "I'm glad we could help." I yanked out my phone from my bag. "Smile," I told Dash, and before he could say no, I snapped a picture of his face. When he looked at me with narrowed eyes, I said, "I'm going to ask around if anyone recognizes you. Hopefully, you're from this town."

"And if I'm not?" asked the werecat.

"Then we'll figure it out," I told him, stuffing my phone into my pocket. "Stay here. Don't go anywhere. Not until we have more answers to what happened to you."

Dash nodded. "Okay."

"I might have some yoga pants and a T-shirt that

would fit you for now," I said. "I'll get you some spare clothes on the way back."

"Where are you going?" asked my aunt.

"To a place I know I'll get some answers."

There was only one place in town I knew where I'd get those answers.

And that was at The Blue Demon.

CHAPTER 9

The Blue Demon was a local favorite hangout. It was a bar and grill where you could get an order of cheeseburger and fries with a pint of beer. Well, it was the last time I was here.

I parked my Jeep at the curb and got out.

A painted sign with faded letters that read THE BLUE DEMON hung over a wood door that might have been painted blue once upon a time, but it was now gray with scratches and boot marks, like a pack of wild cats had attacked it. I pulled open the door and walked in.

The restaurant had all the usual scents of a human diner. The smell of fried food and steamed coffee wafted from the kitchen behind the bar, but there was also the lingering scent of alcohol, sweat, and old spilled beer.

Just like you'd see in a regular human diner, booths were laid out next to the windows with tables and chairs filling out the rest of the space. Men and women, friends and family, hung over tables and booths, shoving pasta, burgers, and fries into their hungry mouths.

On the left side of the room, a long, polished wooden bar spanned the wall with an array of tumblers, rum bottles, whiskey jugs, and vodka decanters decorating the surface. The bar and columns were interwoven with intricate carvings of devilish battles between paranormals.

Seeing as it was still early in the evening, the night crowd hadn't shown up yet. But that didn't matter. The one I needed to speak with was there.

Kolton. The owner of the diner and a werewolf.

I spotted him drying a glass behind the counter.

I trod carefully around a group of werewolves, avoiding any chance of accidentally brushing against them and setting off their quick tempers. One with brown hair and a leather jacket had the nerve to flare his nostrils as he sniffed me.

I kept my pace steady and my emotions in check. The last thing I wanted was to get into a fight with these guys. After all, I had a reputation to maintain.

I reached the bar, pulled out one of the empty barstools, and sat.

"What can I getcha?" asked Kolton as he moseyed near me. He looked exactly like I remembered him, just with a few more wrinkles around his eyes and streaks of gray at his temples. He was still the strapping, handsome black man with muscles to go around and a chest as wide as a fridge.

"Beer. Whatever you have on tap," I said, reaching for my phone and wallet.

I swept my gaze around the bar as Kolton poured me a pint of light beer. I spotted faces staring back. Hell, they were *all* staring at me. Guess they knew I wasn't a regular.

Kolton set my beer on a napkin in front of me. "That'll be six dollars."

I paid the man and took a sip of beer. "Mmm. Good. Heineken?"

"That's right." That drew a small smile from the owner. "Where are you from? You're not from around here."

I smacked my lips together, trying not to think about how well a cigarette would go with that beer right now. "Actually, I am from here. I've just been away for a long time."

"Why'd you come back?" Kolton was surveying my face like he was trying to recall who I was and if I'd ever been in his restaurant. Or maybe he was just wary of strangers.

"Work." I tapped my phone and showed him the picture of Dash. "Does he look familiar to you?"

Kolton stared at the screen of my phone. "Sure. That's Dash."

Relief flooded my body. Good. That meant he was from this town. "What can you tell me about him?" The more I knew about Dash, the better it would be for him and the closer I'd be to finding out what exactly had happened. It wasn't part of my job per se at the moment, but I was very curious about who would put an illegal curse on him like that and why. I wanted to find out.

Kolton eyed me suspiciously and folded his thick arms over that ample chest. "I don't give out information to strangers."

"I'm actually working a case." I grabbed my wallet, looking for one of my cards, and then remembered that Blake had taken my last one. Damn. Now, I looked like a fool, an unprepared fool. "I'm out of cards." I looked back at Kolton, and he looked like he was debating tossing me out on my ass. "I'm an investigator. Lawless Investigations. The Merlin Group in New York hired me to look into the murder of Tim Mason."

Kolton's lips parted at the mention of my name. "You're a Lawless?"

"Unfortunately. I'd thought about changing my name, but I knew my aunt would have turned in her grave." Might as well go with her being dead and all.

Kolton pressed his large hands the size of plates on the bar and leaned forward. His scent of musky aftershave filled my nose. "I can see the resemblance. You look like your mother."

"So I've been told."

"You look nothing like your father."

"Music to my ears."

He leaned forward another few inches and sniffed. If I'd been a human, I'd have been totally insulted. But as a so-called witch, I knew he was only trying to get my scent, my paranormal scent.

"You've got that Lawless mark on you," he said,

seemingly satisfied with my answer. "Why haven't I seen you before in my diner?"

"Well…" I wiggled in my seat. "I have been here before, but I was seventeen. A long time ago." I wasn't worried about my brother seeing me. He would never step foot inside The Blue Demon. It wasn't sophisticated enough for him.

The sound of scraping wood turned my attention around to a male with a forgettable face and allure. I couldn't get a good read on him through the cigarette smoke that surrounded him. It was distracting me. He pulled out the stool next to me and sat. The only thing I noticed was his hair, like he hadn't washed it in a few months.

"I'll have another," said the stranger, motioning to his empty glass of beer.

I watched as Kolton filled the male paranormal's glass with beer. He came back and placed a bowl with some peanuts in front of me.

"So, you're an investigator," said Kolton. "Not a Merlin like your family. But you work for them."

"That's right." It was strange that I was being investigated like this since I was the one who usually asked the questions, but this was a small town, and I understood Kolton's apprehension. I was, after all, a stranger.

"So, what's that kid's murder gotta do with Dash?"

Good question. "I'm not sure. Maybe nothing. But he kinda showed up at my house in a bad way, and I'd like to know why."

Kolton's jaw clenched, the muscles around his neck bulging. "Is Dash in some kind of trouble?" Kolton might not be thirty and in his prime, but I wouldn't underestimate the power in that body—a predator's body. Damn.

"That's what I'm trying to determine. Any information would help."

"You would help a stranger?"

I could tell by the intriguing tone of his voice that it was something he wasn't used to hearing. "I would." Especially the strays, like my aunt would say.

Kolton stared at the counter before answering. "Well, I haven't seen him in about three months. He's a bit of a loner type. Sticks to himself. Decent guy."

I took a sip of my beer. "Is he married? Girlfriend? Boyfriend?" If he was involved with someone, they were most probably out of their mind with worry if Dash had been missing for three months. It would explain why he looked half-starved. Now, I really wanted to find those who'd cursed him.

Kolton leaned back as he thought about it. "I don't think so. I had seen him with a pretty redhead months ago, but then he started coming in alone, so I figured that didn't work out for him."

"Hhmm." I wasn't sure how much I should trust Kolton. Yes, he was the owner of this bar and grill and had been for years, but I still didn't know much about the werewolf apart from the fact that he owned this place. I didn't want to risk telling him too much until I knew I could trust him.

"Do you know if he got involved with maybe… the wrong crowd?" There. That was the most I would say. Too many paranormals had expert hearing in this place. The last thing I wanted was to cause more harm for Dash.

"Like what?"

I tapped my glass of beer with my fingers. "Like maybe some shady characters he didn't normally associate with."

Kolton shook his head. "No. Not that I can remember. But I wouldn't know."

I thought of something. "Do you know where he lives?"

"Sure." Kolton picked up a rag and began to clean the counter. "That big ol' farmhouse out on Stardale Road. The one with the ol' red barn next to it. Can't miss it."

"Thanks." I'd take Dash to his home when he was better in hopes of jogging his memory. Maybe seeing where he lived would help.

"You think you'll find Tim's killer?" asked the large werewolf.

"That's the plan," I told him. The main reason I came back to this town. "I'm going to swing by that house again. See if I missed anything."

I finished my beer and waited for Kolton to return from making a margarita for who I guessed was a fae female with blue hair and yellowish skin.

"Before I go," I said to the large werewolf, "I have another question."

"You do, do you? Maybe I should start charging you."

At Kolton's smile, I asked, "Have you noticed anything strange happening in town over the last few months?" There, my aunt would be proud.

"Apart from the kid that was killed?" asked the werewolf. He thought it over. "Yeah. I did notice something."

I leaned forward, my pulse increasing. "Like what?"

"I didn't think much of it at first, but now that you mentioned it..." Kolton cast a gaze around the bar before leaning forward and lowering his voice. "The pack I belong to, well, we've all been feeling… a bit off."

"In what way?" I asked, matching his low tone.

"Sometimes we can't shift into our wolves," he said. "And sometimes, we can't shift back. It's like our nature is all screwed up. Does that mean anything to you?"

I shook my head. "No." But my new witch neighbors had experienced something similar with their magic. Like something was interfering with it, and now it looked like that same something was messing with the werewolves.

"Who's this lovely creature?"

I turned to my right toward one of the most beautiful men I'd ever seen. His black hair was cut in a modern style with thick lashes that would be the envy of all females and dark eyes that matched his hair. With his straight nose, chiseled jaw, and dark brows, he gave off a Mediterranean vibe. He was in his late thirtics and way, way too pretty. By that confident look on his face, he knew it, too. He knew he could get any female he wanted, anytime. I didn't have to use my witchy instincts to know this handsome fella was a vampire.

I didn't have time for this. "I was just leaving."

"Don't leave on my account," said the vampire. "Miss…"

"Kat," I said but looking at Kolton. "Just Kat."

The vampire smirked, showing off his pearly white teeth. "Kat. I like it. *Meow*."

"I'm sure you do," I muttered under my breath. This vamp was trouble. "But I really do need to go." I wanted to swing by the house Tim was murdered in now that I had all this new information.

I stood up from my seat, ready to make my escape. I spied a pack of matches on the counter, and snatched them up, stuffing them into my jeans pocket.

"Wait," the vampire said, grabbing my arm lightly. "I haven't even introduced myself yet."

I turned to face him and pulled my arm away. "I'm not interested. Sorry."

"Come on, just one drink?" he asked, flashing me a charming smile.

"No, thank you," I said firmly. "I have work to do."

"Leave her alone, Remy," said Kolton, a smirk playing across his lips. "She's not interested."

The vampire called Remy was eyeing me with a

look that promised lots and lots of orgasms. "Nonsense. All women are interested."

I laughed. That was funny. "Well, not this one. I have work to do."

Remy leaned on the bar, his arm brushing up against mine. "What kind of work do you do, Kat?"

"He's annoying but harmless," said Kolton. "Unless he steps out of line, and then, he knows what'll happen. Don't you, Remy?"

The vampire saluted the werewolf. "Yes, sir."

I snorted. He was annoying but funny. "I'm an investigator."

"How undercover-licious." The vampire smiled. "Kat, the investigator. I like it. Sounds… *exciting*."

I rolled my eyes, not amused by his attempt to charm me. "Yeah, it's not that exciting." My life was the opposite of exciting. More like morbid and habitual. I was a creature of habit.

"Oh, I'm sure you have plenty of exciting stories to tell," Remy said, his eyes scanning my body up and down with a predatory gleam.

I felt uncomfortable under his gaze and took a step back, putting some distance between us. The last thing I needed was to get involved with a vampire. Been there. Done that. A few times. Not tonight, though.

Remy chuckled and leaned in close. "You know, I could help you with your investigation. I have some... connections that might be useful to you."

I narrowed my eyes suspiciously. "What kind of

connections?" He did look like he got around, and not in the sexual sense, though that was a given.

"Let's just say I know some people who know some things," he replied with a sly grin.

I sighed, considering his offer. On one hand, I could use all the help I could get in this case. On the other hand, getting involved with a vampire like Remy was bound to lead to trouble.

Before I could make up my mind, Remy leaned in even closer, his breath hot on my neck. "Come on, Kat. Let me *show* you what I can do."

I knew exactly what that meant. "See you around, Kolton," I told the owner as I turned to leave.

"And I'll be seeing *you* around later, Kat," called Remy with that confidence that he never went home alone.

"Sure."

I made a beeline for the door, eager to put some distance between myself and the bloodsucker. I got into my Jeep and drove to the empty house where Tim's body had been found. The house looked the same, but somehow, it looked more gruesome and uninviting now that I knew what had transpired inside.

I parked in the parking lot, killed the engine, and made for the front door. Surprise, surprise, it wasn't locked.

Gently, I creaked the door open and stepped inside. I left the lights off, mindful of the neighbors who could easily be alerted if anyone noticed a light. The kitchen light illuminated the hallway enough so I could make my way over to the living room, where Tim's body had been.

With the new information of a possible group that had planned on killing Tim, I was sure I had overlooked something here. Something important. Something that might give me a better understanding of what was happening to the town.

I expected to find something. Just not someone or, rather, some*ones*.

My thoughts consumed me to such an extent that by the time I heard the rustling behind me, it was already too late.

CHAPTER 10

From the darkness, an eerie hissing sound filled the hallway followed by a seething energy, and then three figures stepped into the light from the shadows near the kitchen.

Yup, not one, but three silhouettes took shape.

A frightful sight of scaly, clawed monsters with a cluster of black eyes lurking in the middle of their flat skulls greeted me. They were like a mix between an alligator and a scorpion, and their tails each ended in a deadly talon that swung from side to side menacingly. Sharp claws sprouted from the ends of their four fingers that most probably carried a toxic venom.

"Hi, doggies. Who's a good doggie?" I tried in my animal voice to see if I could coax them to leave or maybe communicate with them somehow.

They lowered themselves, readying their bodies to spring.

"Right." My skin erupted in goose bumps, and I

slipped my hand into my pocket. Demons weren't my forte, but I made a mental note to read up on them as soon as I got home—if I survived.

But why were they here?

My mind told me to run, but my legs seemed to be cemented into the floor. It didn't make sense that demons would be here. There'd been no evidence of demon summoning before or a demon attack. I'd searched the house thoroughly. If there had been traces of demonic summoning, I would have found it. Demons hadn't killed Tim. So why were they here now?

The only logical explanation was that someone summoned them. And sent them after me.

Looked like they didn't want me investigating Tim's death. Looked like they wanted me dead. Yeah, not going to happen.

I hadn't told anyone I was coming here. No. That's not right. I'd told Kolton.

But I couldn't see how he would be involved in this. I didn't get that impression. But I didn't really know him, and I'd learned over the years that people were pretty much capable of anything.

I'd think about that later. Now, I had bigger problems on the scale of demons.

From what I knew of them, their weakness was light. Demons hated the light, as darkness fed them. Without the protection of a human body or a constant fill of human souls, the light would kill them unless they slipped back to the Netherworld. It was only five past six p.m., but since it was October, we lost daylight a lot faster. Sunset was around six.

I was screwed.

But fire could kill them.

"Are you guys hungry?" Yeah, that didn't sound right. These weren't stray cats. They were monsters from the bowels of hell. "What do you want?" I called out instead, hoping we could negotiate terms or something. Could mortals negotiate with demons? I had no idea. Did they even understand the words that came out of my mouth? Who knew.

These creatures were only out for blood. They wanted to feed on mortal souls. Mine.

"Who sent you? Who is your master?"

Another hiss.

So, someone, a magical practitioner, possibly a Dark witch or mage, had summoned these demons to get rid of me. That told me one thing. I was definitely onto them, and that black van had been a good lead.

Deep, savage, and vicious cries sounded from the kitchen.

And then they charged.

The sound of nails tearing up the wood floors echoed around me, almost like cold fingers at the nape of my neck. These damn things were going to eat me.

I pulled out my antique silver lighter and pressed down on the ignition switch.

A flame flicked into existence.

See, I might not be able to call up elemental fire from thin air, or out of my ass, like most White witches. But I'd discovered ten years ago—after accidentally burning myself while trying to light a cigarette—that if I was in the presence of an actual fire—I could control it.

Holding my lighter in my left hand, I tapped into my magic, and then, using my right hand, I pushed out.

A ball of fire blasted forward from the lighter and hit the first demon.

The creature went sailing back and hit the wall with a frightening crunch. I wasn't an idiot to think I'd killed it, but it slumped to the ground, my fireball extinguishing. It was only out of commission for a few moments.

And there were still the other two.

I let my anger spill inside, the fuel for my type of magic—whatever it was. I still didn't know.

From the corner of my eye, another demon leaped at me and then came the other. Two at the same time. Wonderful.

I steadied myself. "Come on, you ugly bastards!"

With my magic in tow, I pushed, concentrating on the flame of my lighter, and another fireball surged forward. It hit one of the demons, sending it spiraling down the hallway.

But I'd completely missed the other.

Oh shit.

Pain tore through my arm as the creature's teeth dug in. I screamed as searing heat radiated from the puncture wounds. I curled my left hand into a fist and slammed it against the demon's head again and again, yet it refused to release its grip.

If I didn't do something soon, they'd rip me to mortal shreds.

Its grip loosened, and I jerked forward. But my left leg wrenched, and something yanked me back.

Not something. The demon.

I flew across the room like a rag doll, screaming in terror. I collided with the wall, knocking the breath out of me. *Ouch.*

I fell to my knees, blinking away the pretty little stars that danced in my vision, only to be ruined by the vision of a misshapen monster heading my way.

I struggled to my feet.

Fear. Anger. Desperation. All these were wonderful things when you had magic like mine.

With the lighter still clutched in my left hand, I flicked on the switch.

Nothing.

"Shit."

That was the problem with lighters. Sometimes they ran out of fuel.

Not panicking, I pulled out my backup—the matches I'd nicked from Kolton's place.

"Backup." I smiled at the demons. "Should never leave home without it." I struck a match, and a pretty yellow flame danced before my eyes.

And this time, I pulled.

Fire erupted over me, coiling and coalescing like fiery ribbons. I let my magic fuel inside me. It had been a long time since I'd used it. And it felt... good. Damn good.

Strings of fire exploded out of me. It was beautiful as it soared through the air, lighting the house in hues of gold, oranges, and reds.

The first demon howled as my fire magic wrapped around it like a tight rope, burning it, its flesh, its insides, everything.

Horrible screams of pain filled the air, piercing my ears. The fire towered above its victim, blazing like a giant inferno.

I took a step back, feeling the heat radiating from the creature as it raged. The smell of burning flesh filled the air, and then suddenly, it was gone. Lying motionlessly on the ground was nothing but a pile of gray ash.

But I didn't have time to relish in my small victory as the other demon threw itself at me.

Hot anger welled over my skin. The demons were starting to piss me off. I had a case to solve. I didn't have time for this.

The demon's mouth stretched widely with each roar. It rushed me. Black eyes glowing while snapping its huge teeth. I faked to the left, came up behind it, and slammed a blast of fire at it.

But my fire magic never came.

My match was out.

Damn. Before I could light up another match, the demon slammed into me with supernatural strength, and I went sailing over the sofa and hit the wall hard.

"I don't get paid enough for this shit."

I pushed myself up and whirled around. The demon's arms were spread out in an embrace of death before it ate me. Yikes.

I struck another match just as a burst of fire shot out of me and wrapped the demon in a blanket of flames. Its high-pitched wail sent shivers down my spine as it thrashed around the den, trying to extinguish the flames. And then, just like the other demon, it crashed on the floor in clumps of burnt flesh and ash.

The sound of the floorboard creaking pulled my attention back around.

"How nice of you to show up," I said to the other demon as it emerged from its unconscious state and rejoined the fray.

The demon howled as its eyes flashed with hunger. It was so close now the stench of carrion burned my nose. If I wanted, I could reach out and touch it. But why would I?

Using the same flame from the match, a rush of power overflowed my aura. And then I let it go.

The demon staggered back at the impact as the flames rose. It swayed for a few moments, holding my gaze with its dark eyes, and then burst into pieces.

Not ash—that could easily be wiped off with the brush of a hand like the rest of the demons—but a spill of wet, putrid bits of skin and yellow liquid. Lovely.

A wave of nausea hit me as a thick sludge slapped my face, neck, and chest. The rancid smell of carrion filled my nostrils. I spat out the gunk that had slipped into my mouth, trying hard not to vomit while desperately attempting to get rid of it all.

My clothing was completely soaked with the demon goop. It was utterly revolting. I almost vomited when I saw the sticky slime clinging to my jeans and T-shirt.

"This is soooo gross. I'm asking Jack for a raise."

Movement caught my eye.

A tall, slender figure in a black robe, black cape, and black hood appeared from behind a veil of black mist, standing at the mouth of the hallway that led down to the front door. He looked vaguely familiar.

The dude from Kolton's diner. The one who sat next to me.

I glowered. "You. You summoned those demons." Yeah, he did. I was going to fry that SOB. This bastard was mine.

I rushed forward. Was that stupid? Probably. But I was angry that I was covered in demon blood and guts. And I knew this mage or witch was highly skilled in demon summoning, but I was highly skilled in stupid.

The robed figure spun and rushed down the hallway, out the door.

I ran as fast as I could. But by the time I reached the door, the robed figure was gone.

Well, son of a damnit.

CHAPTER 11

Driving home covered in demon guts and blood was a new experience that I never wanted to experience again. Ever.

Not only did I smell like sewage, but I looked like I just crawled *out* of sewage.

I parked my Jeep up my new driveway and killed the engine. I sighed. "I'm never going to be able to get the smell out." I would have to use bleach. Lots and lots of bleach.

The only comfort I had at the moment was that the exterior lights were on, giving the old house a bit of illumination. It was nice to have the electricity back on finally. I was sure my Aunt Luna was grateful. I didn't want to have to think about her maneuvering in the dark these past two years. Unless she'd conjured some witch light at night, she'd have been in complete darkness.

I looked over my shoulder at the neighboring houses, seeing yellow light spilling from the many windows. Peaceful. Something was beautiful about nighttime in this place.

The last thing I wanted was for the neighbors to see me in my sticky state. Luckily for me, it seemed like the coast was clear. I peeled myself out of the car, my butt sticking to the seat, bruised, and feeling a slight fever, but otherwise in better shape than I would have thought, which concerned me. I should have been really sick since the demon claws had broken my skin, but I wasn't. In fact, I was feeling better since I left the crime scene.

Trying not to overthink things, which was like second nature to me, I opted for the garden hose. Yup. I would have to hose myself off. At least, that would get most of the demon guts and blood off. No way did I want to contaminate my aunt's house with demon goo. She'd kill me. I'd have to throw away my clothes, too. No amount of detergent could save them.

I felt like Carrie at the prom as I wandered over to the side of the house. Slips of demon flesh fell from my body as I went. I was leaving a damn trail of demon goop. Nice.

I saw the garden hose and cringed at the thought of how cold the water would be. Ice-cold, that's what. Didn't matter. What mattered was getting as much of these demon guts and blood off me before I got into the house. And before anyone saw me. Maybe I should strip down first.

"Kat? Is that you?"

I flinched. Ah, hell. Why did these things always happen to me?

I turned around very slowly and spotted Annette and, to my horror, Blake staring at me, wide-eyed.

Oh, fuuuuuck.

"Oh my cauldron! What in the devil happened to you?" said the witch. "You're bleeding!"

"Not my blood." I looked at Blake. His posture was stiff, and he looked… angry?

She blinked, coming closer and pointing her cell's flashlight at me. At her wincing, I knew she'd smelled me. "Ugh. What *is* that smell?"

"Demon guts." Yeah, I wanted to die right about now. Why were they here? Why was Blake here?

"Demon?" repeated the witch, looking mildly impressed. Maybe even envious. "You fought a demon? Really?"

"I did. Three, actually." Might as well tell the truth. One was bad enough, but three… three had been a complication, and I'd been lucky to come out of there alive and with all my limbs.

Annette's lips parted, and a strange smile spread across her face. "But why? Where? Here? In this house?" She looked up at the house like she was expecting a demon to show itself in one of the windows and wave down at her.

She was definitely a weird one. "Not here." I wasn't about to tell her where. Annette was still a stranger. She was nice, but I didn't know much about her apart from the fact she was a White witch and lived across the street from me.

"Where?" Blake was staring at me with so much anger and intensity that I wasn't sure whether he wanted to pound my head in. "Where?" he pressed.

Yeah, I didn't do well when people barked orders at me. Part of me didn't want to tell him, but this was such a small town, the news of those demons would eventually catch up to him. Not like I'd cleaned up the scene either.

I reached up and wiped the slop of demon that was covering my left eye. "At the house where Tim was killed. I went back to take another look and see if I'd missed anything. They were inside the house when I got there."

Because of the demons, I hadn't had a chance to look around for more clues. Now that the crime scene was seriously contaminated with demon blood and guts, it wasn't worth looking at anymore.

I licked my lips and flinched. Damnit. I had demon goo on my lips, too.

"They were waiting for someone. You." Blake's expression was terrifying. He needed to calm down before he gave himself a stroke.

I nodded, having reached that same conclusion. "That's what I think. Me or anyone who's looking into the case. There were no traces of demon summoning before. This happened recently." I debated whether or not to divulge the hooded figure I saw and decided that I should. "I saw the summoner. He was probably waiting inside the house for me. Maybe the basement. But he disappeared before I could get to him."

I made a mental note to check the basement later. I hadn't contaminated that area. It might be worth a look. "So, we're dealing with someone who can do Dark magic. Or maybe whoever killed Tim hired them." That was also a possibility. Plenty of weres could pay good money to find witches and mages to do their bidding. I wouldn't rule that out until I had more proof.

I glanced at Blake, but he was staring at my shoes like he wanted to burn them with his glare.

Annette pressed her hands on her hips. "What kind of demons were they? I happen to know a lot about demons. I might be a White witch and a house-wife witch, but that never stopped me from devouring every book I could on demons and demonology. If we know what kind of demon, it might help determine who was powerful enough to summon them."

That made sense. I thought about it. "Big. Claws, fangs, black eyes. They looked like a cross between an alligator and a scorpion."

"That sounds like tuktuk demons," said Annette, nodding. "Evil sons of bitches. And really hard to kill. Their hides are like metal. You're lucky they didn't tear you to shreds. They have a kind of venom in their claws and teeth. Were you bit?" Annette moved toward me but recoiled at my stench. "Did they break the skin?"

"No, I'm fine," I lied, hoping the demon guts hid any traces of my own blood. "I didn't get bit."

"So you used elemental magic to defeat them?"

asked Annette, a smile on her face and her eyes wide with awe, almost like she was going to fangirl over me.

"Something like that." This wasn't the time to discuss my brand of magic. It was never the time.

"Impressive. I don't know of any witch who fought not one but *three* tuktuk demons on her own and survived. Wow. You're going to have to tell me all about it."

"I need to get clean first," I said, hooking thumbs at myself, hoping she'd drop the subject. If I told her how I defeated them, the truth, she'd know I wasn't a White witch. I wasn't like any witch.

"Why didn't you call me?" snapped Blake, yanking my attention back to his intense eyes.

Anger flared in my gut at the way he was glaring at me. "Uh... because I was busy getting my ass kicked." The nerve of this guy. As if I had the time to put the demons on pause, reach for my phone, dial his number—did I even have his number—and then... what? Wait for him to show up? He had some serious issues.

Blake exhaled through his nose. "You should have never gone in there alone."

I gritted my teeth. "I didn't know I was going to have company. Like I said, I was going in there to look for more clues. It's part of my job."

Blake raked his hands through the top of his hair. "You should have called for backup first. That was really stupid of you going in there alone. You could have been killed."

Did he just call me stupid?

I took a step closer to the big beast-like man, hoping to smear some of the demon goo over his pretty body. "I don't remember needing your permission to do anything," I growled, matching his tone. He might be able to order around the paranormals in this community, but not me. "I don't work for you. I do what *I* want *when* I want."

He stepped closer to me, towering over my small frame. "As the sheriff, it's my duty to ensure the safety of my people. And that includes you."

"I'm not *your* people." My eyes locked with his. A humming sensation filled my body, causing my skin to tingle. I strained, pushing my magic down. If he continued to aggravate me, there was no telling what I would do. "I don't need you to protect me. I can handle myself."

"She can," agreed Annette. "She vanquished three tuktuk demons. She's got skill. No denying that."

Blake leaned his face just inches from mine. Damn, he was tall. "Maybe you don't want me to protect you, but you need it. You're in over your head. You're just an *investigator*."

If he had pulled the not-even-a-Merlin card, I would have punched him in the nose.

"I'm good at my job." He was getting uglier and uglier by the second, his sex appeal quickly diminishing. "I don't care what you think of me. I'm not here for you. I'm here to solve a case. I don't need your protection." I clenched my fists, not wanting to show weakness in front of him. If he got any closer, I might have to kick him in his man-junk.

"Is that why you're covered in demon guts?" Blake sneered. "You're lucky to be alive. It was a stupid move, *Katrina*."

How could it be stupid when I didn't know what was waiting for me? I'd walked into a trap. It wasn't a stupid move. A stupid move was what he was doing right now. If he kept pushing, I was gonna castrate the bastard.

A foolish part of me, surely the one covered in demon goo, wanted to give him the finger. Yeah, so I might have gotten too confident in my abilities, thinking I could take on anything that came my way. But I'd been ill-prepared. It's not like I was asking for trouble. It sort of always followed me.

I clenched my jaw. "Just… stay out of my way, *Blakie*. Don't mess with me or my case."

The big man snorted. "Is that a threat?"

Damn straight. I held his gaze, refusing to back down. "It is what it is."

He straightened up, towering over me once again. "You're making a mistake, *Investigator*. You don't know what you're dealing with. You don't know this town… not anymore."

I raised an eyebrow. "Maybe. But the only mistake I can see is getting involved with you. I work alone. Stay away from me."

"Fine," he said, throwing up his hands. "I can't help you if you don't follow the rules."

"Fine by me." Screw your rules.

"But if you get yourself killed, don't come crying to me."

"I won't. I'll be dead." *And I don't cry. Haven't for a very long time.*

Annette looked between us. "Uh… well, this is all very entertaining. And speaking of entertainment, we came over to make sure you hadn't forgotten about my invitation for drinks."

Crap. "I didn't forget." I'd totally forgotten. "I was just getting ready."

"Kat? You all right?" Dash was standing on the front porch, wearing nothing but a pair of tight light-blue yoga pants. Mine. He looked healthier than before. He looked good, damn good. And he was glaring at Blake.

Ah, hell.

"Who's that?" Annette leaned forward—remembered my stench—and jumped back.

"A friend." I just met Dash, but what else was I supposed to say?

Blake cleared his throat, drawing my attention away from Dash. "We're done here," he said, scowling at me one last time before turning on his heel and striding away.

"Who was that?" Dash asked, his eyes following Blake's retreating form.

"Nobody," I said vaguely, trying not to let my gaze linger on him too long.

I glared at the back of Blake's head as he walked away toward Annette's house. "What's his problem?" I asked, a bit too loudly, and I was sure he heard. I didn't care.

"He gets a bit wound up when the safety of the community is involved," answered Annette. "He's built that way. He really does mean well. I swear. He's not usually this rude."

"He's an asshole." I'd had enough of those for a whole lifetime. I didn't have room for another. If he wanted a war, he'd get one. I wasn't afraid of him. I didn't need him. And maybe that was why he was acting like such a douche. He wasn't used to a strong, independent female like me. Tough.

Annette sighed and pressed her hands to her hips. "Well, I won't forgive his attitude toward you. That was just plain dumb, but he's not a bad guy. Just takes his job *very* seriously. He worries about people. That's not a bad quality in a man."

"Maybe, but he has no business bossing me around." Hell no. It was one of the reasons why I started my own investigative company. I didn't take well to others giving me orders.

"Well…" Annette cleared her throat, her eyes moving from Dash, still standing on the porch, and then back to me. "Will you come? I think a few drinks is what you need right now. Especially after what just happened to you. It'll be a nice change for you." Her eyes flicked to Dash again. "Unless you have other plans?"

The way she said "other plans" was like she thought me and Dash were about to have some sexy time together, or that we already had and this was going to be round two. "No. I'll be there." I really didn't want to go. "Let me get cleaned up first."

"Yay! I'll see you soon." She started rushing forward, stopped, and whirled around. "It's that house with the white picket fence and the red door." She pointed to a cute blue cottage with a red door and a multicolored wreath hanging over it. Pumpkins and lanterns were arranged on the porch. It was a lovely home.

"Got it."

She pointed a finger at me. "You better not change your mind, Kat. My girls are very excited to meet you. They can't stop talking about the new witch."

"I've already met Tilly and Cristina," I told her, remembering them both very well.

She let out a small laugh. "No. *My* girls. My daughters."

"Ah. How many daughters do you have?" I tried picturing mini versions of Annette, and that actually brought a smile to my face.

"Five. See you later!" She waved me off and ran across the street to her house.

Damn. Five daughters? And here I thought I had problems.

CHAPTER 12

A half hour later, I stood on the sidewalk facing Annette's house, a cigarette between my fingers as I debated going in. I'd always kept a pack hidden away in my Jeep's glove compartment. I'd never been able to throw it away.

Yes, I'd crumbled and succumbed to the pressure of smoking. I had a moment of weakness.

The events of today, tonight, had taken a toll. The fight with Blake was the worst. I was an emotional wreck. I hadn't been this upset and felt this kind of internal turmoil since I left my home and family twenty years ago. I hated feeling this way. It was like I was losing control, and that wasn't me. I didn't let people get to me in that way anymore. Over the years, I'd built myself a wall, and I never let them in too close. Never. Because that's how you got hurt when you let the wall down.

Damnit. I thought Blake was one of the good guys. But now that I saw his true nature, I despised him. Hated his guts. Okay, hate was a strong word. I unliked him. Disliked him? Whatever.

I took a drag, my fingers shaking slightly, letting the nicotine fill my lungs. I hadn't smoked in over a month, and the smoke burned my throat. It didn't feel as good as I remembered. And I hated myself for being weak. Pathetic.

"Damn you," I cursed, flicked the half-smoked cigarette on the sidewalk, and stepped on it. I felt like I'd betrayed myself, feeling vulnerable and angry. Feeling alone. "I should have stayed home."

When I'd finished hosing myself down and had stripped down to my bra and underwear, I'd climbed back into the house, wet and angry, to meet a shocked aunt, but Dash just looked concerned.

"What in Lucifer's crack happened to you?" my aunt had shouted as I wandered in. "You're soaking wet. Where are your clothes?"

"In the garbage can outside."

"Why?"

"Tuktuk demons. The last one kinda exploded. Got it all over me." I quickly recalled the events leading up to me being covered in demon sludge.

My aunt swung her cane at me like a sword. "That's The Forsaken. I'm telling you. Summoning demons is like taking a walk in the park for them. They go hand in hand."

"Maybe." I looked at Dash. "That witch and the big idiot. Did you recognize them?" Annette and Blake hadn't seemed to recognize Dash, but maybe he did.

Dash shook his head. "No. Should I?"

"I have no idea." I'd realized I was standing in only my underwear in front of a male stranger. A very pretty one. Too late. He'd already seen me. If I tried to cover up now, I would just look like an idiot. "I know where you live. You're from here. Kolton, the owner of The Blue Demon, recognized your picture."

Dash squished up his face. "I don't remember anyone called Kolton. Or a shop called The Blue Demon."

"It's a diner." I sighed. The fact that Dash still couldn't remember much was concerning. "I think you should spend the night here. I'll fix up one of the spare bedrooms for you, and tomorrow morning, I'll drive you home."

"Sure." Dash looked at me, those deep, pene-trating dark eyes shining in the kitchen light. "Why was that guy shouting at you?"

"We could hear him all the way in the kitchen," said my aunt, a frown bringing her brow down so it nearly covered her eyes.

"Forget him. He's a jerk." A big, stupid jerk. "Maybe seeing your house will help you remember." I didn't want to think about Blake right now. Now, Dash was a priority.

"Yes," said Dash. "I think it will. Thanks, Kat."

After that, I'd rushed to my new master bedroom —and lo and behold—I took a fifteen-minute steaming *hot* shower. Woo-hoo. I was in there longer than necessary, but I had to make sure I'd scrubbed all the demon grime from my body and my hair. I didn't want to show up at Annette's with demon guts sticking out of my scalp.

I grabbed a pair of clean jeans and a black top. Dabbing my lips with some lip balm, I smudged some black eyeliner over my top and bottom lids, and with some mascara, I was done.

My hair was still damp, but I didn't care. It would dry. Grabbing the wine bottle I'd gotten earlier at Winnie's Wine & Beer Shop, I left my aunt and Dash and headed for Annette's cottage.

And now that I was here, I couldn't bring my legs to move up the front porch.

I could hear laughter inside, and then a voice, a young girl's voice shouting something I couldn't make out. I smiled. I'd go in if it was just to see her daughters.

With my mind made up, I reached into my pocket, grabbed the mint I'd been saving, popped it in my mouth, and stepped up onto the porch.

I rang the doorbell and waited.

A moment later, the door swung open. Five girls were sandwiched together at the entrance. They were lined up as though in height and age, starting with the smallest one, who was maybe four years old, to the eldest, who looked like she was in her teens, maybe fourteen or fifteen.

I raised a brow. Curious, they gave off witchy vibes but also werewolf. It looked like some took after their mother and some after their werewolf father. Or were they a blend of both? Interesting. I'd never met a witch and werewolf couple. It was rare. Most of the time, witches married witches, and werewolves stuck to their own kind. So, the idea of mixed offspring was uncommon. But the heart loved what the heart loved.

"She's here," said the eldest girl, who was the spitting image of her mother.

"She's pretty," said the middle child, her blonde hair tied back in a high ponytail.

The second to the youngest just stared, her face turning a shade of strawberry red that matched her long, silky hair.

"Is it true you defeated three tuktuk demons," asked the girl standing next to the eldest girl. Her red hair hit her jaw in a perfect slick cut.

"Uh..." I began, staring at these beautiful and intriguing creatures.

"You wanna see me room?" asked the smallest of the children with big, blonde curls.

God, she was so freaking cute. I wanted to grab her and squeeze her.

"Finally," said a female voice. "I thought you weren't going to show." Tilly appeared behind the wall of girls. She wore a tight black dress with spaghetti straps that pushed her breasts out for the world to see. Her hair was up, showing off her fabulous cheekbones and eyes. "Move. Let her in." She grabbed the eldest girl and the middle one and pulled them away to make an entrance. "This is a grown-up party. No kids allowed. Scoot."

"This is *our* house," said the eldest girl, her hands

on her hips, looking very much like her mother and not at all afraid of Tilly. I liked her.

"Yeah, well, tonight it's a grown-up party." Tilly hooked her arm around mine. "This way, hon."

I waved at the girls with my wine bottle. They all looked hurt and disappointed that I was taken away from them, as though their mother had taken away their favorite toy.

"I hear you need a drink," said Tilly, dragging me across the hallway to the end of the house. She pulled me into a large, bright kitchen with white upper cabinets and navy for the bottom. The fridge was decorated with drawings and paintings from the girls. The house was a happy place. I could feel it. Feel the energy. This was a loving family.

The house had an open concept. The kitchen and dining room were one big area. I spotted Cristina and Annette standing next to the dining table stacked with finger food and way more wine bottles than necessary. Blake was there, and I looked away quickly. He was talking to a red-haired man who I assumed was Annette's husband.

"Here." Tilly offered me a glass of red wine. "You like red?"

"Sure." I set my wine bottle on the counter and took the glass.

"So, who was that naked guy on your porch?"

I barked out a nervous laugh. "First, he wasn't naked. Far from it."

"That's not what I heard." Tilly smiled. "I want all the details. Who is he? And why was he naked?"

"His name is Dash. He lives here. That's all I know."

"Wow. And here I thought I moved fast. How is he in the sack?"

"That's not it," I said, mortified that she thought that. Did everyone think that? "He just showed up at my house."

Excitement flashed in Tilly's eyes. "Even better. Banging a complete stranger. It's one of my fantasies."

Damn. This was not going well.

"Who's banging a stranger?" Cristina waded up to us, followed by Annette, who flashed me a huge smile.

"So glad you came," she said.

"Of course."

"Shh." Tilly waved a hand. "Kat was just about to tell us about that stranger she's been having sex with."

At that, I felt Blake's eyes on me, but I ignored him.

I mentally smacked my forehead with an open palm. "No. You've got it all wrong. Remember that stray cat?" I gave them the whole story. Might as well. They might even know him. I pulled out my phone and showed the others his picture, recapping what had happened.

"And he doesn't remember anything?" asked Cristina, taking a sip of her white wine.

"Just his name," I answered.

"From what Annette said, that picture doesn't do

him justice," said Tilly. "She said he had the body of an athlete. Rippling, washboard abs. Smooth, silky skin."

I laughed. "Well. He is handsome, but I'm not thinking of him like that. I'm more concerned about why he's in that state. My aun—I think he was cursed." Damn, that was close. "Cursed to remain as a cat and not be able to remember that he was also a man." I did not want anyone to know that my aunt was alive and well and had been living in her house for the last two years incognito. Well, at least not yet. Not until I knew them better and thought I could trust them with that.

"That's really disturbing," said Annette. She tapped her wineglass with her finger. "You think it's connected to Tim's death?"

"Maybe. I'm not sure yet. I need to do some more digging around before I can connect the two." But I was leaning in that direction.

"Is this permanent? Will he ever regain his memory?" asked Cristina.

I pursed my lips. "Not sure. But I'm making him a counter-curse. It'll help." I had no doubt my aunt could give him back his memory. If anyone could, she was the witch to do it.

"Do you want us to help you with the counter-curse?" asked Annette, looking as though this was something she would like to do.

I shook my head. "I think I can manage. But if I do, I'll ask."

"I'm not very good at curses," announced

Cristina. "I tried a curse once when I was eighteen. Daphne Bernard stole my boyfriend back then. So, I tried a pox curse."

"And?" I had to ask. I was a curious beast.

Cristina's eyes widened. "*I* ended up with chicken pox."

I snorted. "Sorry."

"And I specialize in men," said Tilly as she gave me a wink. "Making them do what I want."

I bet she didn't need help in that area.

"Mom!" a voice screamed.

I turned to see the second eldest girl with a beak. A real bird beak.

"Holy crap." I stepped closer for a better look at the beak. "Is she a bird shifter?"

"No." Annette grabbed her daughter's hand. "Which one of your sisters did this?"

"Emily," said the girl with the beak.

Annette caught me staring. "This is Ella. She's a werewolf like her father. And her sister Emily is a witch."

"A bitch," said Ella.

"Language," warned her mother. "Emily. You come here right now!"

The middle girl I'd seen at the entrance came walking into the kitchen, accompanied by the rest of the sibling horde.

Annette pointed a finger at her daughter. "You change her back this minute, or you'll be grounded for a week. I told you that we had an important guest. No hexes tonight."

Emily looked down at her feet, but she couldn't hide the smile from her face. "Yes, Mom." She lifted her hand, pointed it at her older sister's face, and muttered, "Ad corpus tuum."

With a sudden pop and influx of magic, the beak on Ella's face was gone.

"I hate you," snapped Ella.

"I hate you more," hissed Emily.

"Girls, I'm warning you," growled Annette. "Not in front of our guest."

"Don't worry about me," I told her, thinking I would have loved to have sisters who paid attention to me growing up. "So, some are witches, and some are werewolves? That's pretty cool."

Annette snapped her fingers. "Girls," she ordered, and the five girls lined up in front of us. "Emma, my oldest, is a witch. Ella, whom you've met, is a werewolf. Emily is obviously a witch. Then that's Elanor, a werewolf. And last, we have my little girl, Elsie."

I frowned. "Is Elsie a witch or a werewolf?"

"We don't know yet," answered Emma. "We'll just have to wait and see. Dad said it'll materialize later."

Fascinating. The blondes were witches, and the redheads were werewolves. Wow.

"What about Dad?" said a man's voice.

I looked up to see the redheaded man I'd assumed was Annette's husband.

"Kat, this is my husband, Liam," introduced Annette.

Liam was tall, about six feet, and thick with

muscles. His red hair was cut short, and I could prac-tically see his scalp. He had all the stereotypical traits of a werewolf, from the bulging muscles to predator vibes that were rolling off him. But his eyes were different. They were bright green and kind.

He stuck out his hand. "Nice to meet you, Kat. Welcome to Moonfell."

"She was born here," said Tilly.

"Right," said Liam, his face taking on a shade of red. "Well, welcome back."

"Thanks," I laughed and shook his hand. I wished I could say I was glad to be back, but I wasn't.

Liam took a sip of his beer, leaned his face into his wife's neck, and started sniffing her. "Mmmm. You smell nice." With his free hand, he grabbed her butt.

Annette jumped. "Stop that." She smacked his arm. "Not in front of our guest. You're embarrassing me. What will Kat think of us?"

Liam grinned. "Can't help it. You're so hot. Blake, my wife is hot."

Blake nodded. "Your wife is hot," he repeated, like a robot.

Idiot. But I thought that being married for at least fifteen years, maybe more, and still having the hots for one another, was amazing. And rare. I was happy for them. Truly. Even envious.

Annette rolled her eyes. "Ignore him, Kat. Liam thinks he's funny."

"I am funny," Liam protested, grinning.

I couldn't help but chuckle at his antics. "I can tell."

"So," said Liam, his arm around his wife. "You've met Blake," he said, gesturing to the wall of a man next to him.

"Unfortunately."

He laughed. "Ouch." Liam must have sensed my unease because he cleared his throat and turned to me. "So, Kat. What brings you *back* to Moonfell after all these years?"

"I'm working a case. The death of Tim Mason."

"Ah, right." Liam nodded. "We were all saddened by the news. He was a good kid. A decent werewolf. Any progress with the case?" Liam looked between me and Blake. I wasn't sure what to say, but Blake beat me to it.

"Some," said the large werewolf. "We know a black van took Tim. We don't know who, just that it was rented from some fae prick down in Tombstone."

"A black van?" Annette was staring at Blake; worry etched her brow, making her look years older. "Do you think my babies are in danger?"

Blake let out a sigh. "I can't say for sure. But maybe you should keep tabs on all your kids until we figure out who killed Tim."

I looked over my shoulder, glad the girls were all in the living room watching television. I didn't want them to overhear the gory details of how Tim died.

"I have a team going over the van right now," said Blake. "So far, it's clean. We found no traces of fibers, no blood, DNA, nothing."

I was a bit ticked that he hadn't mentioned that

part to me. Guess I was truly on my own with this case. So be it. "Have you heard of a group called The Forsaken?" There. I, too, could play that game. Blake's eyes snapped to me, but I was looking at the witches.

"I have," answered Tilly, and I couldn't help but notice how she was practically brushing her body on Blake's like she was trying to rub her scent on him. "It's a children's tale used to scare us. My mother would say, 'Come home before it gets dark, or The Forsaken will get you.'"

Huh? I'd never heard that. Maybe it was because my mother hoped The Forsaken would get me.

"Well, I heard they're real," said Cristina. "Aren't they a group of Dark mages from the seventies that moved here from Europe?"

"That's right." Annette's eyes rounded. "I heard about them, too. But they're gone now. Right? You think they're involved in this?"

"Someone mentioned them to me back at The Blue Demon," I said. I wasn't about to tell them my aunt was the one. "I thought I'd check it out." But it didn't look like they were very helpful. I'd have to ask around. Maybe I should ask Kolton.

"I know of a member."

I looked at Blake. "Really? Who?" And would he tell me? Not sure. I hadn't been exactly polite to him.

"His name is Eli Souza," said Blake, surprising me. "And he lives here in Moonfell."

That was very good news. "And what makes you believe he's part of The Forsaken?"

Blake flashed a smile at me like he knew he had something I wanted. "Because I heard him say it."

If this Eli was in the group, I needed to speak to him.

"And you can't speak to him without me." Blake looked at me, a challenge in his features.

Yeah, he knew just how to press my buttons. "I don't—"

"Come on. Let's get some food in you," said Annette, pulling me away from Blake and not a moment too soon. "You look like you could use some."

As we walked toward the dining table, Annette gave me a knowing look. "You and Blake have some history. Don't you?"

I grimaced. "No history. I just don't like his type."

"The handsome, I-like-to-boss-everyone type?"

"Exactly." I let Annette make me a plate topped with pigs in a blanket, chicken taquitos, a few spinach artichoke cups, garlic knots, and some fried cheese balls. That was a lot of food.

I smiled at her as she kept piling on more food, her words lost to me as my mind was on my case.

In the end, it had been a good idea to come here tonight.

And it looked like I was going to pay this Eli a visit.

CHAPTER 13

"Sorry," I said, rolling down my car window. "I know it smells like death. I didn't have time to clean it completely." I chewed my nasty nicotine gum, thinking I probably looked like a cow, like Blake said. I didn't know why I was thinking of him right now.

Having decided to drive Dash to his place this morning, I hadn't had time to do a thorough cleaning of my Jeep. I managed a five-minute scrub down and an entire can of air freshener in the process—but that only made the inside smell much worse than before with a sickly sweet, flowery scent lingering over everything else. So, so gross.

"It is pretty potent." Dash pulled his face toward his open window. "Maybe you should take your Jeep to the professionals and let them clean it."

"Ha. Ha. I'll clean it better later." If I couldn't get the smell out, I'd have to buy a new car. That was not an option. I didn't have the money. "Just pretend it smells like oranges."

"Oranges?" Dash laughed. It was such a beautiful sound. The melody of his voice took me in a whirlwind of chills and thrills, its music cascading through my veins like the best kind of drug. No way was this guy single. He was probably married to some hot werecat female and had ten werecat babies, and they were madly in love and hot for each other like Annette and Liam. His wife or girlfriend was probably worried sick.

"What kind of demon was it again?"

"According to Annette, they were tuktuk. I think she's some kind of demon expert. Or a demon enthusiast." If there was such a thing. Not sure why anyone would be interested in demons. I nearly got my ass kicked by them, and Annette had seemed... envious.

His head snapped my way, and I wasn't sure what I saw on his face.

I slowed my Jeep at the next stop. "Why? Does that mean something to you? Do you know demons?" Maybe he was remembering something. What if a demon had cursed Dash? It was a possibility. There were many different types of demons, just as there were many different types of us paranormals. What I fought was more in the animal range, but some demons practiced magic, just like witches and mages. That didn't explain the connection between what happened to Dash and Tim, though, and I was certain there was one.

Dash's features closed off again, and he shook his head. "No. I don't know."

He was wearing the same yoga pants from last night and one of my oversized T-shirts that fit him well, snug around his chest and showing off all his pretty muscles. I hadn't had time to get him those spare clothes.

He still couldn't remember much, apart from his name, and I was hoping that taking him home would somehow change all that. At least have some of his memory return.

"I still need a day or so with the counter-curse," my aunt had said as Dash and I prepared to leave this morning. She stood next to the stove, sprinkling herbs into her simmering pot, wearing pink sunglasses and a matching pink feather boa. "Make sure to bring Dash back here so we can administer it. I want to be with him when the transformation happens."

"Is he transforming into a table?" I laughed.

"His memory, smart-ass. It'll be like an alteration. A change. I want to be there when it happens."

"Okay, fine. I'll bring him back." I took a sip of my freshly brewed coffee. Now that we had the electricity back on, I could relish in the pleasures of hot morning coffee and hot morning showers.

It was clear that my aunt had grown an attachment to the tall werecat. Looked like I wasn't the only one with a soft spot for strays.

When I'd returned from Annette's cocktail party, Dash and my aunt were in the living room, deep in conversation. By the relaxed, casual look on the were-cat, it seemed like they had a good talk. About what? No idea. But I was glad he had someone to talk to.

"Anything?" I'd asked Dash as soon as he'd walked into the kitchen this morning, hoping a good night's sleep and some more food in him would help jog his memory.

Stormy dark eyes met mine. "Nothing. Same as yesterday."

I drove down Maple Drive and took a right on Stardale Road. The scenery quickly changed from rural to a country setting with mature trees and fields of greens and yellows.

"This area of Moonfell is really beautiful," I said as I stared straight ahead. "It doesn't even feel like the same town. You must really love it here. Surrounded in nature." As a werecat, that didn't surprise me. Most weres preferred to live next to nature, at least in some part.

"I guess."

I cast my gaze on the side of his face, seeing a frown. He didn't remember it, and I could tell it was making him upset. I'd be upset, too.

I chewed harder and focused on the road. I didn't know why, but the close proximity to Dash was making me nervous. I didn't know him at all, but his easygoing smile and calm demeanor were enough to make me like him and trust him. I didn't know who did this to him, but it pissed me off. And I would find out.

The Jeep rocked as the paved street turned into a

dirt road. Branches hit the sides of the Jeep as we headed deeper down the path. We crested a hill, and there, sitting on a small rise surrounded by green pastures and what looked like apple trees, was a white farmhouse. Next to it sat a red barn. There were no farm animals that I could see.

An old, forest-green Land Rover sat in the driveway but no other cars.

I slowed the Jeep when we got next to the house and shut off the engine. I waited for Dash to comment, but he was just staring at the house with an expression like he'd never seen it before. For a second, I thought I'd gotten the wrong house, but this was the only house on this road with a red barn. It had to be it.

I expected to see a gorgeous female come bursting out the front door, screaming his name. But no one came.

"You want to look around?"

Dash nodded and stepped out of the Jeep. I followed him out, glad to get some fresh air into my lungs instead of the stench of demon guts.

"It's lovely," I told him, searching his face. "Do you remember it? Do you remember living here?"

Dash was shaking his head. "No. I don't remember." He gazed around at the barn and out to the fields. A look of sorrow crossed his features, and I felt my chest tighten. "I don't remember any of this. I don't remember this place."

"Let's go inside. Maybe it'll help." I had to make

sure this *was* the place. So I needed to see something with his name on it, like bills or something.

Not waiting for Dash, I climbed the stairs and was surprised to find the front door ajar. "Do you leave your door open?" I asked and then caught myself. "Sorry. It just popped out."

"It's fine." Dash moved past me and pushed the door open like he wanted to go in first in case something or someone was waiting for us.

I could defend myself, but his actions didn't bother me. It wasn't like Blake, who thought it was his right as the alpha or sheriff to always put himself first. Dash did what he did out of concern for my safety. It wasn't the same thing.

The musty smell of the old farmhouse hit me as soon as I stepped inside. It was like a mixture of dust, old wood, and something else that I couldn't quite put my finger on.

The inside of the house was just as charming as the outside. The living room was cozy, with a fireplace on the far wall and comfortable-looking armchairs arranged around it, nestled on a large Persian rug. The walls were painted a warm cream color, and shelves lined one wall, filled with books and trinkets.

I followed him, feeling like we were trespassing on someone's private sanctuary. One thing that struck me was I couldn't get a sense of a woman's touch to the décor. All the furniture was big, leathery, and male. If I had to guess, I'd say Dash was a bachelor.

The floors creaked beneath my feet as I followed him into the living room. He didn't seem to be paying much attention to his surroundings, but I was taking everything in, looking for any clues that might help me figure out what happened to him.

He made his way to the nearest bookshelf. His fingers traced the spines of the books with a delicate touch as if he were afraid they would crumble to dust with too much pressure.

"Do you remember anything yet?" I asked, my voice barely above a whisper. I felt like we were intruders in someone else's home. And there was a small chance we were.

Dash shook his head, his eyes still fixed on the books. "No, but it *feels* familiar. Like I've been here before. My scent. My scent is everywhere."

Weres had super-smelling powers. Well, that's what I called them. "So, this is your place." I relaxed a little and eased up on the gum-chewing before I dislocated my jaw.

"I think so."

"Do you smell any other scent? Like another paranormal? Or maybe demon?" I thought it highly unlikely that a demon did this to Dash, but I had to ask.

The werecat shook his head. "No. Just mine."

We moved to the kitchen, which was bright and airy with a large window above the sink. A small wooden table sat in the center of the room, surrounded by four chairs.

I noticed a stack of mail sitting on the counter and

walked over to it. Most of it was junk mail, but one envelope from Moonfell Bank had the name DASH DREUX written on it. I flashed him the envelope. "This is your home, Dash."

He took the envelope from me. "I can't remember it, though." He tossed the envelope back on the counter, a flash of anger on his face, and his fingers curled into fists. "Why? Who would do this to me?" His gaze traveled around the room as if he was expecting to find an answer to his questions hidden among the kitchen cabinets.

There was so much emotion in his voice, so much confusion and hurt. I wanted to reach out to him and try to offer some comfort, but I somehow knew that nothing I could say would truly help him. Only getting his memory back would.

"I don't know. But we're going to find out. I promise. As soon as my aunt's counter-curse potion is ready, things will start making sense." I was surprised at how angry I was for Dash. Guess robbing someone of their memory would do that.

I walked over to the fridge and opened it. "Good. You have lots of food. Stay put until I come back. I mean… for your own safety. I'm not giving you an order or anything." Heat rushed to my face. I sounded like a moron.

Dash flashed a smile. "I know."

I glanced around. "There's no sign of a struggle here, so I have to assume that whatever happened to you happened somewhere else. I think you'll be safe here." I grabbed the notepad I saw next to the pile of letters and yanked my pen from my bag. "Here's my cell. Call me anytime."

"And where are you going?"

"To find this Eli. If he's really part of The Forsaken group, I need to pick his brain." I'd filled him in along with my aunt after coming home from Annette's. It might not have been smart to discuss my case with a stranger openly, but I felt like I could trust Dash.

He folded his arms over his chest. "You think they're involved with Tim's death?"

I shrugged. "Well, someone in this town is." And my witchy instincts told me they were also involved in what happened to Dash. I just didn't know who that was, but I would find out.

An uncomfortable silence followed as Dash's gaze still lingered on me.

"Well, I better go. You'll probably want to change," I said, flicking a finger at him.

Dash shrugged. "It's comfortable," he said with an added smile. "Just a bit tight."

I laughed. "It is that." I walked toward the front door, hearing Dash's light footsteps behind me. Seriously, the guy was a true werecat.

I stepped onto the front porch. "What's in the barn?" I asked before I could stop myself.

"Let's see." Dash leaped off the porch like it was something he'd done a thousand times. Maybe he had.

I ran after him, cursing his long legs. Dash pulled

open one of the barn's large double doors and walked in.

The first thing I noticed was the smell of wood, maybe wood chips, as though someone had just cut down a few trees. In the middle of the barn stood a large table saw. Workbenches and tables were stacked with knives and wood planers, chairs and couches, and even a dresser and a mirror. But what drew me in was the detailed carvings on some of the furniture —intricate designs with a mix of animals and plant life. The dresser had a carved silhouette of a woman with a plant sprouting from her head, roots weaving through her hair like bobby pins. Carved on the sides were two women, each playing a harp and each with a cat curled in her lap. It was extraordinary.

I envied artists. I was always so amazed at what a person could create with a pencil, a paintbrush, and now, a chisel. I was more of the stick-figure kind of artist.

Dash was walking around, his fingers running over the rough surfaces. I followed him, my eyes flickering over everything.

"This is amazing," he said, almost to himself. "I don't remember building any of this, but it *feels* familiar."

I nodded, not sure what to say. The barn was impressive, and the workmanship on the furniture was outstanding. Dash was a master craftsman.

"Looks like you're a carpenter," I said. "These are amazing, Dash. You're quite the artist."

Dash was smiling, and I could see that this was a good idea to bring him here. His mind might not remember, but his fingers would. Did that sound dirty?

Dash wandered around the furniture and stopped next to a carved bear from what I believed had once been the trunk of a tree. My eyes traveled down to his fine butt. What? I couldn't help it. It was amazingly defined in my yoga pants. I could practically see right through them.

Dash seemed to sense my gaze and turned to look at me.

I gave him a quick smile to recover from my voyeurism. "Dash, if you do remember anything, anything at all, could you call me and let me know?"

"Yeah. Of course. I don't know if I have a cell phone, but I saw a landline back at the house."

"Good." His phone number would have been practical, but I was sure I could find his number on the internet through one of the online search tools. "I'll see you later."

"Thank you, Kat." Dash's words were like velvet sheets, and I just wanted to roll in them.

Control yourself. "You're welcome." I started to walk back to my car.

"And, Kat?"

"Yes?" I turned around.

Dash watched me for a beat. "Be careful."

"Always."

CHAPTER 14

I parked my Jeep on the curb of Death Row Drive. I didn't think I'd be back in Tombstone this soon, but here I was. All because of this Eli, a member of The Forsaken.

And I didn't have to look hard for his address. All I had to do was ask my aunt.

"*Eli Souza*," she'd said last night after I'd gotten back from Annette's. "That dirty, stinky excuse of a man. And the ugliest toes you've ever seen."

Dash spat out his coffee. "Sorry." He wiped his mouth.

I laughed, happy to see Dash so relaxed with my aunt. "Tell me more about these toes. I mean… how would you know what his toes looked like unless…"

My aunt waved a dismissive hand at me. "I never had sex with that snake, if that's what you're insinuating. Though, he did try to get into my pants more than once."

"More than once?" This was a strange conversation, and I'd started it.

My aunt gave me her bulldog stare. "Don't you start with me, young lady. Why do you want to know about him?"

"Well, Blake seems to think he's one of The Forsaken."

"Does he now?" My aunt pursed her lips, her brows lowering as she tossed that new information around inside her head. "That wouldn't surprise me. He was always practicing illegal spells and somehow never saw the inside of a prison. I'd always wondered why that was."

That was interesting. "You think he has friends in higher power?"

"Higher power," agreed my aunt. "Like The Forsaken."

As soon as I got out of my Jeep, I had my guard up. The last thing I wanted was to see that nasty fae and his crew again. I checked my pockets and was rewarded with the thud of my metal lighter. My little buddy. I made sure to refill it before leaving my aunt's house.

A few paranormals across the street from me looked my way, and I did my best not to make eye contact.

I had the feeling that Blake would show up, seeing as he was so commanding last night, but I didn't see his SUV anywhere. Good. I didn't feel like dealing with him right now. I was busy. He and his ego needed to take a number.

My phone buzzed in my pocket. I pulled it out.

"Speak of the devil."

It was a text from Blake.

Blake: We found a body at an old abandoned mill at the edge of town. His name is Samuel Caddel. He was killed the same way as Tim.

Shit. This was the Samuel Cristina had told me about.

I scrolled through the gruesome pictures. Judging by the level of decomposition on the body, Samuel had been killed days before Tim. Was he the first sacrifice? Were there more? I didn't know. But Blake was right. The body had been carved with the same symbols I'd seen on Tim's body. I could clearly read the same Latin letters—ANIMAE. SOUL.

Damnit. Another dead kid. If my aunt was right and these Forsaken were responsible, I needed to stop them.

My eyes traveled over the dingy apartment buildings, all sandwiched together like whoever had built them wanted to put three units where the space allowed for only one. The number 1224 came into view and I made for it.

I reached the building, pulled open the entrance door, and stepped into a small lobby covered with newspapers and flyers. I glanced over at the panel of names. ELI SOUZA was written next to the apartment number 1.

I pressed the buzzer. A moment later, a buzzing sound rebounded, and the lobby door popped open.

That was weird. A bit too trusting. Or was I walking into a trap?

Blake's words from last night about calling for backup rang through my head. It wasn't a bad idea. But then he had called me stupid.

Screw backup.

With my guard up, I stepped through, walked over to the door with the number 1 stenciled above it, and gave it three knocks. A few moments later, the door opened, allowing a faint light to shine out from within. The smell of cigarettes filled my nostrils, making my head spin. I peered inside, expecting an old wizard in dark robes, armed with a staff and magical pendant around his neck. Instead, I saw something entirely different.

Before me stood an elderly man with thin white hair that framed his face and eyes as dark as night that seemed to gaze through me. He looked like he'd celebrated his ninety-ninth birthday a while ago, with bags around his eyes and hollow cheeks, giving him a skeletal look. He had the posture of someone who must have been tall once upon a time, but the years had been cruel. Now he was bent and had probably shrunk several inches in height. He had a horrible scar that took most of his nose and scratched the left side of his face, like some deranged beast had attacked him.

A tiny pair of Spiderman undies was the only garment on his body other than a Batman-patterned robe covering his bony shoulders.

Weird. Magical vibes brushed against my skin. They were limited, but he was definitely a magical practitioner.

The first thing I did was look down at his toes, and I nearly took a step back. I understood my aunt's comments. Those were nasty. The flesh on his toes was wrinkled like he'd just spent three hours in the tub. But his nails… his nails were yellow stained with brown and were easily six inches long.

"Damn, you could poke someone's eyes out with those," I said before I could control my mouth.

He rolled his eyes over me. "I asked for a redhead, but you'll do just fine," he said in a gravelly, scratchy voice, like he was about to lose it at any moment.

I think I just threw up in my mouth. "In your dreams, buddy." It was a strange thought that a man his age was still able to work his machinery. And it was even more disturbing that I was thinking about it.

He squinted at me. "You're not from Gals and Pals?"

I snorted. "No. I'm an investigator. I've been hired by the Merlin Group. I'm working on the case of Tim Mason's death. I need to ask you some questions. May I come in?" Part of me wanted to stay right here in the lobby, but I couldn't risk anyone overhearing this conversation.

Eli tightened his robe around himself, thank the goddess. "And why should I do that?"

"Because if you don't, I'll have to call the sheriff. Trust me. You don't want that. He's in one of his moods."

He seemed to think it through. "Fine." He left the door open and walked away.

I held my breath and stepped inside, trailing after him. The room was scarcely furnished with only with a couple of chairs and a table. For all its simplicity, it exuded an air of mystery that made me feel like I had stumbled on to something far bigger than myself. As my eyes roamed over the shelves lining the walls filled with books and trinkets, I knew more was hidden behind those closed doors than anyone could imagine. Boxes upon boxes held more books than could fit in this apartment. The old witch was a hoarder.

The apartment was dimly lit with long, pretty shadows just waiting for me to use them. Good.

"I don't know why you want to ask me questions about that boy's death. I had nothing to do with it," said Eli, the annoyance of missing out on his lady date high in his tone.

"Seems like you know about it." I let out a breath and inhaled, regretting it immediately. The air smelled of old ashtrays and urine.

"Of course I know. Just like everyone in this stupid town." He made his way to a living area and sat in an old, dingy recliner that would have been in style in the sixties. "What's it got to do with me?"

I moved around to face him. I saw a chair, a wooden one, and decided it was safe, so I grabbed it and sat.

The old man's gaze seemed to linger on me. He

stared a little too long for my liking. If he kept on, I'd have to do something about it.

"Are you a witch?" Let's go with the obvious first.

Eli snorted and scratched his man junk. "Don't confuse me with that sorry lot. They can't yield real magic. I'm a mage. There's a difference."

Not really. Mage was just another term for spell-caster. Just like sorcerer or wizard. The real difference was that they attended a higher level of education at some magical university. It didn't mean witches were lesser or weaker, just that they learned their magic either from their family or on their own. Most were self-taught.

"Are you part of The Forsaken?"

The old man's lips parted, and then he pointed a finger at me. Well, what looked like a finger. The nail was similar to his toenails—yellow, stained, about six inches long, and twisted. I tried to keep my face from showing my disgust.

"Bastards," he spat. "They think they got the better of me. Ha! They didn't. They think they've won this battle." He scoffed. "No one can control me! I don't need them for anything. I'm already tapping into the dark forces. I've gone beyond what any of them could ever imagine. My power is everlasting! I've plumbed the depths and tapped into unfathomable energy."

I leaned forward, seeing the results of someone tapping too much into that type of magic. The more he had channeled the darkness, the more it had taken from him. His skin was pale and shallow, his body emaciated. His eyes seemed to burn with intensity and madness.

"So, you're not part of them anymore?" I asked.

The mage hissed, "Kicked me out."

"Why?"

He leaned forward. "I was too powerful. They could see it, and they were envious of me. They knew… They saw that I was *better*, that I held more power."

I seriously doubted that. I did feel some magical energies coming from him but nothing like a powerful wizard or witch. His energy was… reduced.

He cackled a laugh. "They didn't like the experiments I was doing."

"What kind of experiments?" I figured the more I stroked his ego, the easier it would be for him to give me more information.

He looked over his shoulder, as though checking that he wouldn't be overheard in his own place, and whispered, "The infusion of blood of demons into our blood. Ha! Didn't see that comin', did ya?"

He was mad as a hatter. "And you've tried this? I mean, you succeeded?" Demon blood was poison to us paranormals. If you drank it, you got sick. I didn't see how he could have done this successfully.

He tossed his head back and forth. "They died. But I was almost there. Almost." He reached out and gripped the air like he was holding on to something tangible. "A few more subjects, and the transformation would have been complete."

I hated to ask. "What transformation?"

He raised his fist. "Absolute power. A mage with demonic power. A hybrid."

"You were trying to *make* a hybrid?" Yeah, that would have gotten him kicked out. I'd heard of witches who had demonic powers. They were called Shadow witches. They were extremely rare, but they were born that way. They weren't made.

"I would have succeeded. And they knew. They knew. So they stopped me. They were afraid, you see. Afraid of what *I* was going to become."

Ah. Ha. The idiot was testing his theory on himself. "What can you tell me about The Forsaken?" I figured since he was booted out, he might be more prone to spill the beans. I took it as a good sign that I didn't have to make him tell me.

Eli leaned back. "What do you want to know?"

I thought about it. "Are they all mages like you? Are some witches?" The more I knew about this group, the easier it would be to identify them.

"Mostly mages, but a few are witches. Albert Terbonne was a witch. But he died ten years ago."

"What kind of magic do they practice?" I had an idea, but I wanted to hear it from him.

Eli chuckled sinisterly. "Dark. What else is there?"

Of course. "Do they sacrifice paranormals?" *Here it comes.*

The old man's eyes shone with glee. "Of course. There is no power without sacrifice."

Damn, that was disturbing, but I was surprised he

answered the question. Now, the hard part. "Kids? Would they kill kids?"

Eli's eyes gleamed, and a smile formed on his thin lips. "What better sacrifice than the innocent?"

My stomach churned, and I felt sick. "Right. Do you believe they were responsible for that boy Tim's death?"

Eli pulled his mouth into a bigger grin, revealing his last four rotten teeth and red, swollen, infected gums. "Yes. They did it. I'm sure of it."

Holy shit. I still had no proof, but this was almost just as good. "Why?" The images of Tim's mangled body flared in my mind's eye, and part of me wanted to punch that smile off his face. "Why did they sacrifice Tim?"

Eli watched me, hesitancy on his face. "Why should I tell you? What can you give me in return?" His eyes rolled over my body slowly, and I stifled a shiver. I would need to douse myself with bleach after this visit.

I focused inward and connected with my magic. Not too much, but enough to show the old bastard that I meant business.

I pulled on the closest shadows around me, drawing them in like strings from a web, and flicked out my wrist.

A string of shadows shot out of my hand, knocking the old man and his chair back in a flutter of robes and toenails.

I stood up and looked down at him. "Don't make me hurt you."

He raised his hands in surrender, his eyes wide. "Okay. Okay. I'll talk."

"Good." I walked behind him, grabbed the chair, and yanked him back up. "Tell me," I said as I sat back down. "Why Tim?"

Eli frowned at me. "What kind of magic was that? I've never seen it before."

"Focus, Eli. Why Tim?"

The old man was still staring at me like he wanted nothing more than to rip me open and steal my unique power. "Because. He's part of the big plan."

"What big plan?"

The old mage's eyes widened. "To raise the demon king."

That's not good. "Tell me more."

Eli's face lit up with a wide smile, pleased to have another who was eager to hear what he had to say. "You can only offer the sacrifice of the pure of heart when the stars coalesce in conjunction with the sun and moon cycles once every twenty years," he explained, "to summon the Dark Master."

"The demon king."

"Precisely."

Every twenty years. It had been exactly twenty years ago when I'd seen the body—the victim. Her chest was carved in the same way that Tim's and Samuel's had been. The images had haunted me since I was seventeen.

It was raining heavily that night, and I had run out of my house in a rage after a fight with my mother—one that I couldn't recall now. My destination—my aunt's house. As I passed by the aging Fallburn Bridge, I decided to duck under it to wait out the storm.

That's when I stumbled over Nancy's body. I knew her. She was a local teen witch, and I'd literally stumbled over her. My jeans and shirt were soaked in her blood. I remember her exposed chest and the deep gashes, the letters that had been carved.

And now it was all coming back to me.

"You look like you've seen a ghost," Eli laughed.

Yeah, I was going to punch the old mage. "Why? For what purpose do they want to summon the demon king?" I had an inclination, but I wanted to hear it from him.

Eli spread his arms out wide like he was embracing the demon king himself. "To walk among us. To bring eternal darkness to the world. To extinguish the light, and let the demons rise from their depths and join us."

Motherfrackers. "When is this happening?"

Eli shrugged. "I can't be sure. If all the sacrifices had been made, soon, I would guess."

Sacrifices. "How many sacrifices do they need?"

"Three souls."

Souls. Animae.

Crap. That meant there would be one more victim. "How do they pick their victims?" I had to warn Blake. I had to let him know we had one more kid in danger.

"The stars must be in alignment with their birthdays," Eli said. "It's necessary for the ritual to occur. The Forsaken are on the lookout for these chosen ones and take them away when they find them. It's believed that if the last sacrifice is killed during the ceremony, the Dark Master will manifest in a physical form and have control over us all."

My heart sank in my chest. That didn't help much. How many kids were lost in this horrible plot? They had tried twenty years ago and had failed. I didn't know how, but I was going to stop them.

"I need names." I stood up, anger rushing through me. I knew I didn't have much time left to find this kid and keep them safe before The Forsaken got ahold of them. Maybe Blake could arrest them with Eli's testimony. It was worth a shot.

Eli clamped his mouth shut.

I leaned over him. "Give me their names, Eli. I won't ask you again."

The old man let out a puff of air. "Fine. What do I care." He frowned as though recalling some past argument. He opened his mouth, "J—"

And then something weird happened.

The old man's eyes widened with fear, his face turning red as he clawed at this throat with those horrid nails as though he were choking.

"Stop kidding around," I told him. "Eli?"

Eli let out an ear-splitting scream and fell off his chair, convulsing. I rushed to his side, unsure of what to do. His body contorted in unnatural ways like something was trying to escape from within him. It was like nothing I had ever seen before.

And then, just as suddenly as it had started, it stopped. Eli lay still, his eyes closed, and I couldn't tell if he was breathing.

Shit. Was he dead?

I rushed over, checked his pulse, and found it weak but steady. He wasn't my favorite person, but I didn't wish him dead.

He slapped my hand away. "I'm not dead yet." With great effort, the old man climbed back into his chair. I did not offer to help him.

I knew what this was. He was spelled never to reveal their names. Clever.

"I have one last question, and then I'll leave you be."

Eli mumbled something unintelligible.

"Do you know someone named Dash? He's a werecat."

Eli pursed his lips in thought. "No. That name means nothing to me."

"Would The Forsaken require a werecat for the ritual?"

"No. What is the meaning of these questions?"

Okay, so there went my theory of Dash being involved somehow. "Thanks for your help."

I left the old mage's apartment as fast as I could. I'd gotten more out of him than I had hoped. I might not have their names, but I knew The Forsaken had killed Tim and Samuel. I was certain of it.

And now I had to stop them before they got another sacrifice and raised that demon king.

No problem.

CHAPTER 15

I parked my Jeep at the Moonfell County Sheriff's Department parking lot. I'd walked by the station many times as a kid, but I'd never been inside. It was an ordinary building with a painted brown brick exterior and beige siding. It looked like it had never been renovated since the 1970s.

A few cars were parked next to mine. I spotted a large black SUV. Blake's. He was here.

"Can't believe I'm doing this."

True, I did not want to be here. Yet seeing as Blake had given me Eli's name, I figured I owed him. I didn't like owing favors to anyone, so the sooner I told him what I'd learned, the better I'd feel. Or that's what I told myself.

Besides, as the town's sheriff, he needed to know what The Forsaken had planned. He needed to know about the other potential sacrifices.

Taking on a group as powerful as I believed The

Forsaken to be might not be the smartest idea. I needed backup. Blake was it.

I tapped my hands on the wheel and looked over to the glove compartment. A cigarette would calm my nerves, especially after what Eli had told me. Maybe I could just take a few puffs?

"Ugh." I hit my head on the steering wheel.

"Katrina?" said a voice.

I peeled my forehead from the steering wheel and spotted Helen at my window. "Helen? Hi."

Her face split into a grin. "Are you here to see Blake? I knew the two of you were going to hit it off. I told Gerry that Blake was going to finally settle down."

Oh. My. God. "Uh. We're just friends." And yeah, I didn't think Blake and I would ever be a thing.

Her smile faded. "Oh. *Oh!* Are you here about the *other* affair? About Tim?"

"I am."

"And? Have you found those responsible? The town's a mess. We're all worried sick."

"I have a lead. It's why I'm here."

Helen's eyes rounded, and she pushed her glasses up her nose. "Right. Well, I'll leave you to it, then. I'll see you tonight."

Before I could ask her what she meant by that, the werefox was already halfway across the parking lot.

"How the hell did she do that?"

With a last glance at the glove compartment, I pulled myself out of my Jeep. I was wired tightly. So I grabbed my stack of gum and popped not one but two pieces into my mouth.

"He says I chew like a cow. Might as well prove him right."

Still chewing, I made for the front wood door with glass panels. The sign above the door read MOONFELL COUNTY SHERIFF'S DEPARTMENT.

I climbed the redbrick stairs and went inside.

I took a few steps down the hall and arrived in the lobby, not taking in any of its décor. The sound of muted conversations and clicking keys hit me along with the aroma of freshly made coffee as I passed by the closed doors.

Through the doorway, I could spot more offices. Two men and a woman I had never seen before were sitting at desks cluttered with documents, focused on their screens.

A desk sat at the end of the lobby with an elderly woman seated behind it. She had short white hair, and her face was lined with wrinkles as if she were well past her hundredth birthday. Her white blouse was spotless and pressed, and she had a look on her face that could cut through anything.

"Can I help you?" croaked the older woman in a voice weathered with age. Her tone was friendly and kind. She reminded me of someone's grandmother.

"Yes. I'm here to see Blake. I don't have an appointment."

She waved a hand at me. "No worries, dear. He'll make time."

I liked this lady.

She picked up her phone and pressed a number. "Yes. There's a lovely woman here to see you."

"Kat," I told her.

"Kat," repeated the woman. "Sure." She hung up. "He'll see you. Just down the hall to the left. Can't miss it."

"Thanks."

Following her instructions, I headed down the hallway, aware of the few heads lifting to glance at me as I walked past offices. Blake must be in the last one.

"Kat?" Blake appeared from a doorway. He wore a black shirt and jeans that seemed to be tailored to his impeccable physique. His handsome face lit with surprise. "Never thought I'd ever see you here."

I chewed harder, trying not to think about his words or his attitude last night. I wasn't here for me. I wasn't here for him. I was here for the kids. Only for the kids.

"I have new information."

Blake stood next to a doorway and gestured me inside. "Have a seat."

I walked into an office with a large wooden desk and leather chairs. Paintings of wolves running in the woods hung on the walls along with one with just a white wolf. "These are beautiful," I said, and for some reason, I thought of Dash.

"Thanks." Blake walked past me and sat behind the large desk. "They're from a local artist here. Nadia. Have you heard of her?"

"No." I took the only seat in front of his desk. "She's very good."

Blake smiled. "She is." Something about the way he'd said that seemed like she was good at other things, like he'd slept with her.

Figures. "Look. I need to tell you something."

Blake interlaced his fingers on his desk. "You went to see Eli. Didn't you?"

"Yes." No point in lying.

Blake cursed, a vein throbbing on his forehead. "I knew it. I knew you were going to go without telling me."

And there he went again about controlling what I did. "Then you'll know that I have a lot to say. So, you can calm your ass down and let me say it, or I'm leaving."

The large werewolf took a breath in what I assumed was an attempt to calm his temper. "Fine. What did you find out? Is he involved?"

"Eli? No. He got kicked out years ago. He's not exactly stable. The dude is creepy."

"I could have told you that if you'd told me you were going to see him."

Blah, blah, blah. "But he did give me some very useful information. First, I'm pretty sure The Forsaken are the ones that killed Tim and Samuel."

A muscle tweaked above Blake's brow. "What makes you say that?"

"They're trying to raise a demon king." I did a recap of everything Eli told me, watching Blake's face take on different shades of color every second, every time I added to my story.

The werewolf smashed his fist on the desk, making his mug topple over and me jump in my chair. "Who are they? Tell me?"

Damn. He just loved ordering people around. I sighed and leaned back in my chair. "I don't know. And before you ask, Eli was spelled not to reveal their names. He couldn't. He tried to tell me, and it nearly killed him." Not that I would care if he died. The world would be a better place without that creepy witch. But I didn't want him to die on my account.

"One more sacrifice," said Blake, his voice edged with venom. "I'm not going to let that happen. I'm going to find these assholes and rip their fucking throats out."

I believed him. "And so you should," I told him. "They want to bring the end of the world... well, in a sense. If that demon king should rise, and he causes eternal night... the world as we know it will be gone. For us. For humans. Animals. All of us."

The werewolf set his jaw. "I won't let that happen. We'll find them first. But I need to protect my people." Blake's eyes met mine, and I could see the desperate rage simmering behind them. "How can I protect them when I don't know who the next victim will be."

"I have a theory on that. See, Eli said that they pick their victims according to their birth dates. Something to do with the alignment of the stars and the sun, and some numerical crap like that. Do you have Tim's date of birth? And Samuel's?"

"Yeah." Blake pulled out a file on his desk and flipped it open. "Samuel's October third… and Tim's is October eleventh."

"If I'm right, we need to find the kid paranormals born in October. That's who's next on their list of sacrifices."

"Goddamnit." Blake clenched his hands into fists. "They're just kids. What kind of sick group would do that here in Moonfell? It's a quiet, paranormal town. The humans don't even bother us."

"Crazies don't have boundaries. Doesn't matter if it's a small town or a big city. They're here." But sacrificing kids? That was a new level of crazy.

A growl emitted from Blake as he grabbed the edges of his desk like he wasn't sure whether to toss it across the room or not. Yes, he had a temper to match his big frame. But it was clear this werewolf cared deeply about the paranormals in this town. He wanted to protect them. They were his pack, his extended family, and he was the alpha.

The county did well picking Blake as their sheriff.

"The Forsaken. Are they here, in Moonfell?" asked Blake after a moment of silence.

I nodded. "I think so. It would just make more sense that they're local."

Blake bared his teeth, giving him a more primal edge. "If only I knew who they were. I could stop this right now. Stop the ritual and keep the town safe from these maniacs."

If only. "True. But we don't have names. And for now, maybe we don't need to."

A frown pulled Blake's face. "What do you mean?"

My pulse throbbed at the thought. "If I'm right, if we can keep them from grabbing the last kid, that'll stop the ritual. No sacrifice, no soul, no raising that demon king. Let's focus on that first."

A new vein throbbed on the side of Blake's temple. "No. I want these bastards to pay. I can't just leave them be, in good conscience. And in my town? What kind of sheriff would I be if I leave the threat. Right here in Moonfell? No. I can't. What's to stop them from doing this again in a year? In six months?"

Every twenty years, apparently. "I get it. I really do. But it's like you said; we don't know who they are. They can be anyone here in Moonfell."

"Witches. Witches did this."

Anger tightened my chest. He wasn't wrong, but I didn't like the way he said witches, like we were the scum of the paranormal races. Bottom-feeders. "Maybe. And according to Eli, most of The Forsaken are mages. But let's not jump to conclusions just yet. The point is, we'd be wasting precious time trying to figure out who they are while we should be keeping the kids safe. No kids. No ritual. No demon king. See my point here?"

Blake cocked a brow. "You know you're infuri-ating sometimes?"

I smiled. "Part of my charm?"

"Really?" A smirk crossed his face. "I'd love to see more of that."

"If you give me the list of kids born in October," I blurted, trying to keep the conversation professional, "I can start cross-referencing, and it'll go faster. Is there a safe house we could use? It would be best to put them together so we can keep an eye on them."

"We?"

My irritation perked up. "Yes, we. This is *my* case. That's what the Merlins pay me for."

"But it's *my* town."

"Fine. It's *your* town. But it's still *my* case."

"Good." Blake watched me for a beat too long. "We're going to do it my way."

I narrowed my eyes. "What does that mean, exactly?"

The sheriff's smile widened. "It means you're going to do what I say."

Here we go again. "That's not how I work. I told you before. I'm more of a lone gunman—woman."

Blake crossed his hands behind his head. "Not my problem. In my town, you're going to do it my way. I'm not going to risk another life. Even yours," he added, that damn smile of his returning.

"I'm touched," I mocked. But I didn't respond. I thought it better that he believed I would obey his commands. No way in hell I would, but he didn't know that.

"Who's that guy staying with you? Is he your boyfriend?"

I flinched on the inside. That line of questioning

caught me off guard. Why the hell did he want to know that? "No. Just a friend." I felt a flush rise from my throat all the way to my face.

Blake watched me. "A friend wearing your clothes?"

Crap. I'd forgotten about that. "His were dirty. They were in the wash." I realized I hadn't even tested my aunt's old washer and dryer. Had no idea if they still worked or not.

"Why were his clothes dirty?"

"Why are you so interested?" I wasn't sure what crossed the sheriff's face, and I didn't want to know. I wouldn't disclose what had happened to Dash either. Not until I knew more. It wasn't that I was more loyal to either of them, but I was following my gut. And my instincts told me to keep quiet about that right now.

I stood up. "If you could get me that list of those kids. The sooner, the better." Like yesterday. It was our only lead to that group. We needed to protect those kids.

"I'll have that list for you within the hour."

"Can you email me a copy of the names? My email's on the card you stole."

"Sure." Blake rose from his chair and came to stand next to me by the door. "Listen, Kat. I'm sorry about what I said last night. Had too many beers, and I let my mouth run off."

"Forget it. Not important." But I would *never* forget.

A sly smile spread across his handsome face. "You

think after this is done, I can take you to dinner?"

Well, that was unexpected. "Uh…" Cue in more insta-flush. "I'll think about it."

Blake zeroed in on my face, and I knew he could see the redness, probably thinking he was making me hot for him. "Is that a yes?"

"I'll think about it," I repeated, edging closer to my exit.

What the hell did he want? I was not dating material. I hadn't been on a date since my ex took me to dinner, and that was five years ago. And if he was looking for sex, he was barking up the wrong tree. I hadn't had sex in over a year and a half. The cobwebs down there had sewn everything shut. If he wanted sex, he should be asking Tilly.

Yet it was nice to know that I was still desirable in some way. I wasn't an old crone—yet.

And Blake? Well, he looked like sex on two very fine, muscled legs. I was sure he would make up for any indiscretions on my part. I had a feeling he liked to take control in the bedroom, too.

Why the hell was I thinking about sex? Because I hadn't had it for a long, long while. That's why.

With an added layer of redness, I slipped past Blake and sneaked out the door. "Send me that list," I called out, walking faster than necessary down the hall while keeping my head down.

Only when I got to my Jeep did I start to feel that flush leave my face. This wasn't the time to be thinking about sex or anything else but those kids.

My thoughts were all over the place. Blake. Eli.

The Forsaken. The demon king. I'd have to do some research on this demon king. There were many demon kings. Which one were The Forsaken trying to raise?

I was so focused on that thought that I hadn't seen the man who stood on my porch until I'd parked my Jeep in my driveway and was half up the porch's steps.

My legs locked into place. He wasn't a stranger.

I knew who he was. I hadn't seen him in more than twenty years, but I'd never forget that face.

My father's assistant.

Sykes.

CHAPTER 16

"What are you doing here?" I stepped up to the platform, not wanting to speak to him on the steps. This was my house. I should be level with him.

He had the same forgettable face that I remembered, with a long, pointed nose and a thin black mustache that matched his thin frame. Black, oily hair was parted in the middle and combed back in an old-fashioned style from the 1920s. Dull, light eyes stared back at me through a pair of round spectacles.

When I got closer, I noticed something peculiar about him.

He hadn't aged a day. Now, that was strange.

"I see that a lack of manners still exists in you," said Sykes in that same voice filled with contempt I'd remembered. And his breath? His breath was strong and sour like he hadn't brushed his teeth in days. His body smelled of paper and pencil shavings, like an old school desk. Yuck.

I took a step back. "I see you still wear those ridiculous bow ties." I stared at his frame wrapped in a tailored, dark suit and plaid bow tie. I never understood his choice of style. I still didn't.

Sykes pressed his lips into a thin line, or should I say his mustache. "You were always the most vile of the Lawless children."

I know it shouldn't have, but his comment bothered me. "You've got five seconds to tell me what the hell you want before I toss you off my porch. Don't think I won't." I took a step forward to show him I meant business. "I'm not that same kid anymore. You don't scare me." *And you can't hurt me anymore.*

A memory of Sykes gripping my arm and the searing sensation that followed raced through my mind. This happened whenever my parents found out I couldn't conjure up the type of magic they expected from me. Well, their idea of what magic was supposed to be. My parents thought physical punishment was the answer to making me more magical.

The smell of my singed flesh was seared into my memory. Sykes, a powerful White witch, seemed to draw the most pleasure from using fire on me. His face would light up with joy as I writhed in agony. That was nearly as bad as the pain.

Sykes made a disapproving sound in his throat. "Trust me. I don't want to be here."

"So, why are you?" Ten more seconds, and I was about to go crazy on his ass.

"Your father's orders."

I gave him a mock smile. "Still his lapdog, I see.

Aren't you tired of that? Don't you want to be a free witch?" I wasn't sure what he'd do without my father. Unless some other family was in need of some oily bastard witch assistant.

Sykes glared at me, his eyes burning with anger. "I'm no one's lapdog." He ran a hand over his sleek black hair, and I swear he mouthed the word "bitch." "I choose to serve your father."

"Whatever you say." *Lapdog. Lapdog. Lapdog.*

I crossed my arms over my chest, feeling my temper rising with each second I had to stand here with this creep. Funny. He seemed shorter than I remembered. Either I grew a few inches after I'd left, or he shrank. Yeah, he shrank.

Sykes's pale eyes stared at me without blinking. "Why are you back here? I thought we'd seen the last of you. Well, I hoped to see the last of you," he added with a mock laugh.

I plastered a fake smile on my face. "Thought I'd swing by and check out the old neighborhood." I wanted to grab that stupid bow tie and stuff it down his throat.

He stood with his arms straight down, pinned to his sides, like a rocket about to blast off into space—a familiar pose that always creeped me out. It was unnatural.

"No. That's not the reason." Sykes narrowed his eyes. "Are you in need of money? That's it. Isn't it? You thought you'd come back and try to swindle your family's fortune? I have news for you. They'll never go for it."

I laughed. "I'd rather drink a bucket of cyanide than take a penny from them." I meant it.

"Right." Sykes regarded my aunt's house. "It'll take a fortune to bring this monstrosity back to its former glory." His eyes settled back on me and then over to my Jeep. "You certainly don't look like you've done well for yourself. Why am I not surprised? Are those from a secondhand store?" He wiggled a finger at the clothes I was wearing, his expression one of disgust, like my jeans and T-shirt were crawling with fleas.

I gritted my teeth. "I'm perfectly content. I don't need much."

Sykes gave me a false smile. "Apparently not. But then, you're practically human, and they don't require much in terms of *magical* skill. That's what tells us apart—the skilled and the duds. Those with talent excel, and those who don't, well, they end up looking like you."

I shrugged. "If you want to call torturing kids to get them to do magic a skill, then you excel in that. Top marks."

Sykes made a face like he'd bitten into a raw onion. "All was done for your own good. You can't blame the teacher if the student is a moron."

"Fuck off." My voice rose as I imagined strangling him. Would Blake send me off to jail if I killed this bastard? Possibly.

Sykes laughed. "My, my. Temper, temper. You always had a temper as a child. No wonder your mother couldn't stand the sight of you. It's very unladylike."

"I'm not a lady."

"Clearly." He sneered. "I never had any trouble with your brother. He was always the better witch. The model witch."

"Good for him."

"Your parents are very proud of him, of what he's become. He's a very powerful witch in the community. Very successful. Everyone adores him."

"Awesome."

"He's married now. To Andrea Weber. Very powerful witch family. *Very* rich. Nice to tie all that money and power to the Lawless family."

"Whatever."

Sykes frowned at me. "You should show more respect to your brother."

"How's this?" I flipped him the finger.

My father's assistant's face darkened, and his lips moved as though he was preparing a curse. "You were always such a vile child. Useless and stupid. I've always said it."

"And you were always an asshole." I leaned forward, my eyes locked on his. "But here's the thing. I'm not a child anymore. So if you think you can come here and treat me like one, you're sadly mistaken."

Sykes clamped his jaw, and I felt a prick of magic, of hot energies in the air. The bastard was tapping into his magic. He wanted to fry me.

"Go ahead," I challenged, grinning. "Try it and

see what happens. I beg you. Do it." Okay, so killing my father's assistant might not be the smartest move, but if a slip of his fire touched me, I was going to send him to the grave. And I'd be happy about it. He was kind of asking for it.

The magic dissipated with a pop, and he ran his hand through his hair. "Why don't you return to your human world and leave your parents be. Why come here and stir up all those… unfavorable memories. You shouldn't have come here. You should have stayed in your beloved human world."

I shrugged. "I thought it'd be fun. We could celebrate Samhain and all dance naked around a fire."

Sykes recoiled at my comment. "You were never part of the family. You never fit. You're an outsider."

"Amen."

Sykes's eyes narrowed at my comment. He regarded the side of the Victorian home with distaste like it was about to bite him. "Strange what you think is livable. But then again, you always had low standards. We never expected much from you."

"Well, then. You were never disappointed."

Sykes stared at me, a kind of triumphant look on his face. "No. No, we weren't."

Heat rushed to my cheeks. Okay. I *was* going to kill him. I raised my voice. "Either tell me why you're here or get the hell off my porch. I won't ask you again." A flicker of movement caught my attention. Annette was crossing the street toward me, a dishtowel over her shoulder and concern flashing on her face. Guess she heard us.

Sykes followed my gaze, and I saw a flash of annoyance cross his face. Guess he didn't like Annette. That made me like her even more.

"Your father requests your presence tonight at dinner." Sykes turned to face me. "Seven o'clock sharp. There will be important guests, high-ranking figures of our community, so make sure you select some suitable clothing from your human wardrobe. Don't be late."

"I won't be. I'm not coming." Helen's comment about seeing me later tonight made sense now. Apparently, my family told their guests I would be there. Like hell, I would.

My spine stiffened at the mention of going back home. I'd left home when I was seventeen and never looked back. My parents were powerful and wealthy White witches, but they were also abusive. They believed that magic was superior to everything else, especially their own children. So, I'd packed my bags and moved to the city, where I could be myself without fearing their wrath.

I wasn't planning on returning anytime soon.

"He said you'd say that." Sykes laughed, and it had the hair on the back of my neck rising. He'd used the same laugh right before he'd scorch me with his fire magic when I was a kid.

"I'm never going back there," I spat the words out like venom. "You can tell your master I won't be there."

"You will." He took a breath, his fists pinned to

his sides. "He has information for you… about the case you're working on."

My mouth fell open. "I'm sorry, what?"

"Seven o'clock. Don't be late." Sykes glared at me before turning away and walking off without another word. I watched him go, my heart pounding in my chest.

Annette crossed paths with him, but he completely ignored her, like she wasn't even there. I hated him even more.

She climbed up the steps and joined me. "Isn't that your father's man? Spikes?"

"Sykes. Yeah. Unfortunately."

"Ugh. He always gives me the creeps." Annette shook her arms and hands like she was trying to shake out an evil spirit from her body.

I didn't blame her. I felt like I needed a shower. "That's because he is a creep."

Annette laughed. "From the look on your face, I guess he wasn't giving you good news." She waited, and I could tell she was expecting, or rather, hoping I was going to reveal my exchange with Sykes.

I sighed. "He came to tell me that I'm invited to dinner."

"Oh." Annette's gaze flicked back to where Sykes disappeared into a waiting black sedan with tinted windows. "Well, that doesn't sound that bad."

Of course, it wouldn't, not to her. "I'm really not in the mood for a dinner," I said, watching the car pull away and drive off. "Not to mention that it's really poor taste in timing, with Tim's death and all."

Just like my parents to throw a party in the midst of a murder investigation. It was probably the theme of the night to talk and share gruesome reports of that poor kid. I hated them.

Annette nodded, looking troubled as she folded her arms over her chest. "You're right. Dinner parties are a bad idea right now."

I realized she was thinking of the party she threw last night. "Your cocktail party wasn't the same," I said quickly. "You wanted to do something nice for me. To introduce me to your family. To get to know you better. This… this is different. Trust me. There's nothing nice about this dinner party."

"Are you going to go?"

The fact that my parents knew I was working Tim's case told me that they had asked about me, probably as soon as they heard I was back in town. Knowing them, they probably had me followed. So, now they knew what I did. And now my father had some "intel" on Tim's murder? Part of me felt like this was just a ruse to get me to show up at their stupid dinner party. But I couldn't ignore a lead, no matter who it came from.

"Kat? Are you going to go?" repeated Annette, the curiosity laced in her voice.

I looked at her and said, "Yeah. I'm going."

CHAPTER 17

"And he said your father had information about Tim's death?" My Aunt Luna stood next to the stove, stirring an orange substance that smelled strongly of manure. Thank the cauldron *I* wasn't going to drink it.

The thought of Dash brought a pang to my heart. The man, the werecat, must be going through hell. I had no idea what it must be like to be surrounded by your things and not remember any of them. Not remember where you lived or that you were an amazing carpenter and artist.

And he did *rock* those yoga pants and then some. Just had to throw it out there.

"He did." I broke a gum free from the pack and stuffed it in my mouth. I chewed, thinking over the conversation I'd had with my father's assistant. My heart was still hammering inside my chest. I hated that even all these years later, he still had that effect on me. That *they* still had that effect on me.

"Did you use your powers on him?"

Almost. "I didn't. I was cool." Well, in a way. It had been a struggle not to reach out and strangle the pale bastard.

"Good. The last thing we need is for that snake to be asking questions about you." She stirred harder. "Never liked the witch. Something's foul about him, about his aura."

"Definitely is."

"You can see it in his eyes," continued my aunt. "And his lips."

I pulled the stool from the kitchen island and sat. "His lips?"

My aunt pointed the wooden spoon at me. "I've always said never trust anyone with a thin upper lip."

"Okay." I'd never heard her say that. "He told me to wear something *presentable*." I laughed, chewing my gum like a cow. Loved cows.

My aunt chuckled darkly. "He really has no idea who you are."

"Clearly." And neither did my own parents. I laughed harder.

My aunt dipped a glass jar over the contents of the mix, and I caught a glimpse of what looked like tiny bones that could have been from rats or birds. I didn't want to know.

"Obviously, you're going to wear jeans." My aunt snickered. "And flip-flops."

"Obviously." I smiled. The thought of my mother's scowl at my clothes made me all giddy inside. My aunt knew me better than my own mother.

"I wish I could be there with you," said my aunt. "I'd love to slap some sense into your mother. A good slap might shake her up a bit. The goddess knows I've tried many times. But all she sees is that male witch you call a father. Nothing else matters."

A thought occurred to me. "You could come with me." Having an ally with me at that party would make things less… awkward. And I knew my aunt had my back.

My Aunt Luna sighed and propped a hand on her hip. "How can I? I'm supposed to be *dead*. Remember?"

I smiled with the gum between my front teeth. "Maybe you've risen from the dead recently."

"A zombie?"

I shrugged. "Nothing wrong with zombies. Apart from the rotting flesh and their appetite for *fresh* flesh." I'd encountered a few zombies in my line of work over the years. It was a messy business. But it paid well.

My aunt pressed her lips together and turned back to her potion. "You're on your own, darling. I'm not ready to *come out* just yet. Not sure I ever will. I rather like being dead."

"Fake dead." I figured she'd refuse, but it was worth a shot. She'd been hiding and cooped up for the last two years inside this house. I doubted something as trivial as my parents' dinner party would make her leave the comfort of her hiding place.

"You know," began my aunt as she dropped what looked like strands of hair into the mix. "I thought your brother might turn out to be a decent witch, but I was wrong. Just like his father, that one. Cut from the same cloth."

"I could have told you that." And the fact that he loved to beat on me and encouraged Sykes's torture tactics had been an early indicator of the monster within.

"But you do realize this is just a trap to have you go to the house," said my aunt. "Your father knows you'd never go to this dinner unless it had something to do with the case you're working on. I can bet you my pinky finger he's got nothing."

"You can keep your pinky finger. I know." I tapped my fingertips on the countertop. "And you're probably right. But I can't take that chance. Maybe he heard something? Maybe one of his friends did? I'll go, see if he has anything to give me or not, and then I'll leave."

"It's The Forsaken you should be looking for, not wasting your time with those socialites and poor excuses for witches. The whole lot of them give us witches a bad name. They give me indigestion."

"If I had names, I would. Without names, I don't have much to go on," I said to her. "I told you. Eli couldn't give me names. It was going to kill him." I'd recalled the encounter with The Forsaken ex-member as soon as I'd walked in the door, right before announcing who I'd met on the porch.

"Hmmm." My aunt placed her spoon on the

spoon rest on the counter and turned around. "That's very powerful magic. And illegal. Only the darkest, most powerful magic can curse a person not to reveal a name. You'd need an entire coven of mighty witches to do that… or…"

"Or?"

"Or by channeling *other* means of power."

Now, that was interesting. "Like what?"

"A very powerful demon, or a god."

I stopped mid-chew. "Are you serious?"

"As a heart attack."

I sighed. The Forsaken were more powerful and resourceful than I thought. If they could channel their powers from a greater demon, or worse, a god, this was going to be a lot harder than I imagined. Worse, I was going to need backup, and the only backup I had was Blake.

"How long now till the counter-curse potion is ready?" I asked, trying not to despair or become overwhelmed with the case, though I could feel my blood pressure rising.

My aunt pulled out the stool next to mine and sat, her gold loop bracelets tinkling like bells. "It should be ready tonight. After your dinner party."

"It's not *my* dinner party. Trust me, that's the last place I want to be tonight."

"And *trust me*, they're throwing it because you're here. You do know that. It's all about you tonight."

"It's all about how worthless they want to make me feel, you mean."

"I know." Sadness spread over my aunt's face. "I

wish you didn't have such a hard time growing up. It's made you…"

"Stronger?"

"Hard." A wicked smile spread over her face. "And a bitch."

I laughed, realizing at that moment how much I'd missed her sarcasm and truth. "I'd rather be a bitch than let people walk all over me." I'd had enough of that as a young person and into my adult life.

"Maybe, but sometimes being a strong bitch, you forget that it's okay to be soft occasionally."

I snorted. "Soft will get me killed." And soft wouldn't help me solve Tim's and now Samuel's deaths.

My aunt grunted. "You should call Dash and let him know that the potion'll be ready tonight."

"Right." I grabbed my phone, only realizing that I didn't have his number.

My phone buzzed in my hand.

"Maybe that's him now?" My aunt was staring at my phone like I was holding a giant beetle in my hand and not a cell phone.

I tapped on my screen. "It's from Blake. It's the list of names of the kids born in October." I wasn't ticked that he'd gone through the names without my help. It would save me some time.

"And?" My aunt leaned forward, and her lavender soap scent filled my nose. "What does it say? How many?"

"Two," I told her, reading the text message. "Two names—oh shit."

"Oh shit? Please tell me those are not the names. Parents these days think they have the right to tag their children with the strangest names."

I shook my head. "No. There's a Felix Boudreault, and the other... the other is Annette's daughter. Emma."

My aunt leaned back. "Oh shit."

My insides twisted as my phone buzzed again with another message. "He says he's alerted the parents and told them to keep their kids inside. They're not to leave their homes." I sighed. "Poor Annette. She must be out of her mind." In a way, I was glad Blake had taken charge and alerted the parents. I didn't want to have that conversation, especially after seeing what had happened to Tim and now Samuel.

"This is bad, Kat," said my aunt. "You cannot let The Forsaken take either one of those kids."

I bit my lip, feeling my pulse skyrocket. "I can't believe this. Emma. Emma's on The Forsaken's radar." I'd only just met her, but it raised something primal in me—an intense feeling of protection. I'd kill anyone or anything that tried to harm her. I would.

My aunt let out a heavy sigh and put a comforting hand on my shoulder. "We'll figure this out. We'll bring Tim's and Samuel's killer to justice and put an end to all this chaos."

I nodded, taking comfort in her words. But as I thought about the two names on the list, a knot formed in my stomach. I had no idea who this Felix was, but he was just a kid. And Emma? She was just a sweet, innocent witch. The thought of her being taken had my stomach roll.

"I'm not going to my parents' dinner party. Screw it. Not now. I'm going to stay with Annette and her kids. They need protection."

My aunt opened her mouth just as I got another text.

"I'm on my way to Annette and Liam's," I read out loud. *"I put a team outside to guard Felix's house around the clock. They won't be alone."*

My aunt flicked a finger at me. "Looks like you're going to that dinner party."

"Looks like you'd rather be going than me."

My aunt shrugged. "Wouldn't mind having a conversation with that mother of yours. But I can't. I'm supposed to be dead."

"You can't keep pretending. One day, someone will figure it out or see you."

"Nonsense. I've been doing it for the past two years. The longer I do, the better I get."

I dropped the subject. I had more important things to think about, but she was right. If Blake was on his way to Annette and Liam's, I would just end up being in the way. Liam was Blake's best friend. He would protect their children as though they were his own. Of that, I had no doubt.

Besides, that was just for tonight. I didn't know when The Forsaken would try and abduct one of those kids. I just knew it was soon. Could be tonight. Could be in three days.

"You know what you must do," said my aunt.

I glanced at her, my phone biting into the soft flesh of my palm as I held it tightly. "What do you mean?" I had a feeling I knew what she was about to say, but I wanted her to say it.

My aunt looked at me. "Destroy The Forsaken."

My heart sped up at the tone of fear and urgency in her voice. "That sounds awesome, but I've already told you: We don't know who they are. For now, the best thing we can do is to keep those kids safe and away from this group. They can't perform their ritual without them. It's the best we've got."

My aunt gave a laugh. "Is that what you think?"

"Why do I get the feeling this is a trick question?"

"Do you think The Forsaken have only one agenda?" said my aunt as she stood and went back to her potion mix on the stove.

I narrowed my eyes. "It *was* a trick question."

"Even if you manage to stop this ritual, it won't stop them. They've been at this a long, long time. Longer than I've been alive. And I'll tell you one thing: They won't stop. They'll never stop. Not until they're destroyed. Darkness. Unlimited power. They've tasted it. It's addictive. And it changes you."

I thought of Eli and how twisted he'd seemed. "I know."

"They're as crooked as a dog's hind leg."

I hooked a thumb at myself. "And I'm the one who's supposed to destroy them?"

She leaned forward and tasted the wooden spoon like she was tasting her spaghetti sauce. "You or someone else. It doesn't matter. As long as they're put down for good."

I pointed at her. "Uh… should you be doing that?" I had no idea what tasting that potion would do to a witch without a memory problem.

"Too bad Blake's going over to Annette's tonight," said my aunt, ignoring my question. "You could have asked him to join you at that party."

I snorted. "Why would I do that?" As of now, Blake wasn't my favorite person in town. Yes, he'd proven helpful with my case, but he was still an arrogant bastard who thought his hotness would have me throwing myself, my naked body, at him.

My aunt regarded me for a moment. "When's the last time you had sex?"

I wanted to die. "Yeah. Not going there with you."

"Looks to me like it's been years."

How the hell would she know that? "Uh, well, not that it's any of your business."

"So, there's been no one since your ex, Stanley?"

"It's Jayce. And no." I did not want to discuss my sex life with my aunt. Not that there was much to discuss in that department.

She propped her hands on her hips. "What's wrong with Blake? He's handsome. He's the town sheriff. He's single."

"He's an arrogant bastard."

"Yes, he knows he's pretty. So what? I'm not saying marry the werewolf," she continued. "I'm just saying that it might do you some good to let yourself have some fun. And he looks like sex on a stick, that one. I bet he's *real* good in bed."

Heat rushed to my cheeks. "Can we not talk about this, please?"

"He's the most sought-out bachelor in Moonfell, you know."

"Then he doesn't need me."

A giggle escaped my aunt. "If I were your age, I'd be all over him."

"Not listening." I pressed my hands over my ears. "Not one more word."

"Fine," I heard my aunt say and removed my hands. "My lips are sealed." She laughed again, and I did not want to go there.

I jumped off the stool. "I'm going to see Annette before Blake gets there. She deserves to know what's going on. As the hired caseworker, I think it only makes sense that I talk to her. And see how Emma's doing."

She was probably scared out of her teenage wits. I wanted to tell them that it would be all right, that we would catch the bad guys. But I couldn't. We didn't know who they were. Still, Annette deserved to know the truth so far.

"Don't stay too long," said my aunt. "You don't want to be late for your parents' *special* dinner party."

"Of course." I grabbed my bag and headed out the door.

It was going to be a *very* special dinner.

CHAPTER 18

After my brief meeting with Annette, Liam, and all the girls, I headed back home to take a nice hot bath and get ready to meet my *loving* family.

Annette's face was red, and her eyes were swollen with tears when I got there. Liam was shaking, his body twitching like he was about to beast out into his werewolf form and wreak havoc on the kitchen cabinets.

Emma was upstairs in her room on the phone with one of her friends, laughing and having a good time, not fully understanding the severity of the situation. Maybe it was better that way.

"Promise me you'll find these bastards," Annette had said when she'd cornered me in the kitchen just as Blake walked in.

"I promise," I'd answered, knowing I'd just broken my number one rule again: Never promise the client anything because you can't determine fate.

Instead of a nice, calm soak in the clawfoot tub, it

had been a short, jumpy bath time. I couldn't relax. My mind was buzzing like I had a swarm of bees inside my skull. Not only was I about to have a visit with family members I hadn't seen in over twenty years, but now I had to worry about Emma.

The last thing I wanted to do was go to that dinner party. It was a waste of time. I should be trying to figure out who the members of The Forsaken were, not mingling with the high society in our community. It wasn't my crowd. Did I even have a crowd?

The only reason I was going was because Sykes had said my father had intel on Tim's murder.

With a clean pair of dark jeans and a satin black dress top with capped sleeves, I finished the look with my black flat shoes. Grabbing my shoulder bag, I rushed out.

"I shouldn't be too long," I called out to my aunt, who was sitting at the kitchen island, working on her sudoku puzzle.

"Give your mother a slap for me, will ya?" my aunt called, a smile in her voice.

I laughed. "I will. And I'll add one for me, too."

I shut the front door, and just as I stepped off the front porch, a green Land Rover pulled into the driveway.

I forgot to breathe as a glorious, tall male specimen climbed out of the SUV.

My heart quickened at the sight of Dash's dark eyes staring at me from across the driveway. He looked gorgeous in a fitted gray shirt that seemed to highlight his broad shoulders and strong biceps. His dark jeans gave a hint of his toned thighs. A grin adorned his freshly shaven face as he strolled toward me.

Damn, he looked good.

"It's not ready yet," I blurted out, wondering why I felt so nervous.

Dash smiled, transforming his handsome face to a rip-off-your-panties-and-take-me kind of face. "I know. I thought I'd come early." His eyes lingered on my lips, and I could feel my heart race.

I'd finally found Dash's number and called him to tell him that my aunt's counter-curse potion would be ready tonight. He'd been silent on the phone after that, and I'd wondered why that was. Maybe he didn't want his memories back? No, that didn't make sense.

"Well, my aunt's inside, so you can go right in," I told him, trying to rid my mind of those images of him with his bare chest and wearing only my yoga pants.

Dash came to stand next to me, and a musky scent of cologne or soap rolled over me. "You're going somewhere? I should have called you first."

I sighed. "Nowhere special. Just to my parents' dinner party."

"You don't look enthusiastic about going."

"I don't. Oh well. Guess I'm not as good an actress as I thought. The truth is, I really don't want to go."

"So why are you?"

I looked into Dash's eyes, and I felt comfortable. Something about the way he was looking at me made me feel at ease, and I found myself opening up to him.

"Apparently, my father's got information about Tim's case. I can't ignore that." I looked over at Annette's house, and my stomach tightened at the memory of the fear in her eyes and the desperation that I catch the bastards. "But I'm not staying long. As soon as I hear what he has to say, I'm out of there."

"Would you like company?" A smile tilted up the corners of his mouth as he approached me.

I flicked my eyes back on Dash. I couldn't read his expression, but something in his eyes had warmth pool in my belly. "Yeah. Yes, I would." I suddenly felt less anxious having Dash come with me. I had to brave the lion's den, so an ally was much needed.

"I'll drive," said the werecat.

I climbed into the Land Rover, eyeing the rugged luxury. It was an older model, but it was still a classic that I could never afford. I wondered how Dash could on a carpenter's salary.

The werecat pulled out of the driveway, and with one last look over at Annette's house, we were off.

We sat in silence for a while. It wasn't an uncomfortable one, but it seemed like we were both inside our heads, trying to figure things out. He was still dealing with his memory loss, and I was trying to figure out which of the two kids The Forsaken were after. What I should have been doing was watching over Annette's house or even the other kid. Not attending some stupid party.

"Take a left here," I instructed after a few minutes of driving. I could feel Dash's eyes on me as I stared straight ahead.

"I take it you're not close with your family." Dash's voice flowed like smooth silk, and I couldn't help but be drawn to it.

I coughed out a laugh. "We're the opposite of close." I despised them. "Right at the next corner."

"Is that why you haven't come back here in twenty years?"

The werecat was perceptive. But I had told him a bit about myself that first night he'd spent with us.

"That's partly the reason." The other reason was that I'd been traumatized by that young witch I'd left behind under the bridge. When I noticed her chest rise and fall, I'd freaked out. She was still alive, and I'd... *taken off*, in a way, scared out of my mind. I'd left her. And I'd felt guilty ever since.

I didn't want to go into the details of that night so many years ago. And I was saved from divulging anything else as my family home came into view.

"We're here," I told Dash. "It's that big brown brick house with all the cars." I pointed.

My eyes darted to the brick house with steeply pitched gable roofs, elegant masonry and stonework, and stately wooden beams set in a stucco or stone façade.

Dash whistled. "You grew up here?"

"Don't let the exterior fool you," I said, my heart

207

pounding in my chest, and I hated how just the sight of that house made me feel sick. "It looks pretty, but the inside is rotten."

My eyes wandered to the estate located across from us, a sprawling complex nestled within lush meadows. The three-story Tudor manor house surrounded a central courtyard, and the property was bordered by thick woods leading up to a large pond.

Dash parked his Land Rover at the curb. The house had a long driveway, but it was packed with luxury cars and SUVs.

I yanked open my bag, grabbed two gums, and stuffed them in my mouth. Yeah, the way I was chewing wasn't pretty or sexy, and if Dash thought so, he didn't say anything.

I sat in my seat, not moving, as though my butt were superglued to the leather.

"You don't have to go, you know," said Dash. His hand reached out like he was about to touch my shoulder, but he pulled back at the last moment.

I tried to ignore the fact that maybe I repulsed him or something since he wouldn't touch me. "But I do." I took a breath and slipped out of the SUV.

Chewing my gum, we crossed the street and made our way toward the elegant Tudor home. My boots crunched on the gravel path that separated a garden of rosebushes and boxwoods before leading to the main doors of the house.

As Dash and I approached the grand entrance with its towering double doors, music and voices sounded from the inside, and it took all of my will and strength not to bolt.

I pressed my finger on the doorbell and leaned back.

"As soon as you want to go, just give me a sign, and we're gone," said Dash on the landing behind me. "You don't have to stay a minute longer."

"Thanks," I said as I chewed. I was grateful that he'd come with me. I felt more empowered that I had someone. Bonus that he was easy on the eyes.

The front door swung open, and I flinched, losing my balance momentarily.

I felt a hard chest against my back as I crashed into Dash. His strong hands grabbed my arms and steadied me. I felt myself leaning back into him—just a tad longer than necessary.

I knew then that would be the highlight of my night. And I took it like a champ.

I straightened as a man stepped from the threshold. I was expecting to see my mother or even Sykes, having mentally prepared a clever one-liner should she have attempted to slam the door in my face.

The man towered over me, and I had to crane my neck to take it all in. His hair was black with flecks of gray at the temples, cropped short without much care while his expression was fixed with a faint frown. His long nose gave his face an aquiline look. He wore a black shirt and gray trousers that fit him perfectly.

The faint traces of cold energy and the scent of vinegar and sulfur hit me. He was a Dark witch.

"What can I do for you?" the man asked, a slight

hint of mockery in his voice as he looked us up and down. He crinkled his nose at my choice of clothing: jeans and a simple blouse. His posture was one of disapproval.

"My father invited me to this shindig," I said, feeling the loss of Dash's warmth as he stepped beside me.

"Ah, yes, *the* daughter." The doorman stepped aside and waved us in. "Please, come in. They are expecting you."

Fantastic.

Without a word, I walked past the doorman and stepped into the foyer.

CHAPTER 19

Generally, those who are away from home for a long time get a nostalgic feeling when they return. Not me.

I was instantly hit with a feeling of repulsion. And a deep part of me, that inner child that was still there sometimes, begged me to flee.

But I wasn't a child anymore. And these people, these witches, couldn't hurt me.

We were greeted by wood paneling stretching farther than I could see. A magnificent double-sided staircase split the house into two halves. On the walls, hung paintings and warm wainscoting added to the cozy feel of the space. The furniture was strikingly beautiful in its nineteenth-century design, boasting intricate wood carvings.

The house was beautifully crafted and furnished, and I noted Dash had noticed that, too. As a master carpenter and artist, he was probably admiring all the details. I was surprised he didn't comment on it.

"You okay," he asked, his voice low and soothing.

I forced a smile. "I'm fine." Total lie, and I could tell by the concern on his face he didn't buy it.

We followed the male witch down a hallway to a room on the left. It had a strong masculine vibe with dark wooden furniture and deep-navy walls. A magnificent Persian carpet in rich shades of wine, blue, and gold covered the floors while an imposing limestone fireplace completed the look at the end of the room.

I looked around, feeling awkward now that I was in this house again, which felt alien and filled with strangers. Some were my age, while others were older than my parents and even aunt. They conversed and laughed as they sipped their drinks, accompanied by the melody of classical music.

Voices bustled as the guests all moved around the room. I heard a familiar laugh, and my eyes snapped toward it, my attention back to the crowd.

A woman stood across from me, wearing a cinna-mon-colored, scooped A-line evening gown adorned with lace, sequins, and a sweeping train. Her dark tresses cascaded down to the middle of her back. Her smile reminded me of my aunt's, but she was nothing like her. She took in the room with alert eyes, and when she finally noticed me standing there, she didn't look surprised.

Evangeline Lawless. My mother.

Her gaze flicked to mine momentarily, and then she was smiling and started a conversation with another one of her guests, a woman with long silver hair and electric blue eyes that sparkled in the light, like crystals.

Yup. She hadn't changed. Her interest in me was equal to her interest in dog shit.

"This was a mistake," I said to Dash, whose concern for me showed on his face and had my stomach fluttering. "We should go." If we slipped out now, no one would miss us.

"You made it," said a male voice.

I turned toward the sound of the tone. I knew who he was: the same clean-cut face, brown hair cut in a modern style, the same hazel eyes and mocking smile that never quite managed to reach his eyes. I could never trust that smile, knowing an ulterior motive was lurking, or he was always trying to get an edge over me.

"As you can see," I said.

His brows knotted together, but he was still smiling that cold, deceitful smile. "You got old."

"So did you."

"Damn. You look like life's been hard on you," he said, still smiling.

Prick.

Dash followed the exchange with interest, probably wondering whether he should intervene or not. The thought of him smashing his fist in that grinning face was a great visual.

He stuck out his hand to Dash. "I'm Brad, Kat's brother."

Dash shook my brother's hand and nodded in acknowledgment. "Dash."

My brother looked at Dash with mild interest. "Have we met before? You look familiar."

Dash kept his gaze on my brother. "If we did... I don't remember."

And that was the truth. Though I doubted my brother would associate with a mere carpenter.

Brad returned his gaze to me. "Well, he's out of your league. Tell me... did you pay him to come tonight?"

My blood boiled. "He's my friend."

"Hmm. When father told me you were coming, I didn't believe him," said my brother. "I mean... we haven't seen you in, what? Eighteen years?"

"Twenty."

My brother's brows rose. "So, you can see my surprise. I thought you were dead." He threw back his head in a laugh.

"Still breathing."

He watched me a moment, and I could see plans or insults forming behind his eyes. "Why now? Why, after all this time? You're not dying. Are you?" His smile was chilling.

"Unfortunately, no." Though I was sure, the notion brought him great satisfaction. "I'm working a case."

My brother's eyes widened with mock surprise. "Yes. Yes. The famous *murder* everyone's talking about."

I knew it.

"You're the supernatural police, I've been told." That fake laugh returned. "Better watch myself around you, then."

"Something like that."

"Since you've been gone," continued my brother, "I've done well for myself. I'm rich. I've got a seat on the White witch council next to Father. A gorgeous wife with the best tits you've ever seen… and power. More than you can imagine."

"Oh, I can imagine."

Dash snorted, and my brother's smile vanished.

"Not that you'd know anything about power or magic," said my brother, that cold grin returning. "You never had either. And it looks like you still don't. Born a loser, still a loser."

A growl escaped Dash, which only made my brother's enthusiasm at insulting me increase a hundredfold. Yeah, he loved it. He was hoping Dash would do something.

"Where's your father?" I asked, trying to break up the tension. "I only came to see him." And the sooner I did, the sooner I could leave this place.

"Probably banging that hot fae I saw him with earlier," said my brother, smiling at Dash as though he would agree that cheating on your wife was a good thing. I'd heard the rumors when I was younger, the rumors that my father had had many, many mistresses. Looked like things hadn't changed, or maybe they were just more out in the open.

"There he is."

I followed my brother's gaze.

Through the throng of people, I saw a man walking toward us. He was a tall, imposing man with broad shoulders and thick, dark hair. He wore a sharp suit that emphasized his power and wealth. As he approached us, I couldn't help but feel a sense of unease.

Alistair Lawless. Or should I say, Alistair Vargas.

My father and I had never been close, and the rumors of his rise to power so quickly only added to my distrust of him. How he'd married my mother for her name, her position. There was no love there.

And power, he had. Loads of it. I could feel it thrumming across the room, see it on his face and the way everyone parted, giving him ample room to move. Was that fear I saw on some faces?

He caught me staring. At first, I saw recognition in his eyes, and then anger flashed across his expression as his eyes darted from Dash to me. That was quickly replaced by a blank, businesslike visage. Sykes trotted next to him, his loyal witch servant, his shadow.

"Katrina," said my father as he stood before me. "How good of you to come."

I opened my mouth to thank him for inviting me and then remembered that I hated the witch. So instead, I said, "Can we talk privately? Sykes said you had information for me."

"You've changed," he continued, ignoring my question. "You seem… different."

"That's what twenty years does to a person. This is my friend, Dash," I said, and my blood boiled as my father completely ignored him.

"She's the supernatural police, now," said Brad with a chuckle. He took a mouthful of his drink. "Better watch yourself, Father. Or she might throw your ass in jail."

My father's eyes flicked back to me. "Yes. Yes, I've heard all about it."

I seriously doubted that. "Can we get on with it? I'm very busy." Busy helping Dash with his memory and finding out who The Forsaken were. I didn't have time to play into my father's narcissistic games.

When it was clearly evident that he wasn't going to speak to me privately, I asked, "Do you have information for me or not?"

"Do you have a badge?" Brad looked me over like he was expecting to see a gun holster or something.

"No."

Brad gave me a skeptical look. "Then how do you make people believe you're the paranormal police without a badge? They just take your word for it?"

"Something like that."

Brad choked on his drink, laughing, and my face flamed. I wanted to punch him in the throat. I felt like I was fourteen again and the butt of Brad's and his friend's jokes. Which usually revolved around my lack of magical abilities.

Dash moved closer to me, putting himself between me and Brad, and I felt a flutter in my chest.

My brother wiped his mouth. "Is he your bodyguard or something? Buddy, I can snap your neck with a thought."

A wicked smile spread over Dash's face, something I hadn't seen before—yet, more like it. "You don't have that kind of magic."

My brother's mouth parted, and for a second, I saw a flash of that sixteen-year-old kid with a temper tantrum when he didn't get his way. Looked like Dash hit a nerve. I wondered how he knew this. Maybe it was just a good guess, or maybe werecats could sense magic in a way that we witches couldn't.

I turned to my father, who was watching Dash with deep loathing. "You don't have any information. Do you?"

My father turned his attention back to me, and by the sneer on his face, I knew it was a lie. He had nothing for me. I looked over to Sykes, but his face was blank.

"First, let's play a game, shall we?" said Alistair, an evil gleam in his eye. It was the look he had right before he'd either had Sykes burn me with his magic or found a way to demean me.

"It's time to go," I told Dash under my breath. It was just a whisper, but I knew he'd heard me when he stepped closer and pressed his hand on the small of my back.

"Show us your magic," called my father, his voice loud and commanding, so much so that the entire room went still. All eyes on me. "Show us how *strong* the Lawless bloodline runs in your witch veins, Daughter."

A gush of blood rushed to my face as whispers reached me. Everyone waited for me to show off my magic, the Lawless way.

And then, with a snap of his finger, purple fire sprouted from his palm. It coiled around his wrist like snakes, and the air thickened with power as the magical ringlets burned red.

My hatred for him intensified. He knew I couldn't do what he asked and still wanted to make me look bad in front of his buddies. It seemed as if his goal was to belittle me publicly.

With a flick of his wrist, my father flung the red magic at me.

Before I could react, it wrapped around my neck like a heavy iron chain, choking me. Fear hit as the magic squeezed, cutting off my air supply. I grabbed at the magical rope, trying to pull it off. But it was no use.

Panic soared, and I looked around, searching for a shadow, something I could reach out to for help. But the room was lit like it was midafternoon on a sunny, cloudless day. I was out of options.

Alistair walked around me like he was admiring a sculpture he'd just bought. "If you are truly a Lawless witch, you should be able to remove a nightmare snare with a simple push of your own magic. Your brother could do it at the age of five."

Through my tears, I could see my father's victorious face and my brother's smile. Over the white noise in my ears, I could hear my father's laughter above all the guests.

Dash was next to me in a second. "How do I take this off you?"

I shook my head, feeling lightheaded and knowing that, at any moment, I was about to pass out or die.

I blinked, and then Dash was facing my father. Either he moved with vampire speed, or I was seriously losing it. "Stop. This." I'd never heard Dash's voice like that before. It was lethal, venomous, and promised pain. Lots and lots of pain. His hands were rolled into fists, and he looked like he was about to go all crazy on my father's ass. I would love to see that. Too bad I was going to die.

I swayed to the side and fell to my knees. Yup. I was going to die. And in front of an audience. Great.

Just when darkness plagued my vision, the tension around my throat released. I fell forward on my hands, gasping for breath.

Strong hands grabbed my arms and lifted me to my feet.

"Kat?"

I looked into Dash's eyes. "I'm okay." Total lie. My own father had nearly killed me just to prove a point—that I couldn't manifest his kind of magic. It hurt. I wasn't going to lie. But it hurt more emotionally. It brought a lot of old feelings back to the surface. Feelings of not understanding why I was different. Of not belonging to my own family. Of not belonging anywhere.

"Ladies and gentlemen," said my father as he raised his glass. "My daughter. The human."

Laughter and applause exploded all around, making me feel sick. It seemcd like their laughter was choking me again, like I had a nightmare snare wrapped around my neck again.

My father had only invited me to humiliate me in front of all these people.

A tear escaped my eye, and I brushed it away quickly just as I caught a glimpse of my mother. She was staring at her husband with a mixture of confusion and horror.

I didn't have the luxury to ponder what that was. I just wanted to get the hell out.

"We're leaving." Dash grabbed my elbow and steered me toward the exit.

I stumbled along with him, my heart beating frantically in my chest. The humiliation and pain were too much to bear. I had always known my father despised me for being different and weak, but I never thought he would go this far to prove his point.

As we walked out of the room, I tried to keep my head down and avoid the laughing gazes of the guests. My emotions were all over the place, and I wished I could just disappear. Dash kept a firm grip on my elbow, leading me down the hallway and out the front door.

As we stepped out of the house, I took a deep breath, trying to steady my nerves. Dash's arm was still wrapped around mine, and I leaned into him, grateful for his support.

"Are you okay?" His voice was soft and gentle, which made me feel a little better.

"Like a million bucks," I said, my voice hoarse like I'd swallowed a bucket of razor blades.

"I'm sorry," he said, squeezing my arm. "Your father's a real asshole."

I laughed bitterly. "I couldn't have put it better myself." But he'd also been different, more evil than I remembered. That look in his eyes said he really wanted to hurt me… or kill me.

"You're his daughter. Why would he do that to you?"

"Because I'm different." I took a labored breath. "Because I bring shame to him."

Dash stopped and reached for my hand. His rough, calloused fingers gripped mine, and he looked into my eyes. His gaze was intense but also unexpectedly kind and gentle. I felt I couldn't look away as he let go of my hand. It hadn't been much of a touch, only a few seconds. But he conveyed so much emotion in that brief touch. It was like the motherlode of touches.

He opened the Land Rover's front passenger door for me, and I crawled inside.

"Do you need a healer?" asked Dash as he slipped into his seat and fired up the engine. "You'll have to tell me where to go. I… I still don't remember much."

I shook my head. "Let's get you to my aunt." I swallowed, my throat raw. "The counter-curse should be ready by now. It's time for you to get your life back."

Dash pulled away from the curb and did a U-turn, heading back the way we came. For a moment, I forgot about the pain and humiliation. First, we'd get Dash's memory back.

Then, The Forsaken were mine.

CHAPTER 20

"What happened to your neck?" asked my aunt as soon as Dash and I walked into the house.

I dropped my bag on the kitchen island, noticing for the first time six lit candles placed around the kitchen floor, surrounding hand-drawn runes and a circle. "A gift from my dearest papa."

My aunt stiffened. It looked like she'd changed for Dash's counter-curse spell. She wore a purple top hat fitted with a large purple feather, retro purple glasses, pointy ankle boots, a blue minidress, and a red cape to finish the look. Oh—and a bejeweled, green walking cane.

She looked at Dash as though waiting for him to confirm it. "He did that to you? At the party?" she asked, her cane thumping and her eyes widening as she came closer for a better look. "That's a nightmare snare spell. It's illegal to use it on another witch."

I shrugged. "Semantics." I moved to go near the

stove, but my aunt whipped out her cane and caught me in the stomach.

She pointed a jeweled finger at me. "Don't brush this off. This is serious, Kat. Your own father did this? And what was your mother doing?"

"Nothing." Though she did look shocked. I'd give her that. But she didn't try to stop him.

My aunt looked incredulous. "She didn't try to stop him?"

"She probably didn't want to make a scene. Or break a nail." I looked over my shoulder to Dash. "Dash stopped him." Our gazes connected, and an electric current rushed through me at the intensity of his stare.

"It was nothing," he said. That confidence in his voice almost made me purr.

My aunt rushed over and tackled him into a bear hug. "Thank you! Thank you for having balls of steel and not caring about those stuck-up, good-for-nothing witches."

"Luna!" I said, laughing. "Leave Dash's balls alone." Yeah, that sounded weird as soon as the words left my mouth.

My aunt let him go. "I did nothing to his balls," she said, walking away with a tiny smirk.

Yup, this was a strange conversation.

I cleared my throat, feeling a bit of color hitting my cheeks at the grin on Dash's handsome face. "Okay. Is the counter-curse ready?"

"It is." My aunt moved over to the stove. "It's had time to cool down, so it's just right." She jabbed her finger in the mix, pulled it out, and then stuffed it in her mouth. "Mmm. It's ready."

I frowned, wondering if all witches sampled their own potions. "I'm going to head to Annette's right after." Even though Blake was there, looking after them, I'd felt guilty leaving them to attend my family's party. Now, even more so when I realized I'd been duped.

"I'll come with you," said Dash, giving me a warm smile.

"Thanks. I'm sure Annette will appreciate it." And it might give her something to think about other than The Forsaken.

I watched as my aunt grabbed a mug from one of the upper cabinets and dunked it in the potion pot. "So, I gather that your father had no information about poor Tim's murder? Or that other young man's?"

I rubbed the back of my neck. "No. He just wanted to hurt and humiliate me in front of all his friends." I could still hear their laughter as though I were back in the room with them. Taking a deep breath, I shook off the memory.

I should have listened to my witchy instincts and stayed here. I wouldn't be making that same mistake again.

"Don't you worry about them," said my aunt. "People like that are not worth wasting a single emotion on." She sighed. "Though I am disappointed in your mother. She was always a bit of a floozy and learned at a young age that her beauty could get her whatever she wanted. She looked the other way when your father tried to *force* you to do magic. But to hurt you? And in public like that? After not having seen you in twenty years, and she did nothing? I am very surprised. She was never a good mother to you, but she is still your mother."

It had been a shock for my own father to behave the way he did. I'd expected a few laughs at my expense—to taunt my clothes, my jobs, my lack of love life. For all of those things, I'd been prepared mentally.

But I'd not been expecting to be physically attacked. By my own father, no less. And that icy stare, that look in his eyes was like if Dash hadn't stopped him, he would have killed me and then walked over my dead body to get a drink.

If I'd had any doubts about not coming back in those twenty years, I didn't have them anymore.

"Well, my brother's still a dick, so that hasn't changed."

"Brad is stupid," declared my aunt, making Dash laugh. "He was a stupid child, and he grew up to be a stupid man." She held the mug with the counter-curse potion in her hand. The substance, a now dark purple color, almost black, swooshed. "Well, I am glad Dash was there to put a stop to this madness."

"It was my pleasure," said the tall werecat. Was it me, or did he just *purr*?

"Well, then. Here you are." My aunt handed the mug to Dash. "Drink it all up—every single drop. You better do it in one go, if you get my meaning."

227

Dash stared at the mixture with hesitation. "No. What do you mean?"

"She means it's going to taste like crap," I said.

"Nice." Dash gave the mixture a whiff and flinched. "Well, if it tastes as good as it smells… I'm in for a real treat."

"Oh, hush." My aunt waved a hand at him. "We all know things that taste good are bad for you."

I raised a brow. "They are?"

My aunt patted Dash's arm. "If it tastes bad, you know it's good for you."

"Apple pie tastes good. It hasn't killed me yet."

"I'll need to say the spell first," instructed my aunt, ignoring me. "Once that's done, you drink the potion. Step into the circle over there."

Dash did as he was told. Once inside the circle, he asked, "And I'll have my memories back?" He was staring at the mix in the mug like he was expecting to see reflections of his past.

"That's right," answered my aunt. "You'll remember everything."

"And the person who cursed you in the first place," I said, hoping I was right.

My aunt nodded. "That, too. Okay, now, give me some room." She hooked her cane around her left arm and then spread out her arms and crouched like she was performing a plie squat.

I rubbed my arms, feeling nervous, though I wasn't sure why. But I kept thinking that maybe once Dash got his memories back, I might never see him again. He'd have his life back, his memories, and maybe I wouldn't fit in his life anymore.

It was selfish of me. And I pushed those thoughts away. What was important was that Dash would finally get his memories back and know the person who cursed him and hopefully the reason behind it.

My aunt clapped her hands hard and then rubbed them together like she was trying to start a fire. Maybe she could.

My aunt's voice rose in a solemn chant: "Let us call upon the goddess at this darkest hour. May she undo what has been done with her sacred power. Help him through his agony, and bless him with his memory."

The magical energy was palpable as it swirled around the room. I could feel it in the air, intensifying with each passing moment. The flickering flames of the candles brightened and then dimmed with a sudden gust of wind. With a flash of light, the runes illuminated with a golden glow that spread across the table. It was like they had come alive.

I sucked in a breath, feeling envious that I could never do this kind of magic. My powers just didn't swing that way.

My aunt gave Dash a nudge. "It's your turn. Drink!"

"Let's hope I'm the same person," said Dash, and I thought that was a strange comment. Dash raised his mug. "To crap."

I laughed. Dash's gaze met mine, and I couldn't tell what I saw there.

He tipped his head back and drank the contents of the potion. When he lowered the mug, his face was a mask of utter disgust, and I bit my tongue so I wouldn't laugh out loud again and somehow ruin the spell.

"And?" I asked, my body fluttering with nerves as I watched Dash's face carefully. I didn't really know him, though, so I wasn't sure what to expect.

"Give it a moment to work," said my aunt. Her eyes were closed, and her hands were pressed together in what looked like a prayer. "It's a powerful spell." Her eyes snapped open. "You'll feel a bit groggy, like waking up from a hangover. But that should only last for a few moments."

Dash's eyes were flicking all over the place, not really focusing on anything, the way people do when they are throwing thoughts around their heads. His expression went from smooth and collected to concerned and then dark, as though one of the memories he'd just recalled caused him great distress.

"Dash?" I took a careful step forward, my eyes never leaving his face. Something didn't look right. He looked… troubled.

"Dash?" I asked, worried. "What is it? Do you remember anything? Is it the curse? You remember who cursed you?" I looked over to my aunt, who was watching Dash with a concern that mirrored mine.

"I thought this might happen," she said.

A ribbon of fear wrapped around my middle at the worry in her tone. "What are you talking about?"

She pursed her lips in thought. "I might have added a bit too much agrimony."

"And what happens when you do?"

She gave me a sheepish look. "A lobotomy?"

I was going to kill my aunt, but I needed to help Dash first. I moved forward and faced him. "Dash? Dash? Are you okay?" Damnit. If his mind was mush, I was to blame for it. He sought our help, and I told him my aunt could help. I had to remind myself that my Aunt Luna wasn't young anymore. It was possible that her memory might not be as sharp as it once was, which included her potion-making abilities.

The tall werecat's eyes snapped to mine. "I remember. I remember everything."

My aunt raised her hands in the air like she was offering herself to the goddess. "Thank the cauldron. I still got it."

I let out a shaky breath, focusing on the werecat. "That's good. Right? You remember who you are. Your life." But whatever was on Dash's face wasn't excitement or happiness at remembering. He looked like he loathed his memories or even himself.

He looked away from me. "I need to tell you something."

My pulse throbbed at the dark tone in his voice. Was that regret? Whatever he wanted to tell me, it wasn't going to be good. "What? What's going on?"

A loud bang sounded from the front of the house, making me jump.

"They took her! They took my baby!"

I bolted out of the kitchen and found Annette running down the hall toward me, her eyes red and wide with absolute panic.

Oh, gods, no.

I rushed toward her, only to have Annette crash into me. I tried to hold on to her, but she fell to her knees in a heart-wrenching sob.

I wasn't great at comforting people. It always made me uncomfortable. But seeing her distress, her anguish at losing her daughter, I felt myself going down and hugging her. Her head plopped over my shoulder, and I felt the wetness of her tears soaking through my blouse.

I held her for a moment, waiting for the frantic sobs to diminish, and then I asked, "Tell me what happened. Tell me everything."

Annette pulled back and looked at me, her eyes pooling with tears. She took a deep breath and said, "They took her from her room."

"Holy shit. When?"

"Five minutes ago." She wiped her tears with her hands. "I went up to give her some of that sweet and salty popcorn she loves, and she was gone. The window was open."

"Where was Blake?" As the sheriff, I was surprised he didn't think of barricading the windows and securing all entry points. That's the first thing I would have done—secure her bedroom. But I guess he wasn't used to these kinds of situations like I was. And that had caused Annette to lose her daughter.

"Downstairs with us," she continued. "We were

talking about putting up more security around the house for tomorrow. I never thought they'd take her tonight. I thought I'd…"

I reached out and grabbed her hand. "Whoever took her is strong. You can't climb down a two-story house with an unconscious fourteen-year-old on your back without some serious strength." Not to mention, they had stealth, but my guess was magic. They'd cloaked themselves with an invisibility spell and sneaked up to the second-story window.

Annette's face went pale. "You think she's unconscious? They hit her?"

"Maybe not hit her physically, but they gave her something so she wouldn't struggle. To keep her quiet." Otherwise, Blake would have been up there in a second to smash these bastards' faces, with his werewolf hearing.

Annette leaned back with a sniff. Only then did she look past me. "Is that? Is that your aunt?"

Oh, fuck.

"She's alive? But I thought she was dead?" Annette was staring at my Aunt Luna like she'd seen a ghost. It was a perfectly acceptable emotion. To everyone in this town, my aunt was dead. There had been a funeral and everything.

"I can't be dead if I'm standing right here. Now, can I?" said my aunt, a hand on her hip.

I glared at her with my "I'll deal with you later" eyes. I looked over at Dash, who was staring out into space like he wasn't here in the present but somewhere else.

"It's a long story," I told Annette, and tonight wasn't the time. "What else can you tell me?"

Annette shook her head. "Like what?"

"Did they leave anything behind? Was there a strange smell?"

Annette blinked. "I'm not sure. I can't remember. I just saw that my baby was gone." The last word came out in a sob.

Damn. This situation was getting worse by the minute. "I'll need to see her room, if that's okay?"

Annette nodded but remained silent.

Blake would still be there. Good. I needed to get his version of the events. Plus, I was going to need help. Lots of it.

I looked up at Dash. "Dash. I'm going to need your help." As a werecat, he had sensors and instincts that we witches didn't. He might be able to tell me if a mage or even a shifter took Emma.

A dark cast covered Dash's face. "I have to go."

"What?" My mouth dropped open as I watched the werecat slip past us on the floor and make his way toward the front door.

"Dash!" I hollered, my anger rising, not appreciating his attitude right now. How could he leave at a time like this when a girl was missing? How could he abandon us when we needed him? When I needed him.

"Let him go," said my aunt, watching Dash, her brows low with concern. "He'll come back when he's ready."

I gritted my teeth. I never took Dash as a selfish

person. Quite the opposite. But then again, I didn't know him. I only knew the version of the man who'd lost his memories.

Annette grabbed my hand, forcing me to look into her eyes. "Is my baby still alive?"

Moisture filled my eyes at the desperation in her voice, the frantic plea.

I swallowed, blinking hard. "Yes. I'm going to find her." I squeezed Annette's hand, emotions making my voice raw. "I promise."

CHAPTER 21

E mma's bedroom was exactly what you'd expect of a fourteen-year-old *witch* girl.

The wood floor was lit with several candles. Lacy curtains hung in the window, letting the moonlight shine in. Emma's bed had a canopy with sheer curtains, and the comforter was a velvet deep red.

The walls were painted with a mural of the night sky, a full moon hanging in the heavens. The furniture was a mix of modern and old. One dresser was straight from the seventies, but it was still beautiful. Black shelves, a black vanity mirror, a purple bedspread, and a purple nightstand. A marble black dresser sat in the corner but didn't have enough drawers to store everything. A cat bed sat off to the side of the room, holding a cat toy with a white skull wound around its neck.

You'd expect a girl Emma's age to have a white canopy bed with pink and light-gray bedding, with walls covered in the celebrities she was crushing on, and a floor littered with stuffed animals and clothes and shoes. Not her.

It had a Wednesday Addams' feel. I loved it.

"Has anything been touched since Emma…" I couldn't bring myself to say, "was taken," not when Annette was staring at me like she was about to break down into a bout of sobs—or have a stroke.

She shook her head, unable to find the words.

The air smelled of campfires with a hint of oak, but I couldn't find traces of the scent of a shifter or were or even the smell of the magic that was used. Being as this was a multiple-werewolf residence, it would be impossible to pinpoint the paranormal race.

I walked over to the window, which was still open. The curtains blew in the wind, the moonlight reflecting off the glass.

I called out to the shadows that surrounded me and sensed their magic merge with mine, binding together like strands of webbed energy.

I snapped my wrist forward slightly and pushed out the tiny shadow on the window's ledge, tapping into the energies. The shadow slithered across the sill, ever so lightly, like a black mist, and then disappeared into the light of the room.

Pinpricks of power rolled over my skin that was not part of my magic.

This was someone else's magic.

It was both cold and hot like it was purposely throwing me off.

A glamour.

Whoever they were, they were powerful enough to hide their tracks.

"What was that?"

I cringed and turned to see Annette standing over my shoulder. The scent of rosewater filled my nose. "My magic."

And now *my* secret was out.

It wasn't that I wanted to keep it secret. I just wanted to avoid the looks, the confusion, the never-ending ways I tried to explain that my magic was different from the magic that was known to us as witches. It wasn't White magic. It wasn't Dark. It was… different.

Annette was staring at the spot where a slip of my umbra magic, which is what I had named it, had been. "Your magic? But… what kind of magic is that? I've never seen that before. Is that Dark magic?"

It was in a way. And in many ways, it wasn't. "I'll explain later. We don't have much time." Without as much as a definite read on the magic used or the person or persons who took Emma, I didn't know where to look.

Tim's body was found in an empty house, and Samuel's at an old mill.

Emma could be anywhere.

"Did you get a sense of who they were?" asked Annette. "I tried, but I couldn't get a read. Tilly and Cristina couldn't either."

I looked into her hopeful eyes, hating how it made me feel desperate. "I got something. Not much. But they definitely used some sort of glamour. They hid themselves and took Emma. She might have seen her kidnapper in her room, but it was too late."

"Oh my god." Annette covered her mouth with her hand, tears starting to spill out of her eyes again.

Crap. Maybe I shouldn't have said that.

Annette lowered her hands. "Did they hurt her?" She was watching me like somehow I had all the answers, like she thought I was psychic or my magic was.

"No." Technically, that wasn't a lie, but I wasn't sure either. "She didn't feel a thing."

Annette's body shook with unshed tears. "I can't believe this is happening. Why my Emma? She's such a good girl. She'd never hurt anyone. She's only fourteen!"

I wanted to tell her that it had nothing to do with being good or bad. It had everything to do with her birth date. Or rather, birth month.

"Let's go back downstairs," I said to Annette.

I followed her out, and we made our way downstairs into the kitchen. Tilly and Cristina sat at the kitchen table, both wearing frowns, both looking like they wanted to find these Forsaken and go to town on them.

I did, too.

Blake was avoiding my gaze. What was that about?

Ella and Emily had their hands wrapped around their father's arms while Elanor was hanging on to his right thigh like it was a floater. Elsie, the youngest of their daughters, was on his lap, curled into a ball.

The girls were terrified, and it seemed their father was the only one who could comfort them to make them feel safe.

"Anything?" asked Liam, that same hopeful look in his eyes as his wife's.

"They used magic," I repeated. "But I couldn't pinpoint the type." Which wasn't helpful at the moment, and by the look of anguish on Liam's face, he thought so, too.

"Where could they have taken her?" asked Cristina.

I shook my head. "I don't know. But somewhere in town or the surroundings. Somewhere close." I'm not sure why, but I knew it to be true.

Tilly stood. "There're six houses for sale that are empty. She'll be in one of them. I can take you."

"No." I looked at the confusion on Tilly's face. "They won't use that again. They're too smart." And if I was right, they knew we'd be looking for them. For Emma. They'd take her somewhere else.

"So where?" said Blake. His back was pressed on the kitchen counter, and his hands gripped the edge, looking like he was fighting his inner beast to stay calm.

"Some rural place?" I guessed. "Somewhere hidden and away from the general population. If this is the last sacrifice, it'll be more substantial. They'll need more space. They won't want to be disturbed."

"How do you know this?" asked Liam, his daughters still hanging on to him like a group of baby monkeys clutched to their mother's chest and back. If this wasn't a horrid situation, I might have laughed or taken a picture.

I looked into his eyes, recognizing the wariness there. "Experience. I've dealt with ritualistic killings before." Shit. As soon as the words flew out of my mouth, I wanted to kick myself in the ass.

Ella, Emily, and Elanor started to cry. Elsie, not understanding the words but seeing her sisters sobbing and feeding on their emotions, started to wail.

Damn. Nice going.

Liam cupped his youngest daughter against his chest, whispering into her ear until she finally stopped crying.

I'd have to watch my mouth around the children.

"When are they going to do this ritual?" asked Cristina, and just then, I noticed she was rolling tiny stones in her right hand like you'd see someone rolling dice.

"I'm not sure."

"Guess," commanded Blake.

"Midnight," I told them, hating how desperate that bit of news made them look and how miserable it made me feel. "Witching hour. The time at night when the powers of witches and other supernatural beings are believed to be strongest."

"But that's like in an hour!" cried Tilly, her eyes wild.

"We still have time," I told them, though my voice lacked conviction. The truth was, this whole situation was getting worse by the second. If we didn't find

Emma within the next hour, she'd be lost to us. To her family.

"Wait a minute." Cristina held out her stones. "Annette. You can do a locator spell, right? We could find her this way."

I perked up. That was true. I hadn't thought of it. Mostly because I couldn't do that type of magic. But many paranormal investigators worked with witches who could perform locator spells. I just never could rely on that, so I'd found other ways.

But Annette could. She was a White witch.

Annette dabbed her nose with a tissue. "It'll take hours to complete a locator spell. It took nearly the entire day just to find Elanor's doll."

At the mention of her name, Elanor glanced over to her mother, and the two shared a special look, a bond that I'd never experienced.

And Emma would never get that again if I didn't find her.

"What if you use her blood?" offered Tilly. "I've heard that can speed up the process."

"But we don't have her blood." Annette raked her fingers through her mangled hair. "I don't have her blood," she repeated. "We'll have to try another way to find my Emma." I could see the despair in Annette's eyes as she spoke those words. It was like a dark cloud had descended upon us, suffocating any hope we had left.

I felt the weight of defeat bearing down on us. It was as if the darkness of the hour had seeped into our souls and robbed us of any hope. The feelings of dread and anger constricted my gut into a tight ball.

But then, a glimmer of light sparked in my mind. "What about her phone?" I asked, knowing a girl her age would have her phone on her. "We could try tracking it."

Blake reached behind him, grabbed something, and then tossed it on the table. "Here's her phone. We already thought of that." He glowered at me like I was a simpleton and that should have been the first thing to look for.

Okay, so I wasn't the perfect paranormal investigator. I made mistakes. Lots of them. But he was glaring at me like somehow this was all my fault, or that I should have been able to prevent it.

"So that's it?" Annette looked around us. "You're just going to let my baby die?" Her voice cracked, her lips moved, but no other words would come. She stumbled over to her husband and girls, wrapping her arms around them.

I looked at Annette and saw the wild desperation in her eyes as she clutched her girls and her husband. I couldn't let her suffer like this. I had to do something, anything, to get Emma back before it was too late.

I glanced away. Not because I was scared of what the witch could see written on my face—the pain I felt for them, for example—but out of fear that she would notice the feeling of absolute dread and despair emanating from me.

A slip of hopelessness hit hard. I was here to solve

the case, and I usually did. But this time, it didn't look good.

This time… I failed.

My blood ran cold. I took a deep breath and closed my eyes, trying to calm myself and trying not to picture that girl's body cut and mangled like Tim's and Samuel's. Failure was not an option for me. I had to think outside the box and come up with a plan.

A rush of anger welled inside me. I refused to let Emma die on my watch.

"We'll scout the town," I said, knowing how senseless that sounded. My pulse quickened as a nauseating feeling of dread twisted my gut. "We'll search every abandoned building, lot, house, everything."

Cristina chimed in, "We can split up. It'll go faster."

"Yes," agreed Tilly, her voice shaking with emotion. "We'll cover more ground that way."

I glanced at Blake. "If you can get all your people on this to help, we still have a shot at finding her."

Blake stared at the floor. "It'll take an hour just to organize a search. Otherwise, we'll have people searching the same places."

I glanced at my phone's digital clock. We'd already wasted ten minutes of precious time. It meant we had less than fifty minutes to find Emma and stop the ritual.

The odds weren't in our favor.

I stood there, gripping my phone and shaking, half in anger, half in despair as my eyes burned.

And just when I felt all hope was lost, the unexpected happened.

A buzz came from my phone. I stared at the screen. It was a text message. But that wasn't what had me bringing the phone closer to my face to inspect it like I was losing my eyesight.

It was a text message from Dash.

Dash: 11 Seelie Creek.

"What is it?" Blake was watching me intensely, seemingly having recognized the alarm on my face.

"A text."

"And?" asked the big werewolf impatiently. "Does it help us or not?"

I looked up at Blake and then Annette. "I think I know where she is."

CHAPTER 22

"Who was that text from?" asked Blake for the third time.

"A source." I stared out the window of Blake's BMW SUV. Darkness surrounded us as trees flashed by. We were in the more rural part of Moonfell on the outskirts of town. Here in the countryside, Moonfell ended and the human town of Woodbury began.

The SUV rocked back and forth over the bumpy terrain as we raced ahead. I hunched against the door in the passenger seat. Sitting in Blake's vehicle was like sitting on a sofa made of clouds; it was a luxurious four-by-four, far more comfortable than my old Jeep ever was.

I peered in the side mirror and spotted Tilly's white Buick SUV. Annette and Cristina had opted to ride with her while Liam stayed with the other girls. They were frantic, crying over their bigger sister, and scared out of their minds. It made sense that Dad stayed with his girls. Liam was a great father. They were lucky to have a strong, fierce werewolf protecting them.

And for reasons unknown, Blake *commanded* that I ride with him.

But now I was getting the impression that he'd asked me to tag along so he could drill me about the text message I'd gotten from Dash.

I was right.

"Who's your source?" he demanded, staring at me like he expected me to answer. I guess he was used to people answering him. I wasn't one of those people. His aftershave filled the vehicle with a very pleasant smell… but now it stank.

"That's not important." I didn't want to have to think about what this implied for Dash. If he knew where Emma was, that made him my enemy. It also told me he was involved with The Forsaken.

Was Dash a member of The Forsaken?

It was messing with my head. Was Dash really involved? Had he been implicated in Tim's death? Or Samuel's? Maybe something had gone wrong with the ritual or magic they were performing and had accidentally cursed Dash. No, that didn't make sense. Curses were precise, complex, and one as complicated as the one that Dash was hit with couldn't have been accidental. No. Someone hexed him.

But it didn't explain how he knew where Emma would be.

Damnit. My stomach tightened, and I felt like I was going to be sick. My gut had told me I could trust Dash. Something in his demeanor, in his eyes, said he was one of the good guys.

But I'd been wrong. So, freaking wrong.

His words before he drank the counter-curse tonic came back to me. "Let's hope I'm the same person." It all made sense now. Had Dash gotten a glimpse of his past? Maybe Dash could feel that deep down he wasn't who we thought he was. That he was bad.

He couldn't have been more right.

Blake cast a glare my way. I could practically feel the animosity emanating from him, like sweat. "Really? Then why are we wasting our time going there if your source is not important?"

I couldn't reveal anything about Dash to Blake. Not yet. "Just trust me. She's there." I hoped I was right and not wasting precious time. But so far, it was the only lead we had. We had no names, no real way of discovering who these bastards were or where they would take Emma. And we were running out of time.

If what Eli told me was true, and I believed it was, tonight was the night The Forsaken were going to try and raise some demon king from hell, and by doing so, that would mean eternal night for our world.

I couldn't let that happen.

Finding Emma and stopping the ritual was our only shot. My only shot. I knew. My gut knew. We would find Emma. Dash had given us the way. I just didn't know why.

"You tell me who your source is, or I'll have you locked up."

It was my turn to glare at the werewolf. "Really? Is that a threat?"

"It is."

Bastard. "You're going to go there?"

"Yeah, I am."

Motherfracker. I crossed my arms over my chest. "I'm not telling you."

My rage was like a boiling pot of water that threatened to spill over at any second.

The werewolf let out a breath of air through his nose. "Don't think I won't just because I wanted to have dinner with you. That changes nothing. I'll lock your ass in jail if you don't tell me."

What a swell guy. I should have taken my Jeep. "I need to protect my sources. You do what you gotta do." It didn't escape me that he'd used the past tense "I wanted" and not "I want." Guess I wasn't dating material anymore. Did it bother me? Nope.

"And what about Emma?" growled Blake, his voice taking on a dangerous mien. "Don't you give a shit what happens to her? Or are you a heartless *witch*?"

I'm pretty sure that's not the word he wanted to use. "Of course I do." My insides tightened when I thought about how terrified Emma must have been to find a stranger or strangers in her room. I didn't know if she was conscious or not, and I prayed she wasn't. Whatever The Forsaken was planning on doing to her, it was better that she didn't know. Because if she was awake, it would traumatize her for life.

If she wasn't already dead.

Nope. Not going there.

"I care about Emma," I said, my voice low and threatening. "Don't you dare try to imply that I don't. I'm here, trying to find her." I *will* find her.

Blake tightened his large fingers on the wheel. "If we get there, and she's there..." Another grip around the wheel like he was trying to mold it into a sculpture. "It means your source is involved. How else would they know where they took her? Did you think about that?"

He had a point. But I still wouldn't tell him. I wouldn't betray Dash. Not yet. Not until I knew why he took off the way he did, like he didn't want to help or wanted to get as far away from us as he could. And then this text? It just didn't make sense.

"Then you'll just have to arrest me cause I won't tell you."

The werewolf hit the steering wheel, making me jump in my seat. "I can't fucking believe you. You'd protect scum like that? Over an innocent girl? If she dies... so help me god, Kat. I'm coming for you."

I believed him, and I wouldn't expect any less. But it didn't mean it didn't piss me off. "Like I said, you do what you gotta do."

"I'll *make* you tell me. One way or another, you're gonna tell me. If anything happens to that girl, I'm going to hold you responsible."

"I know."

"Keeping information like that, protecting those bastards? It's not going to end well for you."

I'd had enough of his crap. "I get that you're mad. I would be, too, if Emma disappeared on *my* watch. But let's focus, all right?"

Blake growled, and it had the hair on the back of my neck rise. "Watch it. I'm in no mood for your mouth tonight."

"Sorry." That was a low blow. And it looked like the werewolf might just lose it and lose it on me. I took it that he was close to Emma. Probably knew her as a baby and watched her grow up. This was very personal for him.

I didn't want to pick a fight with the sheriff, but, goddamnit, he was ticking me off.

And Dash was ticking me off.

The Forsaken were ticking me off.

Everyone was ticking me off!

I looked behind me and saw Tilly's SUV right behind us. It was good that Annette had her close friends with her. She needed them. And there was nothing I could do to ease her pain apart from leading them to the right location.

Annette had seen my aunt, seen that she was, in fact, very much alive. Knowing her, knowing women, she'd already told the other witches.

I'd known sooner or later my aunt's secret would be out. Guess it came sooner than she'd expected. She would have to deal with the consequences. It was her idea to play dead. Not mine. I did not have the patience or the time to think of the shitstorm that would bring.

And right now, I had way more important issues to deal with.

"What kind of backup did you call for?" I asked, hoping to break some of the deadly tension between us. It was thick and very ugly.

"Everyone," growled the big werewolf. "All my guys. My team. They're going to meet us there."

"Good." The more, the merrier.

"What kind of threat are we going to face? How powerful are these guys?"

I'd thought about that. "Very. These are not your ordinary witches or mages playing with curses and hexes. This group is smart. They plan ahead. They're organized. Probably have unlimited funds. And they've been around for a very long time." I exhaled. "They've been planning this for over twenty years to get it right. They're prepared to kill anyone who intervenes. If we try to stop them, they'll fight back. They'll be merciless. They'll kill without a second thought."

I teetered to the left in my seat as Blake took the next right at a fast pace.

"What are our chances that we get Emma back alive?"

I sighed. "I'm not going to lie. Not good." It'd be a freaking miracle if we got her back unscathed. Tim's mangled body flashed in my mind's eye, and I forced the images out of my head. I wouldn't let that happen to Emma. I'd die trying.

Blake was silent after that.

The SUV careened around a bend in the road, its

tires skidding against the gravel until they finally found purchase on the old asphalt. The engine howled as the car gained momentum, propelling the vehicle forward with a force that seemed to defy its size.

As the vehicle approached the end of the road, a red mailbox came into view, its paint faded and chipping. The address 11 Seelie Creek had been painted in white on the side, but it was still barely legible.

The road ended abruptly in front of the mailbox as if it had known it would never go any farther. Ahead of us stood only an abyss of trees, their branches reaching out like fingers yet never touching each other. The SUV skidded to a stop, and the sudden silence was deafening. There was nowhere else to go.

"This is it," I said as I double-checked Dash's text. I popped the door open and slipped out.

Darkness surrounded me, and the light of the full moon cast tall shadows from the trees and surrounding shrubbery. A night like this, especially with a full moon, was when my magic was strongest.

When shadows dominated.

The air was thick with the smell of moss and wet leaves. I knew Dash had sent me to this place for a reason, and even though that brought up all kinds of emotions, I had to focus on finding Emma. I listened for the sounds of crickets and other nightly critters but heard none. Good. We were in the right place.

"This can't be it," said Tilly, walking up to me, her high-heeled boots sticking into the soft earth and making it harder for her to walk. Cristina and Annette marched behind her. "Nothing's here. It's just a field."

The moonlight illuminated enough of Annette's face to see the panic written all over it. And Cristina was casting her gaze around, her expression echoing that of Tilly. They thought I'd brought them to the wrong place.

Using my phone's flashlight app, I scanned the area for any signs of tire marks or anything that would suggest multiple vehicles passed here.

And I got some. Wide and deep sets of tracks turned from the road and continued out into the field.

I opened my mouth to tell them, but Blake beat me to it.

"I smell people," said the big werewolf. "Maybe a dozen. Maybe more. Definitely paranormal. Witches or mages. The tire tracks lead this way." The sheriff pointed out into the distance.

Annette turned on the spot, searching the field ahead like she expected to see her daughter emerge from the tall grass. "You think she's here."

"I do," I answered before Blake. I looked between the witches. "How's your magic? Does it feel off? Like you told me?"

"Feels fine," answered Annette as Tilly and Cristina both nodded.

I glanced at Blake. "And your wolf? Can you shift?"

"I'm good," answered the sheriff. "Why?"

"It seems that whatever was disrupting the magical elements here in Moonfell has stopped. So we're fine." I was unsure if this was a good thing or not; it meant that whatever had created the disruption had completed its work.

"How do we do this?" asked Cristina, her hands on her hips with an expression that meant business. "I've got my stones ready to kick some ass."

Good question. I'd always worked alone, so the idea of working with a team was foreign to me. I wasn't sure how to proceed. When I glanced at Blake for help, he knelt close to the ground, sniffing.

Werewolves.

"We've got the element of surprise," I told them, which is what I would use if I were on my own. "We'll need a group to create a distraction while the other group gets Emma."

"I'll get Emma," said Annette, her fingers twitching like she was warming up a spell or a hex.

"I'll help," added Cristina, who tossed up one of her stones.

"I'm very good with causing distractions." Tilly smiled wickedly. "Just you wait."

I smiled. "Good."

"What about you?" Annette watched me.

I looked over into the distant field. "I'm going after The Forsaken."

"Not alone, you're not," said Blake.

"Thanks, but you should be protecting Annette and Cristina while they get Emma."

Even in the semidarkness, I could see Blake's fury.

"I'm taking down these bastards. Nothing you say's gonna stop me."

I looked up at the big werewolf. "These are powerful mages and witches. You have no idea what they're capable of. They can kill you."

"And *I* can kill them." Blake yanked off his jacket and tossed it on the hood of his SUV. His large, manly muscles rippled under his tight shirt. Tilly was eyeing the werewolf like she wanted to lick every inch of his body.

"Fine." I glanced away, knowing it was a lost cause arguing with him. "Don't say I didn't warn you." I didn't have time to feed his ego. I had to be smart. We had to go in there and get Emma without getting any of us killed.

Easy peasy.

"Let's go."

With Blake in the lead, we all marched behind him, our footsteps muffled by the thick grass beneath our feet. The moon cast an eerie glow over the field, making the shadows of the trees appear longer and more sinister.

We came upon a group of black cars and SUVs parked next to a line of trees, where the field ended and the forest began. The deep tracks into the ground told me the soil was too soft. They couldn't go any farther without getting stuck.

Now, I was certain this was the right place.

"They made the rest of the journey on foot," I told them, keeping my voice low. "They're close."

We continued in silence.

I could hear the distant hum of magic in the air, sending a chill down my spine. These mages were powerful. That much I knew. But we had to get Emma back, no matter what.

Suddenly, Blake stopped in his tracks. We all froze behind him, listening for any signs of danger. He sniffed the air, his nostrils flaring as he picked up a scent. "They're close," he growled.

"Can you tell how many?" I whispered.

He closed his eyes, concentrating. "Dozen. Maybe more."

I cursed under my breath. We were outnumbered, and we had no idea what kind of magic they were capable of. But we couldn't back down now. Not when Emma's life was on the line.

"Do we wait for Blake's backup?" asked Tilly.

"No time," I said before the werewolf could answer. And when he didn't, it told me that this time he'd agreed with me.

Blake led us forward again, moving with an eerie grace through the shadows. I could see the muscles in his arms and back tensing as he prepared for a fight.

I was constantly looking around for any signs of danger, ready to spring into action if needed. We eventually found ourselves in an area that was much darker than before; trees grew tall all around us while a slight fog swept through their leaves like white ribbons being pulled along by invisible hands.

The air felt colder here, almost chilled from something dark lingering in between these trees. Despite this fear-instilling atmosphere, no one seemed willing to turn back. Everyone wanted Emma back safely more than anything else at this point.

The smell of wood burning reached me. Blake had probably smelled it back at the road. We stepped into a clearing, a yellow glow pulling my attention.

And then I saw them. The mages.

Wearing heavy, dark, and hooded robes, they were gathered in a circle, chanting and swaying to the beat of their own magic. A ring of fire encircled a massive rock the size of Blake's SUV.

And there, in the middle of the fire circle, tied to that massive rock—was Emma.

CHAPTER 23

With her eyes closed and her body limp, Emma looked as though she was under some kind of spell. I didn't want to think about the other option—that she might be dead.

My heart twisted in my chest at the sight of her. She looked so small and fragile, strapped to that boulder in the midst of those hooded bastards. Just an innocent girl.

I hated these hooded bastards. I was going to make them pay.

"Emma!" screamed Annette as she bolted for her daughter.

"Annette! No!" I lunged to grab her, but the witch was too fast, and I landed face-first in the dirt.

I craned my neck, seeing her run toward her daughter. I didn't blame her. If I'd been that girl's mother, I would have done the same thing, seeing her like this. Annette was only doing what her instincts called her to do. Protect her children.

At Annette's scream, the hooded figures—I counted twenty of them—all turned around. Swell.

Stems of green magic dripped from their outstretched hands. Even better.

"There goes our element of surprise," said Blake.

I pushed to my knees, glad to have the attention of some of the hooded mages, and waved. "Surprise!"

They didn't wave back.

The sound of a belt jiggling pulled my attention around.

Holy fairy farts.

Blake was buck-naked, his man-junk out for a midnight stroll.

As Blake stood before me, I couldn't help but admire his sculpted body and the muscles in his chest that flexed with every movement. Even under his skin, I could see rippling motions shifting his features, widening his head, lengthening his jaw, and revealing carnivore teeth the size of my fingers. Suddenly, a flash of gray fur and a snarl filled the air, followed by a horrible tearing sound. In place of the man was a massive two-hundred-pound gray wolf.

He stood on all fours, much larger than his natural counterpart. You did not want to piss off a werewolf in his wolf form. Especially not this one.

Blake, or rather, the wolf, looked at us with yellow, intelligent eyes. He growled, shaking his head, and I found myself taking a step back. But his sudden aggression wasn't aimed at me. It was a "get your asses ready" kind of snarl.

And then, with a powerful thrust of his back legs, the wolf rushed forward to meet the gathering of mages and witches.

A mage—male with an uninteresting face—lowered his cowl and turned to face the wolf. He waved his hand, and a coil of emerald energy flew from his fingertips, hitting the wolf in his chest.

The wolf stumbled, nearly losing his footing, and I sucked in a breath through my teeth. But then the wolf shook his head as if trying to rid himself of an itch. A moment later, the beast opened his maw and unleashed a roar before launching himself back at the mage.

The mage blasted another stream of green energy, but the wolf leaped to the side at the last moment, the magic hitting a tree with an ear-splitting crack.

The mage stumbled back and raised his hands to launch another attack.

But Blake the wolf got there first.

The large wolf's maw wrapped around the mage's neck. I heard a horrifying snapping sound, then a crunch, and then a tear. The mage's head fell with a thud at the wolf's feet.

The wolf growled, his lips covered in blood. His eyes focused on another mage, and he exploded into motion.

I'd have loved to sit and watch how it all played out. Clearly, Blake was an experienced killer, but I had a ritual to stop.

Tilly gave me a smirk and pointed to Blake. "Isn't he glorious?"

Violent was more like it. "Help Annette get Emma," I told Tilly and Cristina.

I headed for the mages, seeking out their leader. Take out the leader, and the rest will fold, or some crap like that. I'd learned from experience that hitting the leader first left the company without direction. It made them weaker. More vulnerable. I cast my gaze around the magic practitioners. They were all dressed in dark robes.

All except for one.

One stood apart, and over their body was a thick red robe, the color of blood. Nice. The shoulders were too wide to be a woman, so I pegged him for a male.

I went for Red.

A scream pulled my attention around.

Annette stood twenty feet from the boulder that held her daughter, her arms out in a spread-eagle pose. Tendrils of green magic spread over her body. She spazzed like she was having a seizure.

And then she collapsed.

Fear choked me, and I stumbled, righting myself before I face-planted into the ground. Annette wasn't moving. I had no idea if she'd been killed, and I couldn't do anything about that right now.

It pained me to leave her there. But I had to stop the ritual.

Her assailant's shoulders shook, laughter escaping his lips, and my fury soared.

"Bastard!" shouted Cristina. She reached inside her bag, said a few words I couldn't catch, and pitched a handful of her stones at him.

Her aim was perfect, and I suspected there was a little help from magic. I watched, curious as to how her magic stones would work.

The stones hit their mark, landing on the mage's chest.

White fire exploded around the mage.

But he just stayed there, his teeth reflecting in the moonlight under his hood as a wall of white flames soared above his head, illuminating the area like a strong spotlight.

I was impressed. Those were some pretty cool stones.

Cristina's white flames briefly surged and then withdrew. There the mage was again, still beaming that confident grin of his. Despite landing a serious hit with her magical fire, it seemed as if an invisible wall of protection shielded him. It was clear these mages were much more powerful than I'd initially anticipated. They had some serious magical mojo.

The amount of energy in the air was like nothing I'd ever experienced, thick and undulating, as though the entire sky was lit with magic. Like this was ground zero for all magic.

"That should have taken him down and vanquished him," yelled Cristina, eyeing the mage like he was the dog poop she'd stepped in earlier this week.

"It's the demon king," I told her as it all came to me. My eyes flicked around the fire circle, the symbols etched into the stone. "The ritual." When Cristina and Tilly met my gaze, I added, "He's pulling from the demon's magic or something. It's making him more powerful." It was the only thing that made sense. A demon king of hell had supplied the mage with some significant magical resources.

Enough to open a portal for the demon king to rise.

"Your magic is worthless," the mage mocked, his fingers working their way through another spell. The air felt heavy and cold as the power of his magic filled our space.

"Try some of your mind voodoo on him," shouted Cristina to Tilly.

Tilly stood next to her. "He's too far. I need to get closer."

A silent communication passed through them, the kind that only two very close friends could understand. And then, the two witches moved as a unit toward the mage.

Movement caught my attention on the far right.

Red was standing next to the stone. And in his hand was an athame, a ritual blade.

Shit.

I rocketed forward, my eyes on the red mage as he moved toward Emma's left wrist. I had to stop him before he cut her, before he spilled blood.

Arms out, I pulled on the shadows around me, tugging them closer. I was going to rip that son of a bitch to pieces.

A shape stepped in my way.

I skidded to a stop just as a volley of green magic came at me.

I yanked on the shadows around me, catching them in my hands, twisting them like silk strands of a web, and molding them like clay until they formed a shield, similar to what you'd see a medieval knight carrying. Strapped to my right forearm, I raised my shadow shield—and not a second too late.

The green energy hit my shield.

Magic sizzled and popped, and warmth hit my face, but my shadow shield held.

I lowered my shield and straightened. "Didn't see that coming. Did you?"

The mage lowered her cowl. "What do we have here?" asked the female mage with bushy brown hair and buck teeth. Her face was wrinkled in both anger and surprise. "What kind of magic is that?" She pointed a black wand at me. Hadn't seen those in a long time.

"Wouldn't you like to know?"

She stared at my shield with a sort of disturbing longing. Like she wanted it. Wanted my magic. It was eerie.

She took a step forward. "I would. Is that Dark magic?"

I didn't have the time or the desire to explain my magic to her.

"Out of my way, Hermione. I've got things to do." A girl and a world to save. "Don't make me kill you if I don't have to. But I will if you don't let me pass."

The mage flashed her teeth in a disturbing smile that matched the look in her eyes. "Give it to me. I want it."

"Uh… *no*."

Rage flickered over her face. "Mine. I want it. Give it to me."

I glanced over her shoulder. Red was still standing next to Emma, but he hadn't cut her yet. Good.

"It's not how magic works," I told her. "You should know that."

She tsked. "I know of a few spells that'll drain a mage of their power. I've done it before. And it feels sublime. All that power." She moaned like she was having an orgasm.

Ew.

"Listen, Hermione. I'd love to shoot the shit, but I'm busy at the moment."

"Give it to me!" she roared, the fingers of her left hand out like claws.

Yup. She had a few screws loose up in that head of hers.

Without warning, the Hermione-wannabe launched a surprise attack on me. She faked to the left and then kicked me in the side, sending me sprawling. The next thing I knew, my face was being hit with a roundhouse kick. As I flew backward, a million stars seemed to burst in my head. My whole body felt like it was on fire from the beating, but I forced myself to ignore it and get back up, frantically scanning the area.

Okay, so the Hermione-wannabe had some moves.

My head snapped to the mage. "Get out of my way."

She laughed, licked her lips, and said, "I want it. That power." She closed her eyes and sniffed the air like she could smell my umbra magic. "Yes. Yes! It's delicious."

"You're freaking nuts." I knew I had to fight her to get to Red. Might have to kill her. So be it.

The mage sneered. "Give it. I want it. I neeeeed it."

"What you need is an hour with a shrink."

Murderously silent, the Hermione-wannabe thrust out her wand.

Shoots of green magic blasted too fast for my eyes to register. I whirled and ducked, bringing up my shield.

I bucked to my knees under the weight of her assault, but I'd had enough.

Gritting my teeth, I yanked on the shadows around me, and using my free hand, I forged a shadow spear.

"You will give it to me," she howled, moving closer, her green magic spilling out of her wand and hitting my shield.

I shot up, spun around, and using my momentum, threw the shadow spear.

It hit the Hermione-wannabe in the chest. She stumbled back, surprised. But then she dropped her wand and touched the part of the spear that jutted from her chest lovingly, a smile on her face. "Mine," she gasped, blood trickling down her lips.

And then she collapsed.

I shook my head. "Seriously bonkers, that one."

Not wasting any more time, I rushed toward Red. I was so close now, I could hear the dark incantations on his lips as he raised his hands, the dagger still in his grip.

His head whipped around suddenly. But he wasn't looking at me. He was looking past me.

That's when I realized everything was quiet. Unnaturally quiet.

The stillness hit me like a droning hum. A shriek sounded out, and I turned to find Blake, the wolf, tearing a mage to shreds with the speed of a lunatic, his physique looking as if he had been injected with muscle-enhancing drugs.

The mage let out a desperate cry as the werewolf attacked, biting and clawing at his back.

I snapped my head back around. Red's incantations reverberated in the night air. A wave of dark energy burst forth from his outstretched hand and sent the wolf spiraling into the air, flipping end over end before he was hurled against a tree.

The wolf slumped to the ground, but then he pulled himself up again.

Two other mages hurried forward, something silver dangling in their hands.

Chains.

The wolf rushed them, mad with bloodlust and not seeing the threat.

The mages tossed the chains, and they hit the

wolf, eliciting a howl of pain. The wolf collapsed on the ground, restrained by the silver links.

I froze, but my eyes were pinned on the wolf until I saw his chest rise and fall. Slowly, he raised his head, and his eyes met mine. He was hurt. But that insatiable fury still burned in his eyes.

Shit. Part of me wanted to help, but I couldn't. I had to get to Red.

Except, by the time I felt the threat, it was too late.

CHAPTER 24

A jolt of agony shot through my right arm, and I toppled to the ground. My connection to my magic was lost as my shadow shield burst into mist.

I felt the tension building up in my body like a ticking bomb, starting from my toes and moving upward before settling at the base of my neck. A metallic tang filled my nostrils, accompanied by the unmistakable scent of burnt hair.

Was I burning?

Damn. That wasn't good.

I rolled on the ground and pushed to my feet. I checked myself. I wasn't burning. But something *had* hit me.

Red stood facing me, the cowl down over most of his face. He hadn't stepped out of the circle, and I was willing to bet he was channeling most of his magic there with the help of that demon king.

If he stepped out of the circle, his ass was mine.

His ass was mine either way.

"You should have stayed away, Katrina," said Red.

I pulled at the shadows around me. "You know me?" Who the hell was this guy? The voice did sound familiar. Where had I heard it before? I tried to pinpoint the voice, but it was hard to concentrate through the incessant ringing in my ears.

"So you do possess some magical powers," Red uttered in a tone of amazement. "But they won't save Emma."

I frowned, frustrated that I couldn't place the voice. "I'll take my chances."

"Blake's in trouble. He needs our help," cried Tilly as she bounced into view next to me, Cristina at her side. Both alive, and both with streaks of sweat covering their faces.

With a quick glance behind me, I saw a cluster of mages around Blake, a few others making their way toward us. The wolf was still trapped under that silver net.

"Right now, we need to stop the ritual," I said, turning back and focusing on Red. "That's all that matters." *Sorry, Blake, but the end of our world comes before your arrogant ass.*

"What are we waiting for?" Cristina snapped her head in Red's direction.

With a surge of energy, the witches sprang into action.

"That's for Annette!" cried Cristina as she slung what looked like a small blue stone at Red.

With a wave of his hand, he knocked the stone

away, and it hit the ground. Blue flames rose as it landed.

I blinked through my blurred vision and saw Cristina *and* Tilly standing shoulder to shoulder, a large bag at their feet. They kept digging in, pulling out small stones and crystals, and throwing them at Red.

The stones and crystals flew through the air, splitting on impact and creating walls of blue fire that merged with the orange-and-yellow elemental flames. A smoky odor filled the air as the stench of burning reached my nose and stung my eyes.

My heart leaped. *They got the bastard!*

But when the flames and smoke vanished, Red just stood there. Unscathed. As though the witches' magical fire couldn't harm him.

The mage's cackle bounced around the forest, piercing my ears like a sharp pain. "Your feeble spells won't help you," he jeered. "Nothing will. Not even your best efforts will be enough. How dare you think you can stand up against me? You're no match for the master's power. You're all going to die."

I knew that voice. Damnit. Why couldn't I remember?

Tilly stepped forward until she was at the fire circle's edge, her face red and sweaty. "You're the one who's going to die." She lowered her head, her focus on Red. I felt a tingle along my skin, and I knew she was tapping into her mind control abilities.

Red stiffened. His body shook as though he was fighting something, fighting Tilly.

Yes! It was working. I didn't know much about mind manipulation, but go, Tilly.

Red's voice rumbled with words I didn't understand, and a chill spread in the air. I felt the power of the dark magic wrapping around us like a knotted cord. The flames around the fire circle rose, claiming more energy. He was pulling demonic magic through his circle.

He snarled, and tendrils of black energy dripped from his left hand.

Demonic magic.

Blood trickled down Tilly's nose as she kept pushing her magic into Red's mind. She started to shake, and I had a feeling she was pushing too hard. It was going to get her killed.

Red smacked his hands together.

A thunderclap echoed around us. Tilly cried out and fell to her knees, holding her head in her hands like she was experiencing a migraine from hell. More blood spilled from her nose, and I could see some trickling down her ears.

He was killing her.

"Stop!"

I embraced the shadows that surrounded me, filling my being with them and grasping at the tendrils of darkness like a spider spinning its web. I clasped my hands together and pulled out a blade forged from the shadows.

Putting everything I had into my throw, I aimed... and let it fly.

Red knocked it away easily with a swipe of his hand.

"Is that all you've got?" He laughed at the fury on my face. It might not have killed him, but at least he let go of the hold he had on Tilly.

She stopped screaming, but she was still on her knees, cradling her head.

"Laughable. And you call yourselves witches? Not even worth the effort." The mage laughed again. "A two-year-old demon could do better. You're nothing but a bunch of housewife witches."

"How about you step out of your circle, and I'll show you what this housewife witch is capable of," threatened Cristina, raising her fists like she meant to have a boxing match with the mage, magic stones peeking through her clutched fingers.

Red laughed. "You know nothing." He shook his head at something behind us. The mages, like good little soldiers, all stopped at the gesture.

I watched as Red spread out his arms, standing confidently as if he did not consider us females a menace. Clearly, he didn't. His voice rose as unknown words of an enchantment spilled out of him, holding the power of the spell ready to be unleashed.

The mage's chant changed to a cruel and spiteful tone. I noticed thin strands of darkness spilling out from his hands, spiraling around and engulfing his arm.

And then he let it go.

A streak of black power flew toward Cristina.

Moving fast, she threw up her hands and tossed a crystal. A shimmering pink wall of protection rose from her feet and over her head.

I needed some of those crystals.

The dark energy struck, shattering her protective force field. Cristina screamed as she was thrown back and collided with a nearby tree trunk. The sound of her head hitting the wood was loud and sickening, and she slumped to the ground in a motionless heap.

Tilly howled a few words I couldn't catch. I blinked, and she was stumbling forward at Red.

If she was going to try her mind magic on him again, this time he would kill her.

"Like I said, pathetic." The mage chuckled, and the mages behind us all joined in. Below his cowl, and with the light from the ring of fire, I could see white teeth as he smiled.

He straightened, countering with a shot of black flames.

I jumped next to Tilly and molded a shield from my umbra magic, my shadows large enough to cover both of us.

The black flames hit my shield with enough force to knock me to my knees.

But I didn't let go. If I let go, we were both dead.

"Your magic can't save you." I heard Red say as I slowly stood while the black flames dispersed. "Soon, the master will rise, and all you... miscreants will be nothing but food for his children."

"He's insane," croaked Tilly.

"Tell me something I don't know." And what I

didn't know was how I was going to get to him and stop the ritual. Not while he drew on the powers of a demon king. That was a problem.

But I liked problems. I *solved* problems.

Through my shield, I watched as if in slow motion as Red spun his demon magic, shooting blasts of black energy at us. With each hit, I felt a slip on my hold of my magic. I couldn't keep this up forever.

Sweat ran down my face and back, stinging my eyes. It wasn't looking good for me. Nothing we had tried seemed to work against the mage.

He laughed and then tsked. "You're wasting all that energy," he mocked. "You're too drained to keep going. I can do this all day… I can last all night."

"So can I." That was a total lie. I looked at Tilly. Her pale face twisted like she was about to pass out or throw up.

I caught a glimpse of Cristina leaning against the tree where she'd fallen, her face pale, but she was alive. Thank the goddess.

"You don't have much magic left," continued the mage. "Whatever it is, like all magic, sooner or later, you'll run out. *I* have a fountain of tremendous power at my disposal. Limitless."

He was right. I was exhausted just keeping the shield up. Sooner or later, my magic would run its course. Just like all magic, it wasn't an endless well. And then what?

But Red's? It looked like this demon king's magic had its own replenishing well.

"Face it," continued Red. "You never had real magic. Not sure what to call what you're doing. Borrowed witchcraft? Whatever it is, it's weak. You're weak," mocked the mage. "Just like your magic."

"You know nothing about me," I hissed, blinking sweat out of my eye.

"Oh, but I do." Red gave a false laugh. "More than you know. And I know it won't save you."

A gust of wind began to blow around the mage, his ruby-colored robes flapping with its gusts. He slowly lifted both arms, and I felt an icy chill run through my body as the air filled with a strange energy.

I wanted to see more closely. Prepare for what was about to happen, but I didn't lower my shield.

"What's happening?" cried Tilly, fear heavy in her voice.

"Something bad," I guessed, adjusting my shield and trying to get a better look. He was going to complete the ritual.

The cold energy kept pouring in, gushing through his connection to the Netherworld and this demon king's magic. His eyes closed, and he staggered like a drunk, though drunk with immeasurable power.

Dumbass. But this was my chance.

"I'm going to lower my shield," I told Tilly quickly. "I have to stop him." I was going to kill him. "When I say run, you run!"

Tilly nodded.

I took a breath. "Run." Just as the witch ran in the opposite direction, I shot forward.

Yes, it was probably stupid, but I had one shot at stopping him.

And I was going to take it.

I pulled all the shadows I could around me, holding them tightly and molding them into a spear.

Red's attention snapped to me.

I didn't stop running.

"Xtug Znagh!" he cried.

Dark magical shackles materialized out of nowhere, and before I could react, they wrapped around my ankles and pulled me back with a jerk.

I hit the ground hard, knocking the wind out of me, my spear vanishing. The chains moved up my arms and caught hold of my wrists, searing into my skin. The shackles burned, and I felt my energy lessen like they were draining the life force and my magic out of me.

I twisted in agony as my muscles and tendons screamed. Fear washed over me like an icy flood.

I looked up to see Tilly on the ground, the same magical shackles around her wrists and ankles. I could even see Cristina, who hadn't moved from the tree, her wrists and ankles bound.

We were trapped.

"This is what happens when females think they can do magic." Red leaned over me and lowered his cowl.

My blood ran cold.

"You're all mine now," said Sykes.

CHAPTER 25

"You?" I said, completely thrown for a beat. I did not see this coming. Now that I could put a face to the voice, it suddenly made sense.

Sykes—my father's man, his assistant, the average-looking man with the unremarkable face—and just plain forgettable altogether—was the ringleader for The Forsaken.

Damn. I couldn't come up with this crap even if I tried.

Yet he looked different.

The moonlight illuminated his scalp, visible through the tufts of black hair. Even in the faint light, I could make out the dark circles underneath his eyes and how gaunt his face was.

He'd drawn too much of that demonic magic into himself. It was killing him.

Sykes's face cracked into a smile, his eyes wide with a madman's gleam. Now that his cowl was removed, I could make out blood trickling from his nose, and a layer of blood covered his teeth when he spoke next. "Yes. Who would ever suspect poor, little, ordinary, invisible Sykes to yield immeasurable power."

"Good point," I growled out. "You need to stop this." I hoped I could reach him somehow and talk some sense into him. "This demon lord."

"King," he corrected.

"He won't share power with you. You do realize that the most probable outcome here is that he'll kill you just as soon as he steps out. Right?"

He watched me, and his smile became wider, more ghoulish. "My master needs me. Unlike your father, the master promised to give me eternal life and more power than you can ever imagine."

Another idiot who thought demons shared their power. "You're wrong. And you're going to kill us all."

"I'm not."

"But what if you were? Think about it. Is that a chance you're willing to take? To sacrifice billions of people?"

He chuckled darkly. "It is. And when the master is set free, he will reign over us. Those who will follow will live. Those who don't… well… you can guess the rest."

My anger twisted in my gut at the thought of all this clusterfuck because of this asshat. "I won't let you. I'll kill you first."

"How?" laughed Sykes. "With those circus magician tricks you call magic? It couldn't even save you."

I raised my shackles. "If you take this off, I'll show you what my magic tricks can do."

Sykes grinned maliciously as his dark magic filled the space between us. "It's a fair fight. You just don't have the strength I do. Women never do. It's why they're deemed the weaker sex."

"We give birth. I call that the *stronger* sex." Dumbass. "Unless you can sprout a child through your tiny penis."

The air cracked with power. I could sense more of Sykes's magic now—his master's magic, cold and unfamiliar. He might not look it, but he was a powerful witch. He'd fooled me, but I wasn't going to make that mistake again and underestimate him.

"What would my father say if he saw you?"

Sykes snorted. "Your *father*? He's just a man with a title given to him by his wife. He's nothing."

He had me there. "But you were in his employ for years. He must mean something to you. Are you willing to see him die?"

Sykes thought about it. "Yes. Yes, I am."

"Don't do this," I tried. "You don't have to do this." I hated how desperate my voice sounded, but the fact of the matter was I *was* freaking desperate.

His eyes widened with manic glee. "Oh, but I do."

"Why? Why do this?"

"Why? Why? Why?" Sykes guffawed, the sound

of a madman reveling in his own dark genius. He was ecstatic that he had set off his apocalyptic plot, content with bringing an end to the world we knew.

Total psycho.

The demented mage gave out a wheezing cackle. "All my life, I've been ignored and overlooked. Your father was the worst of them. Thinking I was beneath him. Treating me like a cockroach."

"You kinda look like one," I muttered.

"He thinks he's smarter than me, that he has more power. He's not. He doesn't. I hold the power now. *I* hold *everything*."

"Good for you," I said. "You can still choose not to do this. You can stop it. Don't do it."

My skin prickled at the sudden pull of Sykes's magic, and I felt his fury rippling under the surface.

Sykes's eyes narrowed at me. "Of course I'm going to do this, you stupid bitch," he spat. "I've been waiting twenty years, but *you* ruined it then. You're not going to ruin it again."

I blinked. "What? Clearly, you're losing it. I had nothing to do with this." But something in the back of my mind had my blood run cold. A memory that I had pushed back so long ago was making its way back to the surface.

Sykes glowered at me. "Don't you get it? Don't you understand now?"

I wiggled in my restraints. "Clearly, I don't."

"You ruined the ritual twenty years ago."

"How's that?"

The witch's face twitched into a cold smile. "You were the next sacrifice."

I couldn't breathe. It was like one of those shackles gripped my throat, choking me. "You're lying."

By the look of satisfaction that I knew well enough, I knew he wasn't. "You were to be killed, drained of blood, like this little Emma here. But, something happened, and you just... vanished." He looked at me hard. "How did you do that?"

I was shaking my head, remembering how I'd shadow-jumped—what I'd decided to call that phenomenon—remembering how the shadows around me responded to my fear, wrapping around me like a shield of protection just before they'd pulled me away into that shadow portal.

And I'd ended up in a different town.

"No," I said. "I happened to stumble across the ritual to get out of the rain. I wasn't part of it."

"You were. And you were *made* to come."

I frowned. "Like, hypnotized?"

"If you want to call it that. But it was more of a persuasion. Complex magic that only a few possess."

This bit of information hit me in the gut like a freight train. I still couldn't breathe. All these years, I thought I'd abandoned that girl, brought that guilt with me for twenty years, only to realize that jumping into that shadow pocket, that doorway, or whatever you wanted to call it, not only had saved my life.

But the world's.

I'd been part of that ritual those twenty years ago.

"Motherfracker," I hissed, remembering how scared I was, how young I was. He'd tried to kill me.

Sykes laughed. "Well, you won't be pulling that trick again. This time, Emma's going to die. I don't need you anymore."

The mage reached inside his robe and pulled out another dagger. I watched as he sliced it across Emma's wrist.

"Bastard! You son of a bitch! I'll kill you!" I howled, struggling against my restraints and bucking like a wild animal. I tried to call on my powers, the shadows, but they wouldn't come.

I was powerless to stop it, so I sucked in a breath and watched as the red liquid slowly seeped from Emma's arm, staining the rock she was tied to.

Sykes raised his arms, dark syllables hissing from his lips. Drawing himself up, the mage chanted in his demonic tongue and gestured with a flick of his wrist.

I felt a sudden buzz of energy, a pull of magic as a pop displaced the air. I gagged at the choking smell of rot and sulfur. The flames rose around the circle.

And then the stone glowed with a blinding light, so bright I had to look away.

"What's happening?" shouted Tilly.

Sykes was opening the portal to set his master free. He was completing the ritual.

There was a sudden crack, as though the world itself was splitting in two. I blinked as the light dissipated, and I could see again.

The night sky rippled and glimmered as if a living black sea was floating just above the circle. The portal to the Netherworld had been opened. An icy blast of energy washed over me, thick with death, blood, and evil. A steady hum buzzed in the air like electrical lines, and the stench of burning sulfur and rot made my eyes water. My hair whipped around my face in an unnatural wind that was toxic for us humans. This was the air of the Netherworld pushing its way through the gateway. Through the swirling darkness, I could make out thousands of forms rushing for our world.

Shit. Shit. Shit.

Panicked, I pulled on my restraints, feeling the magic cut into my skin and drain me all at the same time.

Angry tears fell from my eyes. I'd never felt so useless except for that one time I'd left that poor girl to die to save my own ass.

This was it. We'd lost. I'd lost.

A blur of motion snapped my head up.

Through my tears, I saw Dash standing next to Sykes, trembling with rage as he looked at me with his features twisted.

Sykes narrowed his eyes at him. "What are you doing here? I thought we told you to stay away." He waved a dismissive hand at Dash like he was a servant. "Leave. You're not needed here."

I saw Dash's face shift. I saw his mind working through his eyes as he made the decision to go after Sykes.

Dash bared his teeth. In the next moment, there was a flash of fangs, claws, and fur as Dash transformed—not into a sweet kitty but an enormous beast that towered around nine feet high. It was completely black with the head of a lion sporting bovine horns, talons as long as a chef's knives, and glowing red eyes.

The creature, Dash, swung a massive clawed hand at Sykes.

The mage fell, scrambling to get back on his feet as the pissed-off monster advanced on him. Curses and hexes flew as the other mages all rushed to his aid.

I felt a release around my wrists and feet. My bonds were broken.

I cast my gaze at Tilly. She was on her feet, her bonds gone as well. Seemed like Sykes couldn't keep his magical hold on us while he was getting his ass kicked.

"The portal!" shouted Tilly. "It's opening!"

The skin on my neck prickled, and I stood horrified as the portal shimmered only forty feet from us. A massive, giant form hovered on the other side.

The demon king.

Twisted, corrupted masses of smaller demons spilled out behind him—his army, no doubt. A king wouldn't show up without his soldiers.

The creature, Dash, roared as I flicked my gaze back in time to see five of the mages attacking him with their magic. Again and again, they hit him, but whatever monster Dash was, it seemed he was somewhat resistant to their magic. Enough that he could fight back.

"I am here, Master!" cried Sykes, rushing toward Emma. "The sacrifice will be completed! Come forward now! Come forth! Rise!"

Fuck.

I charged after him. Almost there.

But Sykes was at the sacrificial stone. He raised the dagger above Emma's chest.

Time seemed to stand still as terror took hold of me. I concentrated on the shadows around me and used my fear and anger to fuel my powers.

My umbra magic pulsed through me like a surge of energy, far more intense than adrenaline.

The shadows responded to my call, wrapping around me like a cloak of protection. I could feel their strength and energy seeping into my pores, empowering me with a sense of calm and confidence I hadn't felt in a long time.

The shadows were mine now, and in their embrace, I knew anything was possible.

Just like it did twenty years ago, through a combination of utter fear and instincts, a shadowed doorway the size of a regular door materialized next to me.

Focusing on Sykes, so I didn't end up in Florida, I stepped into the portal. And shadow-jumped.

One second, I was thirty feet behind Sykes. The next, I was right beside him.

I punched him in the face.

He staggered, dropped the knife, and fell over, giving me the precious time I needed.

Using Sykes's blade, I cut through Emma's bonds, pulled her over my shoulder, and seeing the shadow portal still hovering, I shadow-jumped.

The last thing I heard was Sykes's wail as I took Emma with me. I didn't take her to another town, just far enough away from the ritual.

We popped back next to the line of parked cars, and I settled the unconscious girl on the grass.

Her eyes flickered open. "Kat? Where… where am I?"

"Shhh," I said. "You're safe now." I ripped the bottom of my shirt and wrapped up her bleeding wrist. "Put pressure on that. We'll get you a healer." She was pale but in better shape than I would have thought. She hadn't lost that much blood.

"You're leaving?" Emma blinked slowly.

"I still have a job to do." I kissed the top of her head. "I'll be back. Don't move."

I tapped into the shadows again and, using the same doorway, shadow-jumped back.

I was getting the hang of this.

I focused on the sacrificial stone, but when I popped out, I landed next to Cristina.

"Ah!" she screamed as I appeared next to her. "How did you get here?"

"Long story." Okay, so I needed more practice. I ran forward, where I could see Sykes's red robe. I had to close the portal somehow, and I had no freaking clue how to do it.

I vaulted forward, my eyes on the rift, and saw Tilly kneeling next to Annette. Her eyes were open. She was alive!

With a new surge of adrenaline flowing through me, I aimed for Sykes. He was the only connection left with the portal.

I didn't know if it would close on its own now that I had stopped the ritual from completing—a second time. But I didn't want to take any chances.

"No! This can't be!" Sykes was shouting, staring wild-eyed at the portal as it started to shift and shrink. "Master! Master! Don't leave me!" He planted himself in front of the doorway, his arms flailing in a desperate attempt to cling to the demon king.

But the portal, the gateway from hell, shimmered and started to fold.

It was closing.

I heard a distant yell of rage from the depths of the portal, but it was already too late. Angry bellows filled the air as their cries echoed away. Suddenly, with a release in pressure, the portal evaporated.

Sykes's ugly face turned toward Dash, still in the form of his monster. "You! You did this!" he screamed, spit flying from his mouth. "You're going to pay for this."

The mage hurled tendrils of his black demonic magic at an unsuspecting Dash. It hit the werecat—well, werebeast or whatever—and the creature wailed in pain as he stumbled to one knee.

"Ha! Yes. Yes. You should have listened. You

should have stayed away. Now I'm going to kill you!" Again and again, Sykes attacked Dash.

He was so focused on the creature that he never saw me coming.

I embraced the shadows, feeling their energy course through my body. I wove the shadows together and conjured a single shadow lance—

And drove it into his back.

The mage cried out and then gurgled some words as he choked on his blood. He looked down at the shadow spear perforating his chest.

"No. Impossible." And then he keeled over and never moved again.

"Oh, it's very possible," I said, staring at him as the life left his eyes.

A shape moved in my line of sight, and my eyes found Tilly kneeling next to the wolf as she hauled off the heavy silver chains.

The wolf growled and staggered to his feet. He turned his gaze from me to the motionless form of Sykes lying on the ground. His yellow eyes focused on Dash, the creature.

And then the wolf charged.

I looked at Dash. Our gazes locked for a moment, and at that instant, I could almost see Dash's eyes through the beast's own.

The creature's enormous form began to undulate and contract until he transformed into a solitary crow standing before me.

"What are you?" I asked the crow, not sure he could answer me back. I'd never known of a shifter

—'cause I doubted very much that Dash was a werecat now—who could take on multiple shapes, beasts.

Dash was a mystery.

And then, with a beat of his wings, the crow flew away.

CHAPTER 26

The Blue Demon was packed and as vibrant and noisy as you'd expect a diner to be on a sunny afternoon.

Word of The Forsaken's defeat and Sykes's involvement spread quickly, and it seemed as though a quarter of the town was in the restaurant.

I rested my elbows on the polished wooden bar, my butt comfortably on a stool, allowing the events of the night before to drift away from me slowly.

Echoes of rich voices reached me, and I turned to see many unfamiliar faces. Witches, werewolves, and shifters all crammed into the diner. Among them, I spotted a few familiar ones. Cristina, her arm hooked around the arm of a tall man with an easy smile and kind eyes. Her husband, most probably, whom I hadn't had the pleasure of meeting yet. They were conversing with a short woman with dark skin and waves of curly black hair. The town healer, Sonia Winter.

Laughter reached me over the buzzing voices. Helen, the town mayor, with a glass of white wine in her hand, was laughing at something Annette had told her. I couldn't see Liam, and I had a feeling he stayed behind with the girls.

My heart swelled with emotion as I thought of Emma. After Sykes was killed, and the portal had closed, I'd rushed over to Annette, who was still recovering from whatever hex or spell the mage had hit her with.

"You disappeared with Emma," she'd said to me, clearly having seen me shadow-jump.

"I'll take you to her. She needs a healer."

With Blake's help, back into his human form, we'd taken Emma to the town healer, Sonia. She took one look at us on her doorstep in the middle of the night as she wore a yellow headband and matching nightgown and ushered us inside.

"Quick. Put her on the kitchen table."

Sonia had meticulously stitched Emma's wrist and given her a vial to drink that looked like a vegetable smoothie.

"It'll help her regain her strength," she'd told Annette. "She's lost a lot of blood, but she should be fine. You look like hell," she'd said to Annette. "Here. You drink this."

Sonia had given Annette one of her green vials and another two for Tilly and Cristina.

Once Emma was deemed healthy enough to go home, three hours later, we all piled into Tilly's SUV and drove home.

Blake returned to the ritual scene, where a team of his deputies waited for him.

Apparently, his "backup" had taken down the wrong address, so they ended up across town instead of the field where Sykes tried to kill Emma. Good thing we didn't need them in the end.

I could have joined Blake, but my part of the job was over. I'd found those responsible for Tim's and Samuel's deaths. Yes, some had disappeared on us once Sykes had been killed, but my job was done. Case closed.

For now.

I spotted Tilly leaning on Blake as she rubbed a hand over his muscled arm. I'd recalled that look of panic on her face when she'd rushed over to him to take those silver chains off him. I suspected Tilly was in love with Blake. She didn't just want to bang his brains out. She wanted a relationship.

Blake must have sensed me staring because his eyes met mine. I flinched at the suspicion and anger I saw there. Yup. He wasn't finished with me.

"Can I get you another?"

I glanced up at the voice, shaking me out of my thoughts. "No, I'm good." I lifted my half-empty beer bottle.

Kolton, the owner, leaned forward, his beefy forearms resting on the bar. "You should be celebrating. You saved that girl."

"I'm not really in a celebrating mood."

Kolton looked at me for a beat. "You did good, Kat. Real good."

I wasn't sure what it was about that statement or how he said it, but my eyes filled with moisture. "Yeah. I guess."

"You should be real proud of yourself. Of what you've done. I know Annette is."

I smiled and looked over at Emma's mother. Seeing her smiling at me had me turning away quickly so I wouldn't start crying. Not sure where all these emotions were coming from.

"How much do I owe you for the beer?" I asked, wanting to change the subject as I blinked fast. I opened my bag, my fingers brushing against my pack of nicotine gum. I'd completely forgotten about them.

Kolton leaned back, smiling at me. His handsome face was striking when he smiled. "On the house."

I raised a brow. "Thanks."

Kolton winked. "You're welcome."

I watched as the strapping black man moved away to serve a handsome man at the other end of the bar. Remy.

The vampire caught me staring and flashed me a sexy grin.

I looked away before I got into trouble.

"You okay?"

I turned to see Annette standing next to me.

"You look… sad."

I shook my head. "Not sad. Just grateful Emma's safe." And that was the truth.

Annette let out a sigh and put her empty wine-glass on the bar. "Are you going to leave now that you solved Tim's murder? You know, we'd love for you to stay. I know Emma would. She couldn't stop talking about you to her father all night."

I smiled. I'd thought about it all night, too. And I hadn't made a decision until now.

"I think I'm going to stick around. For a while, at least. We might have gotten rid of some members of The Forsaken, but they're still out there." And I'd make it my mission to remove every single member.

A flicker of fear washed over Annette's pretty face. "You think they'll be back?"

By "be back," I knew she was asking whether they'd come and take Emma again or another one of her daughters. "Your girls are fine. Don't worry. They can't perform that ritual again for another twenty years. But that doesn't mean they're not up to other vile things."

Annette squeezed my hand. "Good. I'm glad you're staying. You bring excitement to Moonfell."

"That's not what I would call it."

A question lingered in her eyes. "Your… aunt? Care to share that bit of news?"

I smiled. "I was wondering when you'd ask me that."

"Soooo, she's not dead," said Annette.

"Apparently not. She faked her own death." I told her the story, and I felt my tension ease as the laughter escaped her. She had an infectious laugh.

"Wow." Annette shook her head. "All this time? Alone in that house. Your aunt is a bit of a nutcase."

I pushed my beer away. "I know. But she's my aunt. And she's my only relative who always had my back. So, she's a bit eccentric? Who cares. That's how I love her."

Annette stared at my half-empty beer. She frowned. "You're not leaving yet? You just got here."

I gave her a tight smile. "There's something I need to do."

Annette watched me. "I'll call you later. I'm making lasagna tonight. The girls would love it if you came."

I smiled. "I'll be there."

I turned and made my way to the exit, my heart pounding as I thought about what I was about to do.

"Leaving so soon?" came a deep voice behind me.

Shit. I'd almost made it.

I gritted my teeth and turned around. Blake, the sheriff, towered over me.

"Yes. As you can see."

He pressed his hands on his hips, staring down at me. "I'm not finished with you."

"This again?"

"This again," growled Blake, and a few heads turned our way. "We still have some of those mages on the loose. If we had the name of your source, we could find them and throw their asses in jail. They killed two teens, Kat."

"I know."

"And you still won't tell me."

I swallowed hard. "I can't."

Blake let out a sigh through his nose. I swore I could see some steam. "I have to tell the Gray Council. You're not giving me a choice."

The Gray Council was the top governing body in our community. You didn't want to piss them off.

"Like I told you, you do what you gotta do. But I won't tell you."

"Damnit, Kat. Don't do this. Just tell me."

I shook my head. "No."

Blake's jaw twitched. "It's that guy. The one I saw back at your house. Your friend, isn't it? That's your source."

Oh shit.

Panic was a white-hot flare, and my heart hammered. I kept my face from showing any emotion. "It's not. I'm not going to tell you."

"I'm going to arrest you."

Anger flared in my chest. "Right now? In front of everyone? After what I did? You think that's going to go well with the town? With Annette? With Liam?" Yeah, I was going there. My voice was loud, and I saw Tilly watching us warily.

Strange how this werewolf had flirted with me at the beginning, asked me to dinner. Now he was looking at me like he wanted to throw my ass in jail. As though *I* were responsible for what happened to Emma.

Fury flashed over his face. "Don't leave town."

"I won't."

Heart hammering, I spun on my heel and strode

toward the exit. My gaze fell upon the metal trash can at the door. I rummaged through my bag for my last pack of nicotine gum and tossed it inside.

With a deep breath, I pushed the door open and stepped out of The Blue Demon.

CHAPTER 27

I sat in my Jeep. The warm afternoon breeze ruffled my hair, bringing forth the sweet smell of daisies, swamp milkweed, and other wildflowers mixed with tall grasses. The sky was a perfect blue, so blue it seemed to be glowing.

Birds chirped happily, flying from tree to tree, while squirrels shouted their displeasure at another trespasser in their territory.

A man worked on a chunk of wood set on a table before a large red barn. Sweat glimmered over his bare chest as he carved the wings of a giant bird. An eagle, from what I could see.

I'd discreetly parked my Jeep just off the edge of his long driveway, concealed by the trees and bushes but close enough to get a good view.

And it was a very good view.

I couldn't help but admire how beautiful he was. His chiseled chest and arms were a testament to his strength and craftsmanship. The muscles on his back flexed as he cut and chipped shards of wood.

Sykes knew Dash. That much was clear. He knew who he was when I was at my parents' dinner party and had pretended not to know him. Had he cursed Dash? Had they had a falling out? Something had happened that resulted in Dash's memory being taken.

Either way, Dash was a member of The Forsaken. Or at least he worked for them.

Dash was the enemy.

It was a hard pill to swallow, like swallowing a dill pickle whole. How could someone who'd been so kind be involved with something so evil?

And what the hell was he? He was no kind of shifter I knew. A shifter who could morph into different creatures. I'd have to do some research on that.

My eyes scanned his every move as he continued to cut and chip at the pile of wood in front of him, his movements slow and methodical, as if he was lost in thought. Something about Dash drew me in, something I couldn't quite put my finger on. Was it the way his muscles bulged with every movement or the intensity in his eyes as he worked? Or was it something deeper, something I couldn't quite comprehend?

Either way, I couldn't give him up. Not when he'd helped us defeat Sykes. Without his help, Sykes would have succeeded in raising his master, the demon king.

For now, it was good enough for me.

Dash snapped his head in my direction, seemingly only noticing me now. If I wanted to hide from him, I would have parked down the road and spied on him through the trees. No. I wanted him to see me.

Our eyes met, and my heart started to pound madly in my chest. For a moment, we just stared at each other, our gazes intensely locked upon one another. I wanted to say something reassuring, but no words formed on my lips.

He watched me with a stoic expression, emotions I could only guess at were swimming in his dark eyes.

It was hard to understand what I saw on his face. Regret? Sadness? Whatever was there, he turned away before I could get a good read on him.

"Dash," I whispered, my words choking in my throat. "What have you done?"

I didn't know if Dash was bad. Or if he was good and sometimes bad.

Either way, what I did know was that my heart ached at the sight of him.

Damn. I was in serious trouble.

Don't miss the next book in
The Witches of Moonfell series!

Magic of Blood and Ash (The Witches of Moonfell
Book 2)

BOOKS BY KIM RICHARDSON

WITCHES OF NEW YORK

The Starlight Witch

Game of Witch

Tales of a Witch

THE WITCHES OF HOLLOW COVE

Shadow Witch

Midnight Spells

Charmed Nights

Magical Mojo

Practical Hexes

Wicked Ways

Witching Whispers

Mystic Madness

Rebel Magic

Cosmic Jinx

Brewing Crazy

Witchy Little Lies

Magic Gone Wild

THE HORIZON CHRONICLES

The Soul Thief

The Helm of Darkness

The City of Flame and Shadow

The Lord of Darkness

MYSTICS SERIES

The Seventh Sense

The Alpha Nation

The Nexus

DIVIDED REALMS

Steel Maiden

Witch Queen

Blood Magic

About the Author

Kim Richardson is a *USA Today* bestselling and award-winning author of urban fantasy, fantasy, and young adult books. She lives in the eastern part of Canada with her husband, two dogs, and a very old cat. Kim's books are available in print editions, and translations are available in over seven languages.

To learn more about the author, please visit:

www.kimrichardsonbooks.com

Printed in Great Britain
by Amazon